In the Eyes of Anahita

An adventure in search of humanity

"Hugo Bonjean's novel is a spellbinding journey of discovery. Magically woven, suspenseful and evocative, it takes us from the world we know into the heart of what it means to be human."

-Diane Dreher, author of *The Tao of Personal Leadership*-

In the Eyes of Anahita

An adventure in search of humanity

To Joe Ceci,
I applaud you for your actions
to make Calgary a more
sustainable city. I hope you
will enjoy the reading.
May it inspire you to
continue on your path.
Hugo Bonjean

Hugo Bonjean

Published by Synergy Books and produced by Eagle Vision Publishing Ltd.

For publishing information contact:
Synergy Books, 2525 West Anderson Lane, Suite 540, Austin, Texas, U.S.A.
Phone: (512) 478 2028 Fax: (512) 478 2117

For production, copyright, or marketing information contact:
Eagle Vision Publishing, A128-1600 90th Avenue S.W. Calgary, Alberta, T2V 5A8, Canada. Phone & Fax. (403) 933 3913

www. intheeyesofanahita.com
info@intheeyesofanahita.com

Editor: Elizabeth Zack, Bookcrafters llc.
Cover & interior design: Suzanne Oel

Published simultaneously in the United States and Canada

ISBN: 0-9747644-9-3 (pbk)

Distributed by Biblio Distribution, a subsidiary of National Book Network

Our Commitment to a Sustainable World

This book is printed on New Leaf Ecobook 100 paper, made with 100% post consumer waste, processed chlorine free. For each 1,000 books of this title printed on this environmentally friendly paper, the following resources are saved:

12 fully grown trees
5,026 gallons of water
8 million BTU's of energy
561 pounds of solid waste
1,105 pounds of greenhouse gases

These numbers are based on an eco-audit conducted by New Leaf Paper for the production of this book.

Traditionally the paper industry has been structured around wood as the source of fiber. According to the Worldwatch Institute, over 40% of the world's industrial wood harvest is used for the manufacture of paper. This has resulted in the decimation of our old growth forests, which are continued to be clear cut to make paper.

We honor companies like New Leaf Paper and Houghton Boston Printers for their commitment to introducing environmentally friendly paper at competitive prices to the book printing industry, while at the same time diverting waste from landfills and addressing pollution issues. May many follow their example!

For information on New Leaf Paper visit:
www.newleafpaper.com
For information on Houghton Boston visit:
www.houghtonboston.com

Acknowledgements

I would like to express my gratitude to all those who have encouraged and assisted me during the birth of this book.

The feedback I received during the writing process from various people, including Judy Setrakov, Tammy Perrault and my dearest wife, Ilse de Wit, provided me with the self-confidence and courage to keep on writing. I would particularly like to thank a friend of mine, who chosen to remain anonymous, for following through on her intuition and presenting me, very synchronistically, with material that helped me see beyond the duality of values and time.

Without my editor, Elizabeth Zack, it would never have been possible to bring this book to market. Very skillfully she polished my language into proper English, without diluting my personal writing style. Paula Kroeker, Anthony Kroeker, John Robertson, Tom Pitoulis and Heather Glazier's proofreading was incredibly valuable, not only for the spelling and punctuation corrections, but also for their feedback on the story which bolstered my determination to publish my work. I specifically would like to thank Paula Kroeker for taking the time to sit down with me and work through the final line edit.

Suzanne Oel, my illustrator, has absolutely exceeded my expectations for the cover design. I cannot thank her enough for having taken the time to intimately understand what I expected the front cover to look like, and then to use her artistic skills and go over and beyond to create this wonderful book design and interior lay-out.

There have been many others that contributed in small ways to the final production of this book and I am grateful for their support in helping me to select the most appealing title, the most attractive cover design and the best way to publish.

But I would not have been in a position to write this book without my parents, Betty and Willy Bonjean, who allowed me to question everything and invested in my education; without the love of my life, Ilse de Wit, who always stands by me when I decide—on another crazy whim—to enter new uncharted territory; without Janice Pasieka, who saved my life; and without some of my friends: Reas Kondraschow, who provide me with an opportunity to develop my business skills and travel the world, which ultimately led to my profound insights; Joe Perrault, who taught me to bow-hunt and be comfortable alone in the forest; Luis Pedro, who took me across the Andes; and Filip and Jef, my missionary friends, who helped me to discover the hidden side of our world.

My life has been blessed with many gifts and I express my sincere thanks to all those people—friends, business colleagues and enemies—who crossed my path for the lessons they brought me, which made me who I am today.

Last but not least, I want to thank my wife and my fabulous children, Bjorn, Fabian and Amber, for their patience, love and support during those long winter months when I was writing and acted like a hermit. I send a special thanks to Fabian for asking me the question that started this great adventure and to the Universal Source for its energy and beauty.

For

Amber, Fabian and Bjorn

And all the children of our world

That they may find

Happiness and Peace

In a Sustainable,

Harmonious Society.

Author's Note

W ake up! "RIIIIIING; Good morning! It is six forty-five a.m., and this is your wake-up call. Your day should be happy and sunny...but if not, ...most certainly read on. Now have an awesome, discovery-filled and creative day!"

"Wake up to what?" you're probably thinking.

To your personal power of co-creating this world! In order to intentionally create the world you live in, you first need to be aware of how it functions, how it developed up to this point and what active—conscious or unconscious—role you have been playing in it.

Next you need to develop a vision. What kind of world would you *like* to see? And last but not least, you need to understand yourself and the people around you: Is your creativity and passion for life vibrant and strong or do you have to remove suppressing barriers? And how can you enjoy focused and intentional co-creation together with others?

I do not claim to have all the answers for you. Actually, no one else other than you can answer these questions for you. However, I will gladly make an attempt to help you discover them. One thing I do know is that in order to allow your spirit within to bloom to its full potential, you require awareness and conscious action!

My exposure to poor farming communities and the slums in South America while doing business as a corporate executive with some of the richest people on the continent, has impacted my perspective of our world significantly, and given new direction to my life. The spiritual journey resulting from these travels has been the inspiration for this book. To turn it into an exciting, captivating story, I have condensed all my fragmented experiences into a two-week adventure through South America. All character names, and some places, have been changed to protect the privacy of those who helped me discover the power of my inner spirit and my ability to co-create in this universe.

This book challenges traditional perspectives and offers alternative viewpoints. While the story contains my personal insights, it is by no means my intention to "sell" these to you. I am merely sharing them to stimulate your personal thinking and allow you to develop *your unique perspective* of our world, take *conscious actions* in your life and *enjoy* this great adventure of being human.

Contents

✦

"*A human being is part of a whole, called by us the "Universe," a part limited in time and space. He experiences himself, his thoughts and feelings, as something separated from the rest—a kind of optical delusion of his consciousness. This delusion is a kind of prison for us, restricting us to our personal desires and to affection for a few persons nearest us. Our task must be to free ourselves from this prison by widening our circles of compassion to embrace all living creatures and the whole of nature in its beauty.*"

Albert Einstein

"*Be the change you want to see.*"

Mahatma Gandhi.

The Mystery Unveils

A Child's Challenge for Civilization

"Dad, why do people have to pay for food?" That is the question my seven-year-old son asked me while I was cleaning off the dinner table. The depth of the question astonished me at first, since it came from such a young child. When I got my wits back, I started to provide the traditional answer about trade, demand, supply and skill sets, but right in the middle of my elaborate economic theory, the profoundness of the question hit me: Why *do* people have to pay for food in an advanced civilization like ours? Why *do* people still experience hunger today? Clearly this seven-year-old was questioning why, in a civilized society, the most basic of needs -food- was not available to everyone. I hesitated for a moment, then looked into Tom's innocent, questioning eyes and said, "I don't know. That is a very good question."

Earlier, on that cold winter day in March, Tom and I had watched a program from Plan International. It invited people to sponsor a child in a developing country so that his or her life circumstances could be improved. For an hour we had been bombarded with the smiling, innocent faces of children against a backdrop of cardboard houses, open sewage streets, and a display of absolute poverty. Kids' bellies were swollen from starvation, and some of the children were crying, while others showed us their purest smiles. But most striking of all were their eyes: There was something about

1

them. They were windows through which you could see deep into their souls. Pure and innocent spirits puzzled by their state of being. At times afraid and sad, but always with this innocent, sparkling energy that lay just underneath.

I had noticed that Tom had been unusually silent during the rest of the day and had maintained this introverted attitude during supper. Now I understood why.

Why *do* people have to pay for food?

A Trip to Argentina

The day after Tom's question I started to prepare for my business trip to Argentina. Buenos Aires, the city in which I would arrive, wasn't really my favorite place in the world. It had great architecture and atmosphere, but its traffic and pollution seemed to overshadow everything.

Each time I was in Argentina it astonished me how macho egos dominated the business arena. Challenged by a growing mountain of economic and organizational problems, Argentinean businessmen were constantly searching for solutions. Ironically, however, when someone from another country shared how other companies or countries had successfully dealt with similar situations, the Argentinean businessmen would almost always reply that such solutions and methods could not work for them. After all, their situation was very unique!

Defensively, they would argue how they had absolutely no hand in creating the problems and issues at hand, then explain why they were truly unique and could not be compared with others. Subsequently, they would discard all the potential solutions that had been offered, and feel sorry for themselves all over again. Not *all* Argentinean businessmen were like that, but I met quite a few in Buenos Aires with just such an attitude.

However, if the focus of the conversation was turned away from business, political and economic issues to social, environmental and philosophical topics, the Argentineans were great conversational partners. They are a great people, but I just wish that their women were more dominant in business and politics. The businesswomen with whom I dealt were always eager to get things resolved. They were smart and not afraid to copy things from other countries or industries if that could solve their problems. I am certain that Argentinean men have the same skills and drive, but many times their macho mentality clouded the issues.

Still, I was excited about this trip since I would have to travel outside of the capital, Buenos Aires, to Salta, a small provincial town at the base of the Andes Mountains in the northwest of Argentina. As I knew from traveling in other countries, the atmosphere and mentality in a country's capital can be very different from the rest of the nation, and this is certainly the case in developing countries. This visit to Salta would give me an opportunity to get to know Argentineans outside of Buenos Aires.

The purpose of my trip was to visit a small hotel and meet with its owners, managers and staff to evaluate the potential of their hotel to join the multinational hospitality corporation for which I worked. As a hotel developer, I had traveled half the globe during the last ten years. Friends and family always offered to come along and carry my suitcases, for no one realized how few opportunities I had to really see something of the countries I visited during these trips. Such travel was merely strenuous on my body and stressful in terms of my family life.

But this trip was different. It would be more than walking through airports, sitting in planes, getting into taxis and meeting with people in conference rooms somewhere in a big city. This was one of those trips during which I would get to see some of the country and meet some of the provincial natives.

Later that day I left from Calgary airport and connected early in the evening in Chicago to Buenos Aires. After takeoff, the monotonous sound of the airplane engine put me to sleep somewhere high above North America. Then, boom! I suddenly woke up. Boom, boom! The plane was going through some heavy turbulence, and I guessed we were somewhere above the Amazon. I had noticed on previous trips there was almost always heavy turbulence above the rainforest.

As I tried to fall asleep again, Tom's question came back into my mind. Why *do* people have to pay for food? Why *do* we allow hunger to exist in our society? Surely there's enough food on this planet to feed everyone! Actually, I had seen an abundance of food in some of the poorest countries in Central America as a result of their tropical climate. How did a minority population in the world obtain the right to the majority of the world's food resources? Why do we allow people—children—to be hungry? With these questions flying through my head, I eventually dozed off again.

Managing Fear

Shortly before landing in Buenos Aires I woke up. It was cloudy and windy. I passed through customs and took a taxi to the domestic airport in order to catch my flight to Salta.

By the time I arrived at the other airport the sky was dark and threatening. A huge thunderstorm, like you see only in Central and South America, was moving in. The wind was blowing ferociously. It was eleven in the morning, yet the sky was as dark as night. Surprisingly we boarded the plane for Salta without delays. However, a few minutes after we were taxiing, the plane was called back, a delay as a result of the thunderstorm. I looked at the sky and saw many more dark clouds moving in. After consultation with the tower and a ten-minute delay, the pilot decided to leave.

The plane made a steep ascent to the clouds and got through the first layer before getting tossed around like a little leaf dancing on the wind. The turbulence above the Amazon was *nothing* in comparison to this. We were thrown up, down, left and right. At times it sounded like the airplane was hitting concrete boulders underneath! Yet the pilot skillfully flew around most of the immense cumulus clouds at our designated cruising altitude.

Meanwhile, a tremendous light show was going on outside of the plane. I sat with my nose pushed against the window enjoying the most spectacular lightning display I had ever seen.

A teenager was sitting next to me. Based on his looks, somewhat darker skin and black hair, I guessed he was Argentinean and about eighteen years old. Indeed, as far as I could tell, I was the only foreigner on board.

The boy's hands were cramped anxiously around the seat's arms, his body completely tense. Fear had clearly taken control of him.

"It's okay," I reassured him. "Nothing is going to happen. If this pilot thought things would not have been safe, he would not have taken off. He certainly would not risk his life just to bring us to Salta, would he?"

The boy relaxed somewhat, turned to me and asked, "Are you not afraid?"

"Afraid of what?" I replied.

"Afraid the plane will crash!" The tone in which he said these words sounded exactly like the tone some teenagers in my community took when they thought you were asking them a really stupid question. Only the words, "You dummy!" were missing from his lips.

A few years ago, I had learned during a coaching workshop about the effectiveness of helping people to grow and develop by way of using questions to lead them to certain answers. I had learned that when people find their own answers to problems and challenges, their growth is more substantial and the results are longer-lasting. I had used these coaching techniques to develop superior business teams, and recognized a great coaching opportunity of a different kind had presented itself here. Therefore, I decided to change my line of questioning. Rather than sticking with my original plan of calming the boy, I reckoned I could help him conquer one of his fears. I received great personal satisfaction by helping those around me in this way, and besides, coaching this boy would give me something to do on the flight.

"Why do you fear this plane will crash?" I asked.

"Because we get tossed around so much!"

"I understand," I said, "but that is not what I meant. Why does a plane crash scare you?"

He looked at me with big eyes and an expression on his face that said, "Where does this guy come from? Does he not get it? These gringos are really stupid!" Finally he found his tongue and said, "Because then we will die!"

"And why are you afraid of dying?" I questioned, undeterred.

For a moment his face turned blank in disbelief at the apparent stupidity of the question. Then a frown appeared on his forehead. Ahh, he was finally thinking.

"Well... because...." He paused for some time and asked, "Isn't everyone afraid to die?"

I was determined not to give him my opinion, but rather to make him analyze the issue further until he found answers of his own. I knew most people in Argentina were Catholic, and I hoped this could function as a useful point of reference that would guide him to a new, fearless perspective on life. "Are you religious?"

"Yes," and he showed me the little golden cross around his neck.

"Well, what does the Bible teach you about death? Was Jesus afraid of death? What about all the martyrs that were crucified or eaten by the lions in the Roman theaters: Were those Christians afraid of death?"

He thought about the question. Distracted from the storm, his fear faded away and his hands relaxed.

"Well...," he finally responded, "No. They knew they were going to Heaven."

"Wouldn't it be a great adventure if you could travel to Heaven and find out for yourself what it is like?" I asked.

"Well...yes, but what if I wouldn't go to heaven?"

"I personally do not believe in hell. However, if that's what you're afraid of, maybe you can think of something you can do right now which could decide your destiny! According to the Bible, who will go to Heaven?"

"Those who believe and have faith in God."

"Doesn't the Bible also say that God is the Almighty?"

With a questioning tone he answered, "Yes?"

"So if God is Almighty, He would not let an airplane crash just by accident, right? It would be part of His bigger plan, of which surely none of us mortals have a complete picture. If we don't want to die, if we are not prepared to leave this earthly plain yet, aren't we questioning

8

His plan and His judgment?" I paused for a second to give him time to think about the question, and then continued, "So is there anything you could still do, according to your religion, that could decide your destiny in death if this plane were to crash?"

He sat there, thinking, until suddenly his face lit up. A light bulb had clearly turned on. "I have never thought about death in such a way!" he energetically replied. "Now I realize that when I can accept whatever will happen to me, I will go to Heaven, because by doing so, I show my ultimate faith in God and my preparedness to follow His greater plan. It is not up to me to question His judgment and plan." He stayed quiet for some time, and then continued in a somewhat depressed tone, "But this is not easy! Fear sometimes just crawls onto me and takes control over me. How do I prevent this from happening?"

His brain was certainly working, and I liked how far he had taken the subject. Meanwhile, the worst part of the thunderstorm had passed and other than the occasional bump, the flight was now going smoothly. "How do you think the early Christians and Jesus managed their fear and did not allow it to take over when they faced death?"

"Well, they were focused on setting an example."

"An example of what?" I questioned.

"An example of how to live, of the values they stood for! An example of accepting their destiny with grace! The ultimate example of their faith!" he said adamantly.

"In other words, you are saying they knew what they stood for, what their values were and that no matter what, they would not give up their beliefs and convictions, even if that meant death. So, would it be fair to conclude that when you know what you are about and always stay true to yourself, when you realize you do not control when or how you will die—and die we will all do—and when you have faith that everything happens for a reason according to one master plan, then there is no reason to be afraid of death, or anything else, for that matter?"

"That is right!" the boy said excitedly. "It is not up to me to question what happens to me. I just need to have faith in God's plan and live like a good Christian. This means I should never betray my values and be open to the lessons God teaches me in all the experiences He presents me with, no matter how bad they seem at first."

"Did you see that spectacular lightning show when we flew through the thunderstorm?" I asked.

"No," he responded. "Fear had taken such control of me that I only saw disaster and death in my mind. As a result I did not see anything beautiful. When fear takes over, it prevents you from seeing the beauty of God's creation. My Incan grandmother taught me that, but despite having that knowledge I have never been able to control my fears. Yet seeing it now, in the context of life and death, it all makes sense."

"Well, I hope this will help you in terms of managing fear in the future. Yet there is another life-obstructing emotion of which you should be aware: worry, which is just an extension of fear. At times of worry and fear we also miss the lessons and opportunities that are presented to us. I think you'll discover fear is the biggest hurdle to overcome on your path towards growth and happiness. Always realize that when you are afraid of something, you will grow and understand another piece of this earthly existence and the divine plan by *challenging your fear and conquering it.* The greatest growth always takes place when you find yourself outside of your comfort zone. Young man, what is your name?"

"Mario," he said, shaking my hand.

"I am Paul. It is nice to meet you, Mario. You are a very smart young man!"

We chatted some more and I learned that Mario lived in Salta and was returning from visiting his grandparents in Buenos Aires. He volunteered to act as my guide in Salta so I would not leave without discovering the town's hidden treasures. I didn't know what the hotel owners had in mind for me, so I told him I would call as soon as I had a better idea of my schedule. I was only going to be in Salta for two nights, so that would not leave me all that much time. Yet deep inside I hoped to be able to take him up on his invitation. It would give me the opportunity to get to know the real Salta and have some conversations that did not revolve around hotels.

Once we landed we shook hands and both of us went our own way. The general manager of the hotel was waiting for me outside of the airport. He was a friendly man in his mid-thirties. In the taxi to the hotel he told me he had moved from Buenos Aires to Salta only two months ago.

"Don't expect too much! Salta is just a small provincial town, nothing like Buenos Aires," he stressed.

I was happy to hear that, but had the clear impression he preferred his probably more glamorous life in Buenos Aires.

Are Human Beings Being Human?

The taxi took us right into the heart of Salta with its small streets and row houses dating from the first half of the 20th century. I detected strong Spanish influences in both the atmosphere and architecture of the town, and I hoped the beautiful hacienda accents would be incorporated in the hotel building we were heading for.

To my disappointment, the taxi stopped in the center of the town before a concrete hotel dating from somewhere around the early seventies. However, my dislike for the building's appearance was compensated for by its excellent location: on the corner of the cross-junction of the town's two main streets. The property was dated, yet too modern-looking in contrast to the colonial Hispanic character of the town. Rush hour was over, and the two main streets were almost empty. The sun was slowly setting, already too low to spread its warming light into the streets.

I got out of the taxi and was engulfed by the dry heat radiating from the pavement and facades, which had been bathed in sunlight all day. When I turned around to enter the hotel an old woman, her open hand begging for some money, stood right in front of me. Her deeply wrinkled face was dry and strongly tanned from the sun. Her hair was covered with a black scarf and she was dressed in typical traditional Incan clothing. She had a small hump on her back and was bending slightly forward, her right hand leaning on a stick and her left one asking for some money. I reached into my pockets but could not find any change at all. I realized I had forgotten to get some cash at the airport upon my arrival.

Until that time I had taken note of what the old woman looked like and how she was dressed, but I had never looked directly at her. The hotel general manager gestured me to walk into the hotel and not give her anything. I was astonished by his blatant lack of empathy for the needs of this old woman. She was most likely someone's mother and someone's grandmother. Like all mothers and grandmothers she was the representative of the Mother of all creation, Mother Earth. We should honor the lives and wisdom of these women, and here I was being gestured to walk by this grandmother and ignore her request. I wanted to tell her to wait for a moment, until I could get some cash at the reception desk, but it was then that I looked into her eyes.

Such deep and dark windows into her soul! No, not her soul, but the soul of humanity. I felt like I was looking into the eyes of the Divine. I had no idea how long I stood there, speechless, my feet nailed to the ground. I would *never* forget those eyes!

Suddenly I felt the hand of the general manager touch my arm. It took me out of my trance-like state, and I signaled to the old woman to stay there as I rushed through the hotel lobby to the reception desk. I was focused, and on a mission. "Can you get me ten pesos and put it on my room account, please?"

The dumbfounded receptionist stared at me with a questioning look. My question must have taken her by surprise. Obviously these were not the first words she expected from an arriving VIP upon check-in.

"Can you get me ten pesos and put it on my room account, please!?" I repeated impatiently.

"Certainly, sir!" she finally stammered, crossing eyes with the general manager to make sure she had permission for this. "Would you like one bill of ten pesos or ten coins?"

"Whatever is easiest, but I would like it fast," I snapped.

In no time I had a bill of ten pesos, and I walked outside to give it to the old lady. To my surprise the street was completely empty. I walked around the corner in the hope of finding her there, but the other street was also totally empty. Where had she gone? There was no way she could have walked down such a long street in such a short time. The stores along both streets were closed, and this certainly did not look like an area where she lived. From the look of her I expected her to live in a small house on the outskirts of Salta, but certainly not smack in its center. I was puzzled and disappointed.

In disbelief I looked down both streets again. Maybe the light had played a trick on me and she *was* walking somewhere further down the street. There was an eerie, silent atmosphere in each direction. This was the crossing of the town's two main streets. It was early evening, and yet there was not a living soul present in either street.

"What is going on?" I heard from behind me.

I turned around and found the general manager staring at me, an inquiring look on his face.

"The old lady," I said. "She is gone."

Still questioning, he responded, "Yes...?"

"I just wanted to give her some money," I explained. "It's wrong when a *grandmother* has to beg like that. I wanted to give her something but had no cash on me. And now she is gone!" I uttered, disappointed. "It's like she vanished from the streets of Salta."

The general manager shrugged his shoulders and opened the door of the hotel for me. I walked in, explained things to the receptionist and apologized for being so abrupt earlier. Then I checked in and went to my room.

I opened the door to a stale-smelling, colorless room with cheap and worn furniture. There was not enough light in the room—a classic problem of most older hotel rooms! I unpacked my suitcase, hung my clothes in the closet, opened my briefcase and put my laptop on the desk.

The first thing I always did upon arrival in a hotel room was try to connect to the internet and download my e-mail messages from headquarters. As was the case in most old hotel rooms, there were no electrical sockets or telephone jacks next to or above the desk. I got down on my knees and found them under the desk.

In this position I also got a good idea of how well housekeeping cleaned the rooms. Right in front of my nose, a few inches under the desk, was a shriveled piece of paper. I picked it up to throw it into the wastebasket when some scribbled letters caught my eyes: "...being human?"

For some reason it made me think about my experience with the old woman, and I opened the piece of paper. Irregular, large letters, written diagonally across the paper, shaped the words, "Are human beings being human?" Some smaller letters at the bottom read, "Want to find out more? Meet me in Ayacucho on March 21st." As it was March 14th, that was in seven days.

I don't know what caused me to keep the piece of paper. Initially I wanted to throw it away, but something stopped me from doing that. Yet I really didn't know what to do with it, so I put it in the breast pocket of my shirt. "Are human beings being human?" What an interesting question!

I realized I did not even know what 'being human' meant. What was the meaning of the word 'human'? Never before had I given this any thought, but I guessed it had its origin in Latin and I made a mental note to look it up as soon as I had some time.

"Where is Ayacucho?" I thought next, not that I was planning to go there. Why would I? There wasn't even a name on the note to indicate its recipient, and of course the question was not directed at me! Still, I wondered to whom it had been posed, and what the context of the question was. "Are human beings being human?" I pondered that thought.

The sound of the phone ringing snapped me back to the business at hand.

"Is everything okay with the room?" the general manager's secretary asked.

"Uh, yes," I stammered. When you're the guest of the house, what else can you say other than that everything is fine, even in the worst of hotels?

15

"The general manager would like to know if you would want to tour the hotel right now or tomorrow morning, and if you would like to join him and the owner for dinner tonight."

"I will meet him downstairs in fifteen minutes for a quick tour, and then we can go straight to dinner afterwards," I replied.

"I will tell him, sir," she said politely.

Taking Care of Business

F irst I quickly tried to connect to the internet. To my surprise, it worked. In most small towns in Latin America and certainly in older hotels, it was impossible to connect to the internet with my laptop, but today I was lucky. After I downloaded a large number of e-mails though, I wondered how fortunate I really was. When did I have time to read all this?

However, while the number of e-mails always looked overwhelming at first sight, it usually proved to be not bad at all because a lot of the e-mails were not directed at me. It was a modern business trend for people to copy everyone they could possibly think of, even on the most trivial of e-mails. It was an easy way for people to cover their backs and spread their responsibility around! Now, nobody could blame them in case something went wrong, because everyone had been informed about what they were doing. If no one complained or stopped them, that meant their planned action was automatically supported. In addition, they copied others to ensure that everyone noticed how much work they were doing just in case management considered cutting their position.

I answered the few urgent e-mails, then headed down to the reception area. When I looked for the stairs I noticed there was only one central emergency staircase. This would certainly become a safety issue according to our hotel chain's standards, which prescribed a minimum of two emergency staircases.

The general manager was already waiting for me and provided me with a quick tour of the hotel. The hotel was dated and worn down. Approximately ten percent of the rooms were refurbished; the rest of them were old and scruffy. The lobby was nicely modernized in art-deco style, but I knew that this partial renovation would not have the expected economic return. In fact, the renovated lobby would *contribute* to increasing guests' dissatisfaction, since it would raise expectations about the quality of the accommodation! Upon arrival, a guest would check into the nice lobby, only to receive an old, rundown room to stay in! Thus the hotel's renovation plan, spread out over a six-year period, was simply not working. Such partial and unsuccessful makeovers happened all the time in hotels, and by the time the renovation of the last room was complete, the first rooms would be worn and the cycle would have to start all over again. So hotel owners would keep pouring money into their hotels, only without ever increasing guest satisfaction or impacting market performance.

During dinner I tried to explain this, but as usual found the owner's mind so set on the renovation plan that it stifled all flexibility and rational decision-making. Before retiring that evening we planned another meeting in the morning with the other hotel partner. There I would try to explain the mistake in their renovation plan once more, most likely to no avail. This hotel would not create a positive guest experience, and so I knew we would not want to incorporate it in our hotel chain's portfolio.

This made me hope that the meeting would be over by lunch so I could explore this nice provincial town during the rest of afternoon and evening. "I should give Mario a call and see if he can show me around," I thought.

Around eleven p.m. I was back in my room. I quickly prepared for bed, but before falling asleep I recalled the events with the old woman earlier in the day and wondered if finding the little piece of paper was just a coincidence. Where was Ayacucho? Would it be close by? Maybe it was a village close to Salta or a meeting place, a bar or someone's name. Without answers, and tired after a long day, I finally fell asleep.

The next morning, before my meeting with the owners, I quickly phoned my teenage friend. To my delight, Mario said he could meet with me at three that afternoon. He proposed to show me around town and take me out for dinner. I found myself already looking forward to it.

The morning meeting went according to my expectations. I toured the hotel again, now with both owners who proudly explained to me their six-year refurbishing plan. I tried to explain to them how to get a higher return from the dollars they were planning to invest, but to no avail. We went for lunch, got to know each other a little bit and all regretted we could not do business together. By around two o'clock I was back in my room.

Mario was going to pick me up in an hour. That gave me just enough time to change into something more casual and download my e-mail again. In reviewing my messages, one in particular caught my attention. It was about a new hotel project in Peru. No details were provided yet, but I liked the idea of having to visit Peru. I hoped to be able to link a weekend to it and visit Machu Pichu. Old archaeological ruins had always interested me, and I had heard that the unique mountaintop setting of this ancient Incan site was spectacular.

Coincidence becomes Mystery!

At exactly three o'clock the phone rang.

"Hi Paul, it's Mario. I am in the hotel lobby. Are you ready to go?" an excited voice said.

"I'll be down in a minute," I replied.

I grabbed my wallet and left my room. In the lobby a broadly smiling Mario awaited me.

"Good to see you again," he said, "I was not sure you would call. After all, why would a gringo businessman hang out with a teenage goof like me instead of the important people in town?" he grinned.

"You cannot believe what a break this is for me," I replied. "Let's get moving! I would like to see the real Salta. Maybe we can take a taxi and you can direct the driver on a tour around town."

"Good idea," Mario replied, enthused. "And afterwards, I will walk you down the center of town and we'll grab a drink and an empanada at Antonio's."

"Sounds good."

We left the hotel and got into one of the waiting taxis around the corner.

Salta is a beautifully preserved colonial town. It has very charming Spanish colonial architecture with white walls and red tiled roofs. Its setting in the Andean foothills with the towering mountains of the Andes guarding the town is breathtaking. We visited the cathedral, the beautiful church of San Francisco and the castle of San Lorenzo. I had never expected such picturesque historic colonial architecture here in the northwest of Argentina.

Mario had not been able to stop talking about his town since we got into the taxi. Like a professional guide he told me about its history and how the Spanish Conquistadors had entered the region, coming down from Peru. They founded the city following the orders of the governor of Peru in 1582. I enjoyed seeing the pride in Mario's eyes as he passionately presented his hometown to me. After a comprehensive taxi tour, Mario directed the driver to stop and we continued on foot.

Twenty minutes later we arrived at the central market place featuring more of the same colonial architecture and covered arched walkways. Around the corner, in front of a butcher, cheese and wine grocery store, Mario turned to me and said, "This is Antonio's. I am going to let you taste the best empanadas, goat cheese and chorizo you ever had in your life!"

I had no idea what empanadas were, but nodded my head anyway.

As soon as we entered we were indulged in a distinct aroma of cheese, meat and wine. In the back of the grocery store were some dark wooden tables and chairs. Along the walls of the long rectangular shop were thick oak shelves loaded with different wines, pates, oils, herbs, cheeses and different meats. Scattered around the dark old wooden floor were stacked wooden crates with more products on display. All kinds of different sausages in varying sizes hung from the ceiling and on the sides of the shelves. Antonio's had a very casual, rural atmosphere. This was one of those places you would never find as a tourist, and I considered myself lucky to have found someone like Mario who would allow me to experience this unique restaurant/cafe/grocery store.

We sat down and Mario ordered some different meats, cheese, empanadas and Argentinean red wine. As soon as the food was ordered, the teenager turned to me, excited but serious, and said, "You cannot believe what happened to me earlier today on my way to your hotel! I passed the church of San Francisco, and in front of the big wooden doors was an old woman begging for money. She was Incan

21

and dressed completely in the traditional dress. I reached for some coins in my pocket, gave them to her and wanted to continue on my way when she grabbed my arm. When I looked at her and my eyes met hers, the rest of the world disappeared. It felt like I was drowning in her eyes. They were so dark... so deep.... It was like looking into the eyes of God. They were like windows right into the soul of humanity."

As Mario was telling his story, I found the hairs on my neck standing straight up.

"Then," Mario continued, "she smiled at me and surrounded my heart with love. It was such a peaceful and serene moment. The rest of the world around us did not seem to exist anymore. Suddenly she pushed something in my hand, stammered in broken Spanish, 'the gringo,' and walked away. I opened my hand and found a shriveled piece of paper with a question scribbled on it."

"What was the question?" I asked anxiously.

"Are human beings being human?"

A shiver ran up my spine. What was all this about? What was going on here?

"As soon as I read the question," Mario continued, "I turned around and the old woman was gone. It was like she had vaporized into thin air. There was no way for her to walk that fast down the street and around the corner. I am sharing this with you not only because it was so mysterious, but because she said, 'the gringo.' ...But there really was no way she could have known I was going to meet you...was there?"

I sat stunned, frozen in my chair. Mario noticed my paralyzed state and a questioning frown appeared on his face. Finally I found my tongue and shared the experience I had had with the old woman upon my arrival at the hotel. Then I pulled the piece of paper I had found under the desk in my room out of my pocket and put it on the table in front of Mario. Speechless, he stared at the scribbles on the paper as he read, "Are human beings being human? Want to find out more? Meet me in Ayacucho on March 21st."

"How can this be?" he stammered. "What is going on here? Somehow it seems this message is for *you*."

"For me?" I objected. "I just found this piece of paper under the desk because housekeeping didn't do a good job, that's all."

"So then why did you keep it?" Mario questioned while he raised his eyebrows. "And why did the old woman tell me 'the gringo?' Certainly all this is more than just coincidence!"

"But why *me*? ...How did she know I was going to stay in that room? How could she get that note there? How did she know you were going to meet with *me*? And what do *I* have to do with this question? Sure, it's an interesting question, but I certainly don't have the answer. I don't even know what 'human' stands for. And where or what is Ayacucho? I am leaving here tomorrow morning, and I don't have the time to stay here until March 21st in order to meet with someone. Maybe she just said 'the gringo' so that I could give you my piece of paper and *you* could visit with her at Ayacucho?"

Mario did not seem prepared to accept the task, and asked, "Don't you know where Ayacucho is?"

"How am I supposed to know? I just arrived here last night! I don't know the region nor this town!"

Mario smiled in response. "Ayacucho is not in this town nor region. It's not even in this country!"

"You know where it is?"

"Of course," he said. "I am a good student and as part of our geography classes we need to know the different cities in Latin America. Ayacucho is a Peruvian town high up on the East Side of the Andes."

"Peru?"

"Yes. Peru. It is a Spanish colonial town, and its name comes from *Quechua*, the Inca language, and means 'corner of the dead.'"

"But I can't go to Peru, and I certainly have no business in a Peruvian town in the Andes known as 'corner of the dead!' Neither can I imagine this old woman to have the resources to travel to Peru and meet me there on the twenty-first. Why would she not meet with whomever she wants to meet with right here in Salta?"

"Maybe she did not write the piece of paper?" Mario tried. "Maybe she was only a messenger…"

"No," I barked, still objecting to my involvement. "All this just doesn't have anything to do with me!"

Mario got a triumphant smile on his face.

"What are you laughing at?" I snapped.

"What are you afraid of?" he responded in reply.

"I am not afraid of anything!" I denied. "This just doesn't make sense."

"Exactly! It's mysterious, it's strange, it's incomprehensible. It doesn't make sense, so it is out of our comfort zone! So doesn't that make it worth exploring? Did you not teach me that the greatest personal growth occurs at times when we push ourselves out of our own comfort zones, and that growth and learning is what life is all about?"

"Uh...yes. But this is impossible!"

"When you say that something is impossible, don't you limit your own learning opportunities?" Mario replied immediately.

Oh, what a good question! This young boy had certainly taken our conversation on the plane to heart, and currently he was turning the tables on me. "Well, science has proven that certain things are possible and certain things are not possible," I hedged.

"Have they?" Mario questioned.

"Well, they must be teaching you other things than geography in school! Most certainly your school program includes physics, chemistry and biology," I answered somewhat cynically.

"Yes, of course," Mario said, "but it seems to me that the basic philosophy which is dominating our scientific era has created science's biggest limitation."

"And that limitation is...?" I asked curiously.

"Well," he explained, "most scientists start from the premise that something first needs to be proven and understood before they support and accept a certain phenomenon. They act like everything outside of the scientific field—that which has not been studied, clinically repeated and proven—simply does not exist and therefore is impossible.

"But what if there is a piece that scientists still have not discovered? What if there is something science does not understand or only *some* people can do, feel or sense. The fact you can observe something but not explain it, or prove how it works, does not make it any less true. It only means it requires more study. I believe that science would progress much faster, and people like Albert Einstein and other great scientists would not have encountered so much initial opposition to their theories if the scientific world would start from the premise that everything is possible until proven otherwise. This would open up people's minds and cause society to support research for that which we do not yet understand."

"That is an interesting observation," I replied.

"In my mind," Mario continued, "'impossible' does not exist. I believe we should be open to everything in order to evolve to our full potential. Once we say 'impossible' we limit our own potential. Certainly the Romans would have thought it impossible to walk on the moon, but we did. From my point of view everything is possible as long as there is enough focus, resources, passion, perseverance and time committed to what we want to achieve or explore."

"So give me an example of science-limiting attitude," I challenged.

"Take, for instance, witching. Throughout the centuries and still today, farmers in the Andes have used witching, also called dowsing, to find water. Not all of them can do it, but in each

25

community there's usually one person, in a lot of cases the healer of the area, who can find water with the use of a forked stick. Those who are good at it can even say how much water there is and how deep you have to dig to find it. I have read that a lot of people around the world have this skill, and that some have even found oil and gas with it. However, science does not understand how dowsing works. They have not proven nor explained this process to find water. As a matter of fact, scientists are at an absolute loss. They have no idea how it is *possible* to find water with such primitive tools. Therefore, they declare dowsing to be superstitious and non-scientific. It's *impossible* because the methodology has not been scientifically proven. If scientists would open up their minds to such phenomena and explore the subject seriously, more funds could become available for researching the topic. Ultimately we could discover how this low-cost method for finding water really functions, and who knows what else would be revealed in the process?!"

"I never considered this," I admitted, "but I understand your point of view."

"So you will go?" Mario asked, excited.

"Go where?"

"To Ayacucho!"

"Why? No!" I shouted.

"But you should explore this mystery. You told me in the plane that we should not question the Divine plan, and that we should learn from the growth opportunities which life presents to us. You told me that everything happens for a reason. So you have to go!" he said passionately, almost commandingly.

Mario was using my insights against me! But had I really meant what I had told him? Would I be able to live up to those insights, or did I only have a good understanding of them?

"I will consider it," I eventually answered.

In the meantime the food had arrived and I was enjoying a delightful feast of all different kinds of sausages, cheeses and some excellent Argentinean red wine. An empanada turned out to be a sort of meat pie turnover or pastry in the shape of a half moon. It is available in a variety of fillings, and we were having both pork and beef empanadas.

"So how was your meeting?" Mario asked, changing the topic.

"Ahh, a bit disappointing." I explained what had happened, and how it frustrated me when people would waste their money, despite my professional advice, instead of investing it in solutions that had a proven return on investment.

When I was finished, Mario reflected thoughtfully on my words and after a pause asked, "Why does that frustrate you?"

While I had recognized a great coaching opportunity on the plane when I met Mario, this boy was now coaching me!

"Why does that frustrate me? I don't know," I admitted. "I guess if I had that kind of money I would make much better use of it."

"Still," Mario said, "whether they follow your advice or not should not make a difference to you. They have the right to make their own choices! You have no control over that."

"Yes, but it's frustrating because I know what the outcome of their choice is going to be, and it is not going to be what they expect. They asked for my advice, and I gave it to them based on my experience and knowledge of this industry. Yet instead of valuing the information, they are going to do things their way, like thousands have done before them."

A deep frown appeared on Mario's forehead in the painstakingly long silence that followed my last words. Just when I started to think that I was done with being put on the spot and wanted to change the subject, Mario said, "Well, maybe that is a learning process they have to go through. We don't know where somebody else is in their personal growth process. Maybe they need to have an experience where they disregard advice that was given to them, stubbornly follow their own course and burn their fingers in order to learn some important lessons and become wiser people. Couldn't that be possible? ...Still, I don't understand why this made you so upset, upset enough to release such negative emotions."

"It did not release negative emotions in me!" I snapped.

"Oh. Well then, what *is* frustration, according to you?" Mario cleverly asked.

This boy was getting way too good at this, and it just wasn't pleasant to look into the mirror he was presenting! "Well, okay, I guess frustration is a negative emotion," I conceded, "and I probably should not have let it get to me."

"That is right. You shouldn't, because it only affected your own mood and energy level in a negative way. It probably did not concern them at all. ...So why exactly did this upset you? ...You still have not answered the question as to why it frustrated you," Mario tried again, carefully but tenaciously.

He was not giving up, and while I did not enjoy looking into this mirror, now that the subject was on the table I might as well think about it and deal with it for my own good. What Mario was pointing out had been happening throughout my entire life. When people did something wrong, chose not to follow my advice or did not understand what I was trying to explain to them, I would get frustrated. Such emotions always reduced my own energy level and negatively impacted my positive outlook on life. Mario was probably correct that it was not really affecting anybody else but me, and this because I allowed it to. But *why* was it happening?

"I guess I am getting frustrated because I have the underlying expectation when I provide advice that people will value this and follow it. The same occurs when I try to explain something to someone. I expect people to understand what I teach and sometimes they just don't because we are all different."

Mario certainly had me thinking. He was actually a good coach!

"So can you *make* people understand you or follow your advice?" he asked.

"No..."

"Why not?"

"Well, because I do not control them," I replied.

"So what do you control?" Mario continued his line of questioning.

I had to think about that one. What Mario was pointing out was that most of my feelings of frustration, and sometimes anger, were the result of my attempt to control others or certain events. And of course that falls outside of our control.

"We only control our own actions and choices," I said.

"Right!" he smartly confirmed. "And how does faith relate to that?"

I finally caught on. He was using the insight of faith, which I had helped him to discover on the plane the previous day, and had linked it cleverly to my emotions of frustration. "Well, we have to have faith that the reality that presents itself to us is presented to us for a certain reason. It's like we discussed yesterday," I smiled, letting him know I had understood.

"We should discover the learning in it," I continued. "We can control only how we personally will deal with this reality to the best of our knowledge and ability. Once we have done this we should detach ourselves from the outcome and just be open to whatever is presented to us in return. For we only control ourselves; any other perceptions of control are merely an illusion. We don't control our environment or the people in our companies, family or society. And we should have faith that whatever happens to us is happening for a reason. We should learn and grow from life's learning opportunities and move forward on our journey.

"You know, Mario," I said, "this all makes sense from a rational point of view. It is exactly the same thing we talked about yesterday, but it is difficult for me to leave my emotions out of it because I really care about what happens to these people."

"So when you start loading yourself up with negative emotions," Mario pursued, "does that change the outcome of their actions?"

"No!"

"Does it make you feel good, increase your energy and put you in a caring mood?"

"No!" I reluctantly admitted again.

"Just as it was difficult for me yesterday to manage my emotion of fear, it probably is not easy for you either to manage the negative emotion of frustration. I understand you care," Mario said, "but that's still no reason to allow this to affect you in such a negative manner, because as with me on the plane, it prevents you from seeing the beauty around you and learning the lesson. Once you have done the best you can, according to your knowledge and abilities, there is nothing more you can do, is there? ...So when others decide to continue their course you can only acknowledge and respect their freedom of choice. If this leads to a negative outcome, then empathize with that. That is about all you can do. If your actions do not lead to your targeted results, the only thing you can do is learn from the experience and move on. I believe that when you recognize this, you will be able to detach from the outcome of your efforts and be content in the knowledge that you have contributed your maximum efforts to your cause."

"But that logic sounds like we are never responsible for the outcome of things," I protested.

"Well, let's explore this together." Mario said, undisturbed in his newly discovered role of coach. "Are you responsible for developing hotels for your hotel chain?"

"Yes," I answered, curious to see where he was taking this.

"Did you make the decision to spend time with these owners of the hotel in Salta?"

"Yes, but I was told this could potentially be a really good hotel conversion," I protested.

"But was it your choice to follow through with it, or did anyone force you to it?"

"No, it was my choice and my decision to fly to Salta and spend time with these people. And all for nothing!"

"So who is responsible for allocating time to this and not getting the desired results?"

"I am," I admitted reluctantly.

"And who is responsible for getting the desired results for the investments in the hotel?" he continued.

"The owners are," I said understandingly.

"So responsibility is with those to whom it belongs," he concluded smartly. "But never say 'all for nothing!' You did not get the desired business results here in Salta, but the two of us have had some great conversations, and now you have this fascinating mystery to solve! All this would not have happened if you had not decided to come. As you taught me yesterday, we must have faith and understand that there is a reason for everything."

"I have enjoyed our conversations and you are right: Everything has a reason, and I need to pay better attention to my own teachings. But I am not so sure how happy I should be with this mystery! I'll have to see where it leads," I replied.

It had gotten late and the conversation too heavy for that time of the day. Mario and I switched to some lighter topics like the quality of the Argentinean wine and life in the Andes. Then I asked Mario where he had gained such wisdom and maturity at his young age.

He shared with me that our conversation on the plane had refreshed the teachings of his grandmother on his mother's side with whom he had spent a lot of time the previous winter. She was Incan, still spoke the traditional Quechua language, and was living in a small village up in the Andes not all too far from Salta. She was the medicine woman of her village and, according to Mario, very wise. From the way he talked about her, I could tell he really admired her.

After Mario and I agreed to meet for breakfast before my departure the following day, I returned to my hotel room. It was close to midnight. Upon my arrival I decided to quickly download my e-mail again so I could work on it the next day on the plane. I rapidly skipped through the e-mail subject descriptions to check for anything urgent. One message captured my attention. "Hotel Development, Peru." I opened it and read as follows: "Paul, can you possibly change your flights and make a stop in Peru for a few days? A small Peruvian hotel group called Primus Hotels, with four hotels throughout the country, has expressed interest in our management services. It would be great if you could meet with the owners in Lima, visit all the hotels and start negotiations if you think a relationship with our hotel chain could be beneficial for both companies. Someone from the Primus company will drive you to all the hotels and show you around. Their hotels are in Lima, Ica, Nasca and Ayacucho." Ayacucho! In disbelief I stared at my computer screen. "Well," I thought, "whether I like the meaning of the town's name or not does not seem to matter anymore. Now I *have* to go. It seems like an invisible hand is leading me there!"

And from that moment onwards this mystery gained my full attention. I was actually becoming curious as to the next clue on this all-too-strange journey.

Synchronicity at Work!

When I entered the breakfast room in the morning the sweet aroma of fresh coffee greeted me. While I hadn't drunk coffee for at least ten years, I always enjoyed the smell of it. Somehow its aroma alone seemed to heighten the senses and instigate all kinds of interesting discussions. Mario was already waiting for me and smiled when I approached his table. His greeting was enthusiastic, as always. We got some food from the breakfast buffet and sat down.

"You would not believe what happened last night when I walked into my room," I said, excited, and told Mario about the e-mail I had received regarding the Peruvian hotel chain.

"Too cool! That is real synchronicity at work," he almost shouted when I finished my story. "See? I told you, you have to solve this mystery!"

"That is *what* at work?" I questioned.

"Synchronicity."

"Explain synchronicity to me. I am not familiar with the term."

"Did you never read *The Celestine Prophecy*?" Mario asked.

"No. Is that some ancient Inca manuscript or something?"

"No, it's a book!" Mario said with an expression of disbelief on his face. "That book made the concept of 'synchronicity' known among the broad public. I can't believe you haven't read it."

I started to feel old and out of touch.

"The term 'synchronicity' was captured by Carl Jung, a Swiss psychologist and philosopher," Mario continued. "Synchronicities are meaningful coincidences that help us progress on a certain path in life.

It is like what just happened with your e-mail for the Peruvian hotel development: You are dealing with this mystery which requires your presence in Ayacucho, and then suddenly you get this e-mail providing you with a reason to go. It's fabulously divine!" Mario cheered. "The universe wants you there! Now you just need to make sure you will be there on the right date!"

"I'm still not sure I understand," I said. "Certainly, the e-mail was a mysterious coincidence, but coincidences happen to everyone all the time."

"Of course," Mario responded, "but the point is they are not really random coincidences. They are meaningful coincidences, events or people that cross your path to direct your life, provide you with new insights or teach you a lesson. You are attracting those coincidences!"

"I *attracted* this e-mail?"

"Exactly! During our conversation on the plane you explained that we should not question the Divine plan. We should have faith and learn from the reality that presents itself to us. Well, synchronicity fits right into that. We all have a purpose in life. We are here for a reason. When our actions are in alignment with our purpose, we attract meaningful coincidences that help us along on our path. It is like the entire universe collaborates with us to make us succeed. As long as we are in sync with our purpose, we attract our own luck!"

I took a moment to consider different synchronistic events that had taken place in my life. I remembered when my wife and I wanted to move from Belgium to Canada. We had tried to play things safe and find a job and a house before moving with our three children. We had to feed them, after all! Yet it simply was not working and it seemed our North American dream would stay just that: A dream!

But neither of us were prepared to give up that easily, and so we decided to be bold and go anyway. Essentially we burned our bridges in our home country and moved to Canada with no security at all. I resigned from my company in Brussels, after which we sold our house, shipped our furniture and bought one-way plane tickets for the entire family. Once we had made that ultimate commitment, everything suddenly fell into place. Miraculously within a week I got a job with a company that reimbursed all my moving expenses and we found our dream house in the foothills near Calgary.

I also thought back to the only time that I had taken a job out of greed. It was a job with great responsibilities and tremendously good pay, but from the start I knew my learning would be limited since the function did not stretch my skills. On top of that, I was well aware that the required time commitment was going to keep me away from my family and would therefore conflict with my personal priorities. Well, during that year, nothing seemed to go right. When I finally decided to quit and follow my heart and dream again—even when it made no economic sense at all—everything fell into place. I started my own consulting business and had my first big consulting contract within the first three months. Ultimately this led to an executive position with a global company that allowed me to explore Latin America. Actually, I would not have been on this trip if I had not decided to follow my dreams in the first place! So synchronicity was certainly making sense to me. From now on, I was going to pay more attention to where my heart was leading me, and observe the meaningful coincidences on my path.

"I have observed such coincidences in the past," I replied to Mario, "but never did I consider that I was attracting them! Though looking back at my life with this perspective, it all makes sense. I have done some crazy things from a security and financial point of view. Each time before I do such stuff, I am afraid and try to build a safety net. That usually doesn't get me anywhere. It only distracts my attention from what my heart tells me to do. Once I finally make the decision to jump off the cliff into the darkness, things always work out and everything falls into place."

"That is synchronicity at work!" Mario said. "My grandmother told me that when you follow your heart and your dreams you enter a state of flow. Your focus attracts that which you need to succeed. Being in flow allows you to be more open and see opportunities you did not expect and which can help you reach your goals."

"Flow? You mean like what we call in sports, entering 'the zone?'"

"Exactly! All people go into flow with certain activities in their life like sports, music, acting, computer programming, constructing, dancing and so on. My grandmother taught me that once you become aware of your purpose in life and start to align your activities with it, your entire life can enter into flow or 'the zone,' and synchronicity is ever-present. I am so glad I met you yesterday and that you coached me through my fear. I spent the summer holidays in Buenos Aires and somehow, while there, lost my purpose and state of flow. I became afraid of losing things—like my life—and anxious to acquire things. And due to that newly-acquired fear I forgot to enjoy the beauty of life altogether! You got me back on track yesterday. The purpose of meeting you, at least for me, was to return to the path, on which my Incan grandmother has been leading me for years.

"She taught me—but I forgot—that whenever flow is *not* present, you should examine *yourself*, determine how you are blocking the universe from helping you and execute changes in your life that allow you to enter a state of flow again. I would think everyone finds it more attractive when they are in flow and the universe works with them instead of against them. What prevents people most commonly from following their dreams and attracting synchronistic events, though, is fear, just like what I was experiencing over the last few months. When fear kicks in people lose their focus and synchronistic events come to a halt."

"I guess in a certain way I have always sensed the existence of synchronicity," I responded, "but I was never quite sure how it all worked. I knew my fears were my biggest obstacles to success, growth and learning, but I had never linked them to following my dreams and living from my heart. When I am back home I am going to read more about Carl Jung. I find this synchronicity phenomenon very interesting!"

It was time for me to go and pack my bags. I had to catch a flight back to Buenos Aires. So I said goodbye to Mario and promised to stay in touch.

"Don't forget to let me know what the answer is!" Mario shouted as I walked out of the breakfast room.

I stopped and turned around. "The answer to what?"

"To the question, 'Are human beings being human?!' I want to know where this mystery will lead you," he explained. Then he laughed.

I smiled back and went to pack my bags. The general manager had arranged a taxi to the airport. I said goodbye to the hotel staff and left.

Exploring the Meaning of 'Being Human'

On the flight back to Buenos Aires I rearranged my schedule to include the Peruvian visit in such a way that it would bring me to Ayacucho on Tuesday, March 21st. I also decided to spend the remainder of the day in Buenos Aires itself to rearrange my flights and hotels. I had a weekend to kill before I had to work again, and I did not want to stay in Argentina. Nor did I fancy spending it in Lima since I didn't know anyone there.

I knew that an old friend of mine, George, whom I hadn't seen for fourteen years, was a priest in a small farming community near Santiago, Chile. I decided to call him and find out if I could visit him for the weekend. I had tried several times to meet with him on my previous trips to Chile, but somehow it had never worked out. He was studying at the university and was very busy with community activities. I thought it would be neat to stay in a local Chilean farming community before moving on to Lima on Sunday night. I also planned to call the Primus company from Buenos Aires to let them know I would be in their offices on Monday morning and had allocated time to travel to Ayacucho that night so I would be there on Tuesday, March 21st.

As soon as I landed and got to my hotel I started making phone calls to rearrange everything. I first moved the meetings I had planned for the following week. Then I phoned my wife and told her I would not be coming home just yet. I called George, who welcomed me for the weekend, and I spoke with Pedro from Primus Hotels to arrange my Peruvian visit.

Pedro was a very friendly man and was totally prepared to accommodate my time schedule. I told him I wanted to keep my time in Peru as short as possible in order to be home with my family the following weekend. He assured me we only needed four days to visit all the hotels. This schedule allowed me to take a night flight out on Thursday, March 23rd, which would bring me home on Friday, in time for the weekend. As planned we would travel to Ayacucho on March 20th, stay there the following day, and leave for Ica and Nasca on the 22nd. After my conversation with Pedro I booked the necessary flights and hotels. Rarely did my schedules work out so well and fast! "Synchronicity at work!" I thought.

That evening I had dinner alone. When I got back to my room, I started to ponder the question again: Are human beings being human? Since I had answered all my e-mails earlier that afternoon and had a good internet connection, I decided to explore the subject on the world wide web.

It did not take me long to find an online etymology directory for the English language at www.etymonline.com. I learned that the origin of the word 'human' stems from the Latin word 'Humanus,' which means 'man' or 'earthly being.'

Discovering the Latin root, however, did not help in relation to the question at hand. "What would 'being human' mean?" I wondered. I discovered that the words 'human' and 'humane' were used interchangeably until early in the 18th century, after which 'humane' became a word with its own meaning, namely 'the qualities befitting human beings.' What I wanted to know now was what those qualities were.

I wasn't impressed with my progress, and decided to try my luck with www.dictionary.com. Human was described here as 'a human,' member of Homo Sapiens, which again didn't get me any further. However, I did get some more insight into the meaning of 'humane,' which was described as: characterized by kindness, mercy or compassion and evidenced by an emphasis on humanistic values and concern. I found that *The American Heritage Dictionary* listed 'humanness,' 'compassionate,' 'humanitarian' and 'merciful' as synonyms for 'humane.' And *Webster's Revised Unabridged Dictionary* described 'humane' as 'pertaining to man,' 'having the feelings and inclinations creditable to man; having a disposition to treat other human beings or animals with kindness; kind; benevolent.' Its synonyms, according to *Webster's*, are 'kind,' 'sympathizing,' 'benevolent,' 'mild,' 'compassionate,' 'gentle,' 'tender' and 'merciful.'

Gradually I was getting a better picture! However, before turning my computer off, I searched for an online Latin thesaurus to find out the meaning of the word 'humanus' and its opposite, 'inhumanus.' I found my answers in the Latin On-Line Lexicon where 'humanus' was described as 'human,' 'of human beings,' 'a human being,' 'of good qualities,' 'humane,' 'kind,' 'educated,' 'civilized' and 'refined.' 'Inhumanus' was described as 'cruel,' 'barbarous,' 'inhuman,' 'rude,' 'uncivil' and 'uncivilized.'

I was glad my web search was shedding some light on the question. 'Are human beings being human?' meant are we, species of Homo Sapiens, earthly beings, being kind, sympathetic, mild, benevolent, compassionate, merciful, gentle, tender, and civilized, and do we live according to the values pertaining to humans? If we were to behave differently—be inhumane, cruel, barbarous, rude and uncivil— then why would we call ourselves human beings?

But what was civil, what were human values and who had determined those? Those were questions I would still need to answer. However, I was tired and it was already late at night. Happy with the progress I had made, I went to bed and had a good night's sleep.

Social Analysis of a Taxi Driver

The following morning, I got up, packed and left for Chile. I decided to skip breakfast in anticipation of a meal on the plane.

I checked out and waved a taxi down around the corner. By calling a taxi on the street rather than taking a hotel taxi I could reduce my fare by fifty percent or more. It was an attractive young female driver who pulled over and stopped right beside me.

"Where are you going to?" she asked with a beautiful smile on her face and sparkling energy in her eyes.

This was very unusual. Most taxi drivers in Buenos Aires drive old cars, seem bored with life, constantly curse traffic and are male. They just do their job without taking a lot of joy in it. But this young lady was different.

"To the airport, the international airport," I replied.

"Guess you did not want to pay the expensive hotel taxis," she giggled as she got out of the car and opened the trunk to load my baggage. "I don't blame you, and it is good business for me!"

I got in the taxi and off we went.

"So how was your stay in Buenos Aires?" she asked in the same joyful tone.

"It was good," I answered rather shortly.

"Where are you going to?" she said, not letting my cool response disturb her attempt to start a conversation.

This nice young lady seemed a pleasant and intelligent conversation partner. I just did not feel like talking about my work, my travels and certainly not about this mystery I had gotten tangled up in. Therefore, I decided to start *asking* questions in order to lead the conversation to a topic of my interest.

"I am going to Santiago," I replied. "How come an energetic young lady like you drives a taxi in a city where most taxi drivers seem to be middle-aged men?" I continued.

She smiled. "I am a university student," she said, "and this is a pleasant way to pay for my studies. The flexible times allow me to fit the job in with my course schedule, and besides, I meet a lot of interesting people."

"What are you studying?"

"Political science and economics!" she giggled.

"Why are you laughing about your studies?" I asked, a little confused.

"Don't you think it's ironic to learn about politics and economics at a university in Argentina when the entire political and economic system is in shambles?"

"Well, now that you are putting it like that, it does seem rather funny. So why did you choose this line of studies?" I asked, intrigued.

"Something has to change," she said, determined, "and if we have to wait until the men are getting it right, even my children will not see a change in their lifetime!" She joked on, but then continued more seriously, "If I want to enter politics in Argentina, I need a degree from the best university in Buenos Aires. It is not important what or how much I learn there; I just need the degree. I study a lot on the side and follow the politics from other countries in order to learn their best practices."

"So why is Argentina in such a precarious political and economic situation?" I asked.

"Well, you have the immense debt of the country and the contrasting social and economic situation between Buenos Aires and the rest of the country," she said. "But really all those elements, in which the politicians continuously get bogged down, are not the root cause of our situation. They are just problems, challenges to be dealt with! Unfortunately though, they are not being solved, and that is the real issue. Our politicians, and for that matter, a lot of business leaders as well, spend more time in fighting and arguing about possible solutions than creating and executing them! All their egos are in the way! They're more concerned about losing face than solving challenges!"

"Does that not happen all over the world?" I asked.

"I guess to a certain extent, but it's really taken to the extreme when Argentinean machismo gets involved." She grinned again and then continued resolutely, "It kills all creativity!"

"How do you come to the conclusion that egos kill creativity?" I questioned.

"What's the source of creativity?" she asked in return.

"Uh, I guess I don't really know. I have never given that any thought. I know creativity is necessary for our evolution, but I don't really know how it originates."

"Creativity finds its source in the duality on which all life is based," she said factually. "If everyone thought in the same way, nobody would think about doing something different. If that were the case, nobody would ever have thought about using a round object to roll things on and we would not have invented the wheel. So creativity originates from people's different perspectives."

"So following that logic, should you not have tremendous creativity in Argentina with all those different views the politicians and business leaders allegedly have?"

"We would if all those egos were not in the way," she replied, "and that is where our real problem is. Let me explain," she continued passionately. "What is conflict?"

"Is that not the process people go through when they have a difference?" I replied.

"No, not really," she commented. "You and I can have different opinions about the fastest way to get to the airport, but that does not mean we need to have a fight about it. We can talk about it, listen to each other, and try to discover the underlying grounds that support our unique perspective. Such conversation would help us to understand each other. As a result, we would both learn and come to a mutual conclusion about the fastest way to get to the airport. This could be either one of the ways we originally described, or a combination of both, depending on what we learned from our conversation. Solving a difference is a *constructive* process," she concluded categorically.

"So what is a conflict?" I asked.

"A conflict is an emotionally-loaded difference," she firmly stated. "It usually occurs when people are afraid of losing face, when they look at the situation from a 'win/lose' perspective rather than from a 'let's be constructive together' point of view. In conflict people don't listen to each other anymore. They have no interest in understanding the other's point of view. They're only focused on defending their personal position.

"A difference also becomes a conflict when someone gets frustrated with others' opposing opinions. This results from a lack of understanding of how unique we all are. When egos are involved, the emotions of fear, frustration and anger get immediately attached to the differences in opinion, and they then turn into conflicts. And as long as conflict rules, creativity has no chance to develop. The fear of losing face or of losing control, which is an illusion in the first place, turns differences into endless and fruitless win/lose games. Meanwhile, no real lasting solutions are found! It is only when people understand and respect that we are all different that we can learn from each other's unique perspectives and work out constructive solutions together. That is when we experience creative and constructive progress, which is also called evolution."

The silence she entered into then, most certainly with intent, emphasized her last statement and the power of her theory. "What a smart young lady," I thought. "With her determination to make a difference and such understanding of people, she could go a long way. Will she make history?" I wondered. Evita Peron came to mind. I did not remember the exact historical details of it all, but it seemed to me that female leadership had been important in Argentina's past and possibly could repeat itself.

"I am glad to hear such determination and energy," I praised. "It seems that you have thought things through really well. With young people like yourself, Argentina is sure to have a bright future."

A smile appeared on her face as a modest sign of accepting the praise.

"We are almost at the airport,' she said suddenly, changing the topic.

We remained silent for the last minutes of the ride, both of us in thought about the profoundness of the insights we had discussed. After what I had learned from Mario and from this young woman in her early twenties, I was convinced that Argentina would see tremendous change over the next ten to twenty years as this new generation rose to positions of power in both business and politics. "How exciting to see how young people evolve further and faster with each new generation. I guess that's what evolution is all about," I thought.

"We are here," she said energetically when she stopped at the entrance to the airport.

As she handed me my bags, I thanked her for the enjoyable conversation and inspiring insights, left her a good tip, and entered the airport.

The World Depends On Me!

Travel to Chile

I checked in at the Lan Chile counter and went to the gate. I enjoyed flying with this particular airline. Based on my previous experiences, they offered the best in-flight service in Latin America, which still included delicious hot meals. All the North American airlines had been cutting back on such a service.

The fully-booked flight left on time. As I expected, we received a good breakfast. A little later the stewardesses came around with the tax-free items. Because I was unable to open my laptop during the meal I had leisurely screened through the catalogue of offerings. A pair of sunglasses had attracted my attention, for I had lost my old glasses during my last trip in Mexico.

"Could I please have a look at these sunglasses?" I asked the beautiful Spanish-featured flight attendant.

"Of course," she replied sweetly.

Lan Chile always had friendly attendants. She handed me the glasses so I could try them on. They felt good. Then she handed me a little mirror so I could see what they looked like on my face. But rather than using the mirror, I turned to her and asked, "What do you think? How do I look?"

She smiled and said, "They look good on you, but why would you trust my opinion?"

"Why not?" I replied, astonished.

"Well, I am the one selling these glasses to you, so it could be in my interest to just *tell* you that they look good!" She laughed, then said, "But honestly, they look really handsome on you."

I laughed along with her, while deciding that she had made a very good point.

"I will take the glasses." I smiled and handed her my Visa card.

"Why do we trust someone?" I then questioned myself. "And what actually is trust?" I thought about the young taxi driver and wished she were sitting next to me. Certainly she would have had an answer to those questions!

But for now these questions had to wait. My meal tray had been picked up, which allowed me to open my laptop and work through the e-mails that I had downloaded that morning. I had to get this done now because I knew that by the time I would be able to connect again later in the day, I would have more e-mails to answer.

Half an hour later the pilot asked the cabin to prepare for landing. I always enjoyed the approach to Santiago due to the beautiful vista of the modern-looking city set against the backdrop of the Andes Mountains. Santiago was so different from Buenos Aires...actually, Chile was so different from Argentina, and there was absolutely no comparison between the Argentineans and the Chileans either!

Although the Chileans were more reserved, I had found them to be perfect gentlemen who were awesome to do business with. They were honest and open to new ideas. They played with their cards on the table, and constructively worked together to find solutions that would work for all parties involved. There was stability in the country, the economy was strong and Santiago had the look of a sophisticated, high-tech city. In that aspect it was actually unique in Latin America. But Chile was still a developing country, and visitors to the city would always be reminded of that when the drive from the airport to the city took them through the outer ring of Santiago. The slums! They did not look as bad as the slums around Sao Paulo, Brazil, or Mexico City, but for a Westerner the stark contrast between the high-tech riches and the living circumstances of the poor always created confusing emotions.

Today, however, I would not take that route. George would pick me up and take me west to the village where he lived. I was excited because it was the first time I would get to see something in Chile outside of Santiago.

The landing was smooth. I got through customs and picked up my luggage. As in any other international airport a lot of people were waiting at the exit. George wasn't amongst them. He had warned me he might be late due to some classes he had in the morning. It was only 12:15 though, and he had indicated he would be there around 12:30. I decided to sit down at a coffee shop across from the international exit and order one of their chocolate croissants. Some of the things I missed in Canada were the great Belgian and French chocolate pastries. To my delight, as I was a real chocoholic, this little coffee shop at the Santiago airport had real French pastries.

While I was waiting for my order, my eye fell on a pamphlet on the wall. It read, "The rise and fall of humanity." It was advertising a theater performance in Santiago. The title fascinated me, most definitely in the context of the question I was dealing with and my mysterious upcoming meeting in Ayacucho. As soon as George arrived, I would ask him if we could attend this performance. Maybe it could provide me with some further insights.

As I gazed over the group of people who were waiting at the exit for travelers to appear, I suddenly saw her. There she was! The old woman! She was completely dressed in traditional Incan clothing. I could not see her eyes since she was focused on the exit. I only saw her profile. "No...she cannot be the same woman as the one in Salta," I reassured myself. "No, this woman is waiting for someone; she did *not* come off the plane! There must be a lot of old women in the Andes who look like that...although the resemblance is striking." The entire encounter with the old woman in Salta suddenly was right in the forefront of my mind again.

"Here you are," an enthusiastic voice said beside me.

I turned to my left and George greeted me with a broad smile. I stood up and shook his hand. It had been more than fourteen years since I had seen him. I offered him a croissant and we sat down. I quickly glanced over to where I had seen the old woman, but she was gone. She had mysteriously disappeared, just like last time! She could have moved into the crowd, but somehow I knew there was more to it than that.

George and I updated each other about our life situations without going into any detail. Just the headlines: family, job, living circumstances, interests. Besides his job as community priest in three small farming villages, George was studying philosophy now at the University of Santiago.

"Can you take me to the play, 'The Rise and Fall of Humanity'?" I asked. "It is an intriguing title, and the topic is currently of great interest to me."

"The title is actually deceiving," he replied. "The play is not all that great. However, if this type of topic interests you, I am sure you are going to enjoy this afternoon."

"What have you planned?"

"We are invited to a barbecue at the house of two university professors. They also live in San Cristobal, my village. A few years ago they moved to the country because they did not like city life. There will be a bunch of interesting people there; the conversations are always stimulating. What else would you expect from a group of intellectual philosophers?" He smiled and added, "And you are 'the gringo,' so that will certainly stimulate the conversation!"

I was shocked. "What did you say?" I cried.

Worried, he looked at me. "Did I say something wrong? Don't you want to go to the barbecue?"

"No, about the gringo!"

"Oh, only that you are 'the gringo,' and that your presence will stimulate the conversation."

"What do you mean by that?"

"You'll see," he smiled.

I decided to drop the issue and follow Mario's advice: Go with the flow!

While we drove to George's village we talked some more about my family, our move to Canada, my work and my travels. After a one hour journey along the highway I saw an exit sign for San Cristobal. A few minutes later we were driving on a dirt road. Pure sand, no gravel. There was lush vegetation on the sides of the road, and in the distance the first houses started to appear.

Human Dominion Questioned

"That is my village," George said.

The village seemed to consist of one main street without pavement or sidewalk. Kids, barefooted and scarcely dressed, were playing everywhere. As we approached them they ran up to the car and waved to George. I noticed some finger-pointing at me, which each time resulted in some cheerful giggling. Their eyes followed us for a while, but then they continued their play.

To the right of the main street were some side streets laid out according to a grid system. In contrast to the surrounding area they lacked lush vegetation, and all the houses situated on them looked identical in style. They were simple square cubes constructed from concrete blocks with one door and one window facing the street. They seemed extremely small.

"That is where the farmers live," George explained. "A number of years ago the government executed a social housing plan and they constructed these houses for the farmers. It was a great improvement from what their living circumstances had been."

I could hardly imagine anything smaller and less comfortable, but George explained that having electricity, water and a sewage system was a tremendous improvement.

We drove on and I noticed some nicer houses ahead of us. They were not really big, but certainly nicer both in size and finish. They also had beautiful green gardens. We turned right and pulled into a driveway.

"This is where the professors live," George said.

Before I could get out of the car, a friendly, smiling, middle-aged woman came from around the corner of the house and walked up to George.

"Father George," she cried excitedly, "I am so glad you are joining us!"

When I got out she looked at me, came over and embraced me.

"And this must be 'the gringo.'"

There it was again: 'the gringo!' It was like I did not have a name. Why did people keep referring to me like that?

"I am Luciana. Welcome to my home," she said warmly.

"Thank you," I replied politely.

In the meantime the rest of the company had come around the house. They all greeted us warmly. George was clearly a popular guest. We were invited to follow the party to the backyard for the barbecue. As we walked towards there I asked George if he always got such a welcome when he went to a party. He explained it had to do with his job. Being a priest was held in high respect by this culture.

In the backyard I was offered a chair and immediately thereafter the Chilean traditional drink, Pisco Sour. I am not a great fan of strong alcoholic drinks, but with all eyes pinned on me in expectation, it was fairly obvious I had to try it. To their delight I drank it. Cheers and confirmations of how good their national drink was went through the room as I did so. I had drunk Pisco Sour and approved of it, so now everyone could relax.

Next I was served a large plate with vegetables, a big steak and as a beverage, some Chilean wine. During the meal it became clear that the Chileans were very proud of their wine, their beef and of course their Pisco Sour. They also wanted to know everything about me: where I lived, how many kids I had, what kind of work I did and what I thought of Chile.

In return I learned that Luciana was a renowned South American biologist and her husband, Luis, a philosophy professor. Both taught at the University of Santiago. There was Rosa, Luciana's mother, an older woman with a mysterious sparkle in her eyes. She lived with Luciana and Luis and continuously smiled at me during the entire party. She did not really involve herself in the conversation, but seemed to understand everything that was going on.

Pablo and Andrea, who were also present, were good friends of Luciana and Luis and also worked at the university. However, I did not get to know in which capacity. The last two completing the guest list were Sergio and Maria. Maria was a teacher at a high school in Santiago, and Sergio was a retired philosophy professor who had started a small wine business.

"Did you see that play at the theater?" Luciana asked Sergio.

"Yes, I did, but I really did not like it."

"Why not? It seems to cover an interesting topic," she replied.

The conversation immediately caught my interest. "Are you talking about 'The Rise and Fall of Humanity'?" I interjected.

"Yes," Luciana said, surprised. "Have you heard about it?"

"Well, I just saw a pamphlet about it at the airport. It does sound interesting."

"Well, as I said, it was not what you would expect," Sergio continued. "The play was good but it merely was a walk through history and the evolution of civilization, which then got abruptly destroyed when a comet hit the planet. I am sure there were more people like myself who expected to see a play worked out around the theme of humanity's self-destruction."

"That is indeed different from what I expected it to be," Luciana answered. "Like you, I thought it would be all about how our sense of superiority would lead to our self-destruction."

"What do you mean by 'our sense of superiority?'" Andrea asked.

"Well, it seems to me that we humans think the world, even the universe, revolves completely around us. We act like we are the center players in this vast cosmos and the captains of this planet," Luciana answered.

Pablo cleared his throat and entered the conversation. "Illustrate your point with some examples of what you mean exactly, Luciana."

"Well, take for instance the way we see our relationship with animals. As a result of the domestication of animals and the scriptures of some mainstream religious institutions, it is generally perceived that human beings are more advanced creatures—more civilized, sensitive and creative—than animals."

"And are you suggesting we are not?" Pablo asked skeptically.

"Absolutely!" Luciana stated adamantly. "In most of the world's old cultures they made no distinction between humans and animals. They referred to the human people, the eagle people, the deer people, the whale people, the horse people and so on. They even referred to the plant people! As a result these indigenous cultures managed to live in balance with their surroundings because they did not exploit any other beings. They understood the continuous cycle of life, which is built into the fabric of all that is."

"Which is?" Pablo questioned.

"The process from seeding and thinking to growing and creating to harvesting and declining to resting and death. You will find this cycle in everything under the sun, and throughout the entire universe. You will find it in farming, in plant life, in human life and even in business. But you are sidetracking me. What I was going to say was that those people of the old cultures understood how all these individual cycles were interconnected. They valued the life that the plant people, the deer people and the llama people offered to them so they could live. They understood too that their life was dependent on something else dying. This created respect and a bond of interdependence between humans and their animal and plant brothers and sisters. As a result they only took what they needed to survive and respected the land from which they lived. They knew that if they would hurt Mother Earth, sooner or later, due to the interdependence of all living things, those actions would come to haunt them, their children and their grandchildren."

"You are not seriously suggesting that we are equals to this yucca tree in the corner!" Pablo snorted.

"And why not?" Luciana questioned, slightly agitated.

I was enjoying this conversation and listening carefully. Luciana had some unusual perspectives and profound thoughts.

She continued, "In recent years science has caught up with the 'primitive' views of tribal societies and discovered that plants do have a nervous system. Experiments have shown that a plant's health improves when people genuinely care for it and talk to it. Biologists have discovered complex, low-wave communication among elephants, creativity in apes and a clear sense of self-consciousness in dolphins. With such discoveries being made in these fields, I think it is not too far-fetched to imagine that plants and animals are absolute equals to us. I personally believe they just have a different intelligence, a different experiential frequency maybe. After all, we've known for a while already that we are all vibrating energy. Maybe they just vibrate at a different sequence, which gives them a different experience."

"But clearly their communication skills and general abilities are inferior to ours!" Pablo tried.

"According to whom?" Luciana replied. "If more advanced beings from another place in the universe would land on earth and communicate telepathically, it would appear to us like they could not talk at all. Just because we do not understand or recognize a certain way of communication doesn't mean that such communication is inferior to ours!"

Pablo stayed quiet for a while. While he had been skeptical and made some ironic comments, he had been listening carefully to what Luciana had to say and did not seem to be as attached to his original perspective. I actually had to admire him for that.

"I am starting to see where you are taking this," he finally said carefully. "I had not considered that perspective. Go on; I would like to understand more."

In a more relaxed atmosphere, Luciana started to describe how she perceived the relationship between humans, animals and plants.

"Well, I believe each living thing on earth has its own unique way of communication, procreation, growth, creativity, emotional life and consciousness. I also believe that all living things have their own unique set of gifts. Dogs have a phenomenal sense of smell, horses their speed, elephants their strength, cats their flexibility, birds of prey their sight and humans their brain. Our analytical skill is unique to our species, but our specific gift does not make us better or worse than the others who possess equally valuable, but totally different, talents.

"Science has already demonstrated that both whales and elephants have the ability to communicate with other members of their species at great distances. We also know that coyotes, wolves, dolphins and apes each have their own language. I love riding horses, and have been experimenting with directing my horse by thought rather than by the bridle and my seat. Already I've found the results to be phenomenal! From what we have scientifically discovered up 'til now, it is not difficult to make the leap and assume that all living things have a way to communicate. We are in no position to judge the complexity of other species' language until we understand how they communicate and what they are saying."

"I can see that," I offered. "I am a bow hunter, and have spent a lot of time in the mountains in Canada."

"Do you mean they still hunt with bow and arrow in Canada?" Pablo laughed.

"Well, some hunters do," I replied. "It is like fly fishing in the world of fishing: It adds a level of patience and requires the hunter to develop a connection with nature in order to harvest an animal."

"So what do you hunt for?" Sergio asked.

"Deer and elk," I said. "The reason I am bringing it up is that I have observed animals communicate like Luciana described," I continued.

They all listened with the same attentive respect they had given to Luciana earlier.

"Elk are a challenging animal to hunt because they are so sensitive. As a bow hunter I only take a shot when the animal is within a thirty-yard range. Getting so close to a herd of elk doesn't happen all that often.

"It has happened numerous times to me that the elk were approaching and detected my presence before I was close enough to take a shot at them. On several of those occasions the herd split into two groups and ran away for a short distance. Then they would stop and start talking to each other. I have always been fascinated by those conversations, for it seems that a number of different animals in the herd are participating in it. And the variety in tones and sounds is enormous! Often they continue such conversations for fifteen to twenty minutes. Then suddenly the voices stop, and both parts of the herd move off into the same direction. It's like they have had a lengthy discussion about where to go and reach a collective agreement about what to do."

"That is exactly what I am talking about!" Luciana cheered, glad to get some support for her point of view.

"I also believe that animals have emotions," I continued. "I have noticed several times when I shoot one deer out of a small group, the other deer gather around the fallen one and some mourning experience seems to take place. When I then step out of my cover and approach the dead deer, the others run away for a short distance. Then they turn around like they are waiting for the fallen one to follow them. It usually takes quite some time before they reluctantly move on."

"Most certainly these animals have emotions!" Luciana joined in. "Have you never heard the cows calling all night long after their calves get weaned? Have you never observed the eyes of your dog when she is happy or when she has done something wrong? You can read the emotions in their eyes. Science has now confirmed that dolphins, gorillas and chimpanzees have an emotional life. So, simply because we have not been able to conclusively prove the emotional life of other living beings yet, doesn't mean they don't have one."

"I guess we can all see your point, Luciana," Pablo conceded, "but how would our sense of superiority lead to our destruction? After all, that was your original statement, right?"

"Well," Luciana started, "because we feel we are superior, we do not respect the animal and plant life around us and fail to learn from it. We might study them from a commodity point of view, but we fail to learn from their unique strengths and weaknesses. Because we do not recognize as a society the great potential for learning from our animal and plant brothers and sisters, we handle them as a commodity. From our superior perspective they're there for our use, period! More often than not, people see certain animals, insects or plants as pests and just kill them without purpose! This possessive mentality is at the basis of the destruction of the rainforest. We use the wood to make fancy furniture or floors, and farmers gladly clear the forest in order to increase their farmland so they can graze more cattle and supply the rich with yet another steak or burger."

"What do you mean with that last statement?" her husband asked.

"I am saying that the destruction of nature, which is occurring at a worldwide scale, is all for the sake of providing more and cheaper food and material wealth for the rich on this planet. I hope it is quite clear to everyone that destroying a piece of the rainforest so that more cows can graze makes absolutely no impact on the latest statistic from the United Nations, which has determined that twenty-five million people are dying from starvation each year. To put this in perspective: approximately seventy thousand people just died today because they did not get enough food to stay alive! This all happened while we, and the other rich people around the world, are enjoying an abundance of food!"

There was a silence of frustration and powerlessness in the garden. With some feeling of shame we looked at some of the leftover food. I oddly noticed that this gloomy statistic did not seem to diminish the whistling of the birds.

"As you all know, nothing will be wasted on *this* table!" Luciana lightheartedly broke the silence. "That is why we live in the country: so we can keep pigs and chickens that will be happily feasting on all the food *we* leave tonight!"

I admired Luciana for her deep insights and her ability to stay cheerful after discussing such a heavy subject.

Then she suddenly turned to me and said with a deep and serious voice. "But now 'the gringo' is here. That brings us some hope!"

I sat glued to my chair, unable to believe what I just had heard. All eyes were fixed on me, and I noticed Luciana's mother's eyes were sparkling even more brightly. I had this uncomfortable feeling that a great responsibility rested on me. "Why me?" I thought. "What do I have to do with this? How do they all seem to know? And why are they all calling me 'the gringo?'" I decided to try and get some answers. This mystery was getting on my nerves, and the people surrounding me right now seemed to be pretty open and intelligent.

"Luciana, why are you, and others, calling me 'the gringo' in such a way like I am the only gringo in the world? You make it sound like it is my name!" I tried.

She looked deep into my eyes and said, "I am afraid that if you have not found out yet, you still have most of the journey ahead of you. Unfortunately for you, it is not up to me to tell you more. Be patient. You will get your answers all in time."

While she did not answer my question, Luciana just had acknowledged there was a reason for which they all called me 'the gringo.' This also meant I seemed to have a task, and a number of people in South America apparently knew what that was. Still, I wanted to know more, to question more. It was like a great conspiracy, which everyone on this continent knew about, except for me. And I was the central character, or so it seemed!

"We should go," George said while getting up. The afternoon had progressed fast. "I still have to finish some work today," he explained.

Everyone stood up and in turn embraced George and me. The way people hugged me and shook my hand told me they wished me strength and good luck. I just didn't know with what or why.

Dilemma of Different Perspectives

We got into George's car and drove in silence for two blocks. We then turned left, where halfway down the street was an elegant wooden church. On the left side of the church was a little community building with a small playground. "It was a donation from the local landlord," George explained. On the right side of the church was a wooden house with a small treed and flowering garden behind it. George pulled up into the driveway and stopped.

"This is my home," he smiled.

That evening we had a modest supper together and talked some more about how different our lives were. After the meal we both concentrated on getting some work done. I downloaded my e-mail again, dealt with the important things and deleted or filed those items that did not require my input. Tired, we both went to bed early.

I was struck by George's modest way of living and wondered what it was like to constantly live with the contrast of extreme riches and real poverty right in your face. As the community's spiritual leader, he certainly had to deal with this contrast all the time. "I will have to question him tomorrow on that," I thought. While mulling over the afternoon's conversation, I fell asleep.

At breakfast George asked me what I wanted to do for the day. I explained to him how unusual it was to have some 'empty' days on a business trip in my fast-paced life, and therefore I just wanted to enjoy the day without loading it up with too many activities. We decided to go for a short drive in San Cristobal's surrounding area to give me a glimpse of the countryside, and then hang out in the garden during the afternoon.

When we left on our drive we encountered the same children playing on the street again. My appearance triggered similar finger-pointing and giggling reactions as it had the day before, upon my arrival in the village.

San Cristobal was located in a beautiful river valley. The river irrigated the fields where all kinds of vegetables and fruits were grown. The avocado and artichoke crops were very important for the village. Not far to the east a large barren mountain rose up from the flat valley bottom. It was covered with small exotic trees. George explained to me that all this land belonged to the landlord who employed most people in the village. During our drive I shared my experience in Salta with him—the encounter with the old Inca woman and the intriguing question, 'Are human beings being human?'

While the ride through the countryside was beautiful, I just had too much on my mind to really enjoy it, and we returned earlier than planned. We made ourselves comfortable on the porch in George's backyard. I enjoyed the dry heat of the sun on my skin, a nice break from winter in Calgary. Then I explained what I had learned about the meaning of the word 'human' on the internet.

"You have to be careful," George warned. "Dictionaries tend to give the impression that there is a certain right interpretation of a word, that everything has one correct definition. However, depending on people's cultural background, the definitions and interpretations may vary significantly."

"Why is that important in finding the answer to my question?" I asked. "Shouldn't we always look for the *intended* meaning behind the words, rather than that what might be commonly accepted by the general population?"

"Well, let's take the word 'human' as an example," George began, "Your research has indicated it means being kind, sympathetic, mild, benevolent, compassionate, merciful, gentle, tender, civilized and living according to values pertaining to humans. The opposite of being human would be displaying cruel, barbarous, rude and uncivil behavior, right?"

"Right," I answered.

"So this raises several questions with relation to the interpretation of these words," he continued. "What is 'civilized' and what are 'human values?'"

"Well, those are two questions I still have to find the answer to," I admitted.

"This is where it gets tricky," he continued undisturbed. "Most people in the West would think that being human means being civilized. Yet the majority of people there would not share Luciana's perspective on our relation to plants and animals. They consider civilized as being educated, sophisticated and superior. A Western perspective would view tribal and indigenous societies as primitive and subordinate. Yet if you would ask what being human is to people in a tribal, indigenous society, they would talk to you about being hospitable, caring, being good stewards of Mother Earth. If you would ask the farmers in this particular village what being human is, they would talk to you about equality, about those who spend their time in an attempt to improve their life circumstances, about empathy, friendliness and helpfulness. As a result of these different perspectives, each would think from the other that they would have to mature, learn and grow further in order to behave as a human being."

"I hadn't thought about it in such a way," I admitted. "But doesn't this ambiguous situation simply emphasize the need to go back to the original meaning of the word?"

"Not really, since the original meaning of the word is based on the interpretation of the word by those in power at that time. Since a lot of words come from Latin, they reflect the worldview of the Romans at the time, which was distinctly different than the perspective of their slaves. Yet you have to start somewhere, and your approach is a valid one. Still, be aware of people's different perspectives, not only in your analysis but also when you try to explain your findings to others," George counseled.

I could tell he was talking from experience.

"It will get much more complicated when you try to find out what human values are," he continued. "Moral philosophers have never come to a clear conclusion on that, as values are culturally determined. The values that are at the basis of a culture are simply those values that the majority of the people in that society support. Does that make a certain set of values better than another? Absolutely not! And this is important to realize—that values and what is deemed to be right or wrong can be entirely different from one culture to another."

I thought I had made great progress in my research about the meaning of being human, but now I felt I had tumbled all the way back to the bottom of the hill.

"Can you illustrate your last point with an example?" I asked.

"Let's take homosexuality," George started. "In most countries in the West, it is perfectly acceptable for people to freely express their sexual preference. Homosexuality is generally accepted in the Western culture, although people who live in urban societies tend to be more accepting of this preference than those who live in the country, where values evolve less rapidly. However, it would be totally unacceptable for someone to declare openly that they are homosexual in the Middle East; even here in Chile it would be a stretch! On the other hand, if a woman walked topless on the beach in the United States, a country that accepts the free expression of sexuality and protects the rights of gay minorities, she could be criminally charged because such behavior is considered sexually offensive in that country. If that same woman walked topless on the beach in France, people would hardly take notice of it because such behavior is commonly accepted. It isn't viewed as sexually offensive, and it certainly would not be considered a legal offense!"

"I see your point," I responded. "However, the fact that the dictionary refers to a behavior according to human values suggests that there is a specific set of values that are considered to be human. And a number of those values have been listed, such as being kind, sympathetic, benevolent, compassionate, merciful, gentle and tender. Or am I seeing things incorrectly?"

"All I am saying," he explained, "is that the question you have to solve is a difficult one, and you have to find an answer that is acceptable from different cultural perspectives. Just look around in this village and try to understand the contrasting world perspectives of the Indian farmers and their Spanish landlord. The contrast between the 'haves' and the 'have nots' is right in front of you, and not too much has changed in the last four hundred years! We might not call those farmers 'slaves' anymore, and the landlord might not legally own them, but in practice the line between legal slavery and economic slavery is very thin. When you are born in one of those little houses as the fifth child of a farmer who barely makes enough money to feed his family, there really are not a lot of options. When grown up, your choice is limited to farming the land and living in the village—that is, if the landlord has work for you—or going to the slums in Santiago and finding a way to survive there! So not much has changed since the Spanish and Brazilian conquerors colonized South America, and why would it change? All people in power, both here and in the West, and most of the people in the rich world, benefit from this situation."

I could see the frustration in George's eyes. He had worked in these communities in Chile for the last 10 years. It must have been very difficult to be confronted day in, day out with this blatant contrast between rich and poor. As a missionary he tried to improve the life circumstances of the farmers with the limited means available to him, and all the while the landlord's decadent wealth was staring him right in the face.

Then George told me how difficult it had been to get even a few pennies from the landlord to construct the playground at the community center!

I thought back to my first trip to Central America, when I traveled through the Dominican Republic, Panama and Guatemala. The tropical climate of that region allowed almost anything to thrive. There was an abundance of fruit and vegetables growing absolutely everywhere, but at the same time, the majority of people in those areas were extremely poor, and I knew that malnutrition was prevalent in the region. It was hard to understand this situation existed with all that food growing in abundance!

It was only after I questioned a Mexican business colleague about this that I started to comprehend how it was possible. He explained that most of these poor people did not possess any of the land on which the fruit and vegetables grew. These large farms belonged to rich landlords who sold their harvest, which was grown and produced by the farmers for slave wages, to large, multinational food corporations. As a result many Westerners could afford to buy bananas in their stores, and have a cup of coffee for less than a dollar!

Just think about what is involved to get a banana, grown in Ecuador, into a store in North America! Native people take care of the trees and the bananas during their growing season. Then they pick the fruit, load them onto trucks and store them somewhere on the farm. From there they get transported to a harbor and stored again. In the harbor they get loaded onto a boat and shipped off to one of the ports in North America. Upon arrival there they are unloaded and stored again. Once the produce clears customs, they are distributed via train or truck to different wholesalers throughout the country. Again, they get off-loaded and stored. The last shipment, for which the fruit needs to be loaded on and off again, brings them to a local grocery store, where someone puts them on the shelf. And how much do we pay for that banana? Less than a dollar! Such a thing is only possible because those people who grow and pick those bananas for our enjoyment are hardly making enough money to feed their family.

I had never realized what I now considered to be 'economic slavery' was at the basis of the life standard I was enjoying. And it had not happened until I was confronted with food abundance and poverty both in the same place. It made me feel really bad.

I thought about how conveniently those economic slaves remained out of sight and out of mind for the majority of the rich world. If people in our civilized northern countries, on a daily basis, were confronted with the blatant poverty that resulted from slave wages, things would have been changed long ago. Rich, developed countries are all, in their own way, setting up systems to protect their citizens from such extreme poverty. However, if we are the beneficiaries of the labor of poor people in developing countries, should we not make it our responsibility that such poverty, on a global scale, be eradicated?!

Changing the subject I asked, "George, why are people referring to me as 'the gringo?' Even you called me that at the airport!"

"I don't know why," he said, "but you are right: there is a reason. They seem to have an expectation of you. I myself called you that because when Luciana invited me for the barbecue I told her I was expecting a friend and she replied, "Yes, we know ... the gringo." When I questioned her about her response, she did not give me any explanation but just told me to bring you."

I remembered Mario had told me to go with the flow, but not understanding what was going on was driving me *crazy*! It seemed patience was required, but I certainly had none in this case.

"So when am I going to find out?" I snapped, agitated.

"Just be patient," George soothed, understanding my frustration. "Luciana is a very smart woman, and she said you will find out in due time!"

I decided to try and put my mind to something else, so I took my book and started to read while enjoying the late afternoon sun.

Is a Global Society a Social Globe?

The phone rang and George went to answer it. When he returned he told me we were invited to a young girl's 18th birthday party that evening.

At around seven-thirty we left George's house and walked two blocks through the farmer's social housing community.

"This is the place," George said as he turned, walked through a small front yard towards a little house, and knocked on a door. A young, smiling woman opened up.

"Father George," she said excitedly, "how great that you can join us!"

The door gave access to a room approximately three by five yards. Its walls of concrete blocks had no finish on top. Next to the door was one small window that provided a view onto the street. Apart from a little cross between the door and the little window there were no pictures or any other wall decorations. The furniture consisted of one white round plastic table and five plastic chairs. They were the cheapest kind, the kind we use in the United States and Canada as common patio furniture.

The wall opposite to the entrance had two doors, or really two door openings that gave access to two tiny bedrooms. A rag that functioned as a curtain partially concealed the view into the rooms. On the right was a bathroom door with the same shaggy cover. The floor of the room was covered with old carpet. The entire house must have been one square block of five by five yards. Its impersonal, cold feeling was a stark contrast to the warm energy radiating from the two young women in the room.

The girls both kissed George on the cheek. During my travels I had learned this was the traditional greeting by women in Latin America.

"Hi, I am Ethel," a beautiful, dark-haired young woman with fine features said to me. Her voice echoed off the walls, but still had a sweet tender tone to it. She embraced me, kissed me on the cheek and looked me in the eyes. When I noticed her eyes my feet got nailed to the floor. These were the same eyes I had seen in Salta. Capturing eyes, in which I instantly drowned. Dark, bottomless windows into the heart and soul, radiating love, mystery and passion, full of life!

"And I am Claudia." Another voice blasted me out of my hypnotic state. The other girl had moved next to Ethel. I turned to her and we greeted each other in the same traditional way. We sat down on the chairs around the table. There was a bag of salted chips and a large bottle of coke. I learned Ethel was the birthday girl. Her parents, her two younger brothers and her sister were visiting some friends so she could have the house for her party.

I was astonished that six people lived on a day-to-day basis in such a small house. George explained to me later that most houses were actually occupied by larger families, including grandparents and sometimes grandchildren. This apparently led to appalling family fights, violence, incest and a breakdown in family values. He did not want to go into any further details, but I could tell from the look on his face that dealing with all this as the spiritual leader of the community had been very difficult for him. After ten years he was clearly tired of it.

The conversation started somewhat awkwardly. Both girls were talking with George about some community events, but while they were very friendly to me, it seemed my presence created some uneasiness. Eventually Ethel broke the ice.

"So where do you live?" she asked in her sweet voice.

"In Calgary, Canada," I answered.

This opened a conversation about the climate in Calgary in comparison with Santiago, and the fact that it was the end of winter in

Canada for me, while for them it was the end of summer. I told them about my family and a little bit about my work.

"I also want to travel," Ethel said with dreamy eyes.

Someone knocked on the door and walked in. I was introduced to Alejandro, Ethel's boyfriend. A few minutes later another knock sounded and another boy entered, who was introduced to me as Carlos. Ethel looked embarrassed, yet I had no idea what was going on or what had made her uncomfortable. She turned to George and whispered something to him. He reassured her and told me Ethel needed to ask me something.

"I have invited a number of my friends to my party," she started hesitantly, "and today I found out you, 'the gringo,' were staying with Father George. I am so glad that you are able to attend my birthday party, so I hope my request will not offend you."

By now, I had gotten somewhat used to people referring to me as 'the gringo,' but I had no idea where Ethel was going with this.

"See," she continued, "we only have five chairs, and now that Carlos arrived, we cannot seat everyone around the table. Would you mind if we put the table in the corner, stack the chairs on top of it and all sit on the floor?"

I laughed. "Of course not! I am honored to be invited and am quite comfortable to sit on the floor."

A smile of relief quickly appeared on Ethel's face.

We all sat down on the floor around two lit candles in the middle. I noticed that the glimmering light seemed to accentuate the depth and mystery in Ethel's eyes. "The old woman and this beautiful young girl both have the same depth and purity of soul," I thought. The atmosphere seemed more relaxed now that we all hung together on the floor. It reminded me of my teenage years, which I had never been able to shake completely out of my system. I felt truly welcome, and was very comfortable.

"So what are your plans in life?" I asked Ethel who was sitting next to me.

"I have been very lucky so far," she said. "With the help of Father George I have been able to complete high school. Most kids around here only study until they're fourteen."

I could detect a sparkle of pride, but also some sorrow in her eyes and voice.

"Father George even lent me some books from university, which I have studied. I would like to go to university and study some more," she said, "but my parents and I are not able to afford it. And I don't want to stay here in San Cristobal, even if Senior Castillo had work for me. I have seen what life is like here, and I want something better for my children and myself in the future. Therefore, I have no other choice than to go to the slums in Santiago, try to get a job and work my way up. Alejandro, my boyfriend, has studied mechanics, and because people in Santiago all have cars, we think he will be able to get some work there. We are actually leaving next week, as I just wanted to stay with my friends and family in San Cristobal to celebrate my birthday. So this coming Wednesday is the start of our adventure to build a better life."

She paused in thought for some time, and then continued, "I tell you, it really scares me for I don't know anyone in Santiago. Father George has told me he will help us to find a place to live and will provide us with references to find work. I am lucky. I have had a good education, better than most kids, so my chances to get out of the slums are much better than they are for most of my friends. Their choice is mostly limited between the same life as their parents here in San Cristobal or a life in the slums around Santiago." She paused for a while, then said with a dreamy gaze in her eyes, "Maybe one day I will be able to afford to study at the university."

"It must be hard," I thought. "This girl certainly seemed to have the ambition and the intelligence to make it through university, but she cannot attend because she is born in the wrong part of the world." Something did not feel right about this.

"I have a message for you," Ethel suddenly said as her sparkling eyes, full of life and energy, locked onto me.

"For me?" I stammered.

"Yes, for you. Manuelita asked me to tell you something."

"Who is Manuelita?" I asked curiously.

"She is an Indian medicine woman who lives up in the mountains. I went to visit her a month ago. She read my future in the sand and told me I would study at the university one day and find happiness with Alejandro," she said, glowing with excitement.

"How did she know a month ago I was going to be here?" I asked, astonished, "I only planned this visit two days ago!"

"She knows a lot of things," Ethel replied confidently.

"Yeah... but how could she...?" I stammered. This was too much. How could someone I had never met or even heard of know that I would visit this place and meet this girl, even before I had planned any part of this trip? "Are you sure the message is for me?" I asked.

"Oh yes," she said convincingly, "it certainly is for you!"

"How do you know it is for me?" I still questioned in disbelief.

"She told me I would meet 'the gringo' before I would leave San Cristobal at an event that would be of great importance to me. She said the gringo's presence would capture and inspire me." With a shy tone in her voice and a smile on her face she continued, "All this has just happened tonight!"

"But maybe there has been another gringo?" I tried.

"Apart from Father George, no gringo has ever visited San Cristobal as far as I know," she replied. "There certainly hasn't been one at my house during a time that was important to me." Then, shyly, she confided, "And you inspired me."

"How?" I asked, still rejecting the thought that someone could have known a month ago that I would be present here.

"Just by your presence. It is a real honor to have you here. You have traveled the world, followed your dreams, and here you are in my house on my 18th birthday party. You made time to listen to me, and are interested in my story. You are fully present with body, mind and spirit. You really listen, and your eyes tell me that you genuinely

71

care and understand our life circumstances without pitying us. You give us respect as people. Yes, I am certain. You are 'the gringo!'"

I was not sure how to take so much praise all at once.

She put her hand on top of mine and looked into my eyes. "Thank you," she said warmly.

Once again her eyes, expressing humanity's love and the purity of her soul, captivated me. Just like with the old woman in Salta, I felt like I was gazing through some windows right into the soul of the Divine. I wondered what it would be like to step through those windows and immerse myself fully in that unlimited love and vastness of soul. Then her hand left mine and I gazed uncomfortably around the room to see who else had been following this conversation. Other than George, no one else was paying any attention to us. Antonio, Carlos and Claudia had their own lively discussion going.

The door opened and two more girls and a young man walked in. They stepped over the other people in the room in order to reach and greet Ethel. Ethel introduced me to Sanchez, Julia and Andrea. They sat down beside Alejandro and Carlos. When we were all sitting down again there were nine people in the room; the floor was full. I wondered what would happen next when another person would join the party.

"I still have to tell you the message," Ethel reminded me with a twinkle in her eyes.

"I am listening," I said, calmly accepting something was going on which was beyond my understanding.

"Manuelita told me that in order to solve the first riddle, it might help if you would try and answer this question: 'Is a global society a social globe?'"

"Well, that is an easy one for a change," I blurted ironically. "Just look around here! Clearly the answer to that is no."

"The message is not finished yet," Ethel said politely. "Manuelita told me you have to understand why, and that you should go to Salvador, Bahia, at the big ocean in Brazil."

"But I have been told to go to Ayacucho," I protested in disbelief. A little bit embarrassed, I reminded myself that I did not even know by whom! And now this Manuelita, whom I had never met and whom I didn't know really existed, was telling me to go to Salvador as well.

Undisturbed, Ethel continued, "When you are in Salvador, you have to visit a friend and he will lead you to the one you need to see."

"I don't have any friends in Salvador," I sputtered. "I haven't even been there!" I had been working on a hotel development in Salvador, but all meetings with the investors had taken place in Sao Paulo up till now.

Ethel took my hand again and looked into my eyes like her life depended on it. "Don't always try to understand what the wise ones know. Maybe it is not for you to understand. You just have to follow their advice."

How could those eyes tell me anything other than the truth? And how could I not follow the request of this message? After all, it shouldn't be that difficult for me to plan a trip there with this hotel project I had been working on. Still, I got the feeling there was more, and that Ethel might have some of the answers I was looking for.

I nodded understandingly and said, "I will take the message to heart and plan a visit to Salvador, although I have no idea whom to meet there. I will also think some more about the question that you related to me in the context of the first question I am trying to solve."

Ethel's eyes signaled her relief.

"Ethel," I asked, "why are people referring to me as 'the gringo?' It's almost like it's my name! I have been addressed like that by people I have never met before, but they all seem to know who I am."

"Has nobody told you yet about the old Inca prophecy?"

"No," I replied hesitantly.

"Manuelita has taught me about it," she explained. "The elders of the Inca descendants have told for generations that when the age of Aquarius would commence, a white one would come from the far

North. He would have presence and inspire people. He would be granted the teachings of our wise ones, elders and medicine people so that he could use their insights and wisdom to create a following amongst the conquerors with whom our wise ones cannot communicate. By providing 'the gringo' with understanding, wisdom and insights, eventually the imbalance in the world will gradually shift so that humanity can further develop to reach its true potential."

"...And I am that 'white one', 'the gringo?'" I stammered.

"Yes, you are!" Ethel said determinedly, with eyes full of hope.

"Why me? I don't think I want to *be* 'the gringo!' I am just an ordinary guy who happens to work in Latin America. I don't want to create a following or save the world from an imbalance," I whined.

"You mean you would rather see things stay the same around here?" she challenged, a little bit offended.

"No, no, that is not what I meant. Of course I would like to see your life circumstances improve and see a better balance in the world. But why me?"

"Why not?" she replied. "It is not up to us to always understand where life is leading us. It is up to us to live our lives to their full potential. That is what Manuelita has taught me."

We sat for a little while in silence as I considered the maturity and wisdom of the young people I had met on this trip. If this was a worldwide trend, then the Age of Aquarius was about to see some real change in the world! I couldn't wait to see these young people take over and create the society of which they dreamed.

"What is your sign?" Ethel asked.

"What do you mean?"

"Your astral birth sign, your horoscope?"

"Aquarius."

In silence she smiled at me.

The rest of the company was engaged in pleasant and relaxed conversations. Ethel, George and I joined in, and we had a great evening with lots of laughter and joy. At midnight, George indicated we had to go since he had to lead three church services in the morning.

We said goodbye to everyone and Ethel walked us to the door. After embracing George, she embraced me, looked me in the eyes and said warmly, "Thank you for attending my birthday."

"No. Thank *you* for inviting me and educating me," I responded. "I am sure you will work your way through the slums and one day study at the university. I wish for the sake of the world that there are more young people like yourself!"

She smiled and George and I left. In silence we walked back to his house. I had a lot to think about.

Before we went to bed, George told me he would be leaving early in the morning because he had to drive to two other communities to perform mass. He invited me to attend the service in San Cristobal at eleven o'clock. I told him I would be there.

Yet while I had been raised Catholic, I had turned my back on the Church in my teenage years because it was, in my opinion, too judgmental and had rules for which I could find no ground whatsoever in the Bible. I also had a hard time with all the blood that had flowed throughout history in the name of the Church, and the lack of acknowledgment and responsibility the Church had taken for that. After all, the conquering in South America was done in the name of the Catholic Church and saving primitive people from Satan. Currently I was witnessing the results of what I considered a religious 'power trip.' However, I did want to attend the service in order to understand more about George's life and the community he lived in.

That night when I went to bed it took a while before I could quiet my mind. It was only when I thought about the depth of Ethel's eyes and could see them in my mind again that I fell into a deep and peaceful sleep.

Good Intentions from the Rich and Powerful

When I woke up I noticed George had already left. "What time is it? Nine forty-five! I've slept long!" I thought. I took a shower and had breakfast in the garden while enjoying the warmth of the morning sun.

By ten forty-five George had not returned yet so I decided to make my way to the church. I had concluded he probably didn't have time to stop at home before the service.

When I arrived at the church it was already more than half full. It was a nice wooden building and had a warm light brown satin color on its inner walls. The sun was entering through a row of windows just under the roofline. There were two aisles; approximately fifteen wooden benches stood on either side. Each bench could seat about ten to twelve people. There was a modest wooden altar up front, which was decorated with bright red and yellow flowers.

More people were entering the church as I walked in. Most people would try and find a seat as close to the front as possible.

I could not detect Ethel and her friends anywhere. Then again, finding them amidst approximately 150 dark-haired people who were all sitting with their backs to me was not exactly easy. I noticed that all the farmers were surprisingly well-dressed. I could see how some of the congregation curiously looked at me. In an attempt to avoid attention I decided to take a seat in the last row.

Avoiding attention as a blond, white tall guy in an environment where most people were a foot smaller, dark-skinned and black-haired was not exactly easy. However, George then made sure my attempt truly failed! Right at the start of the service, he announced my presence to the rest of the community. With all eyes locked on me he then officially welcomed me.

The mass was not all that different from any other service I had attended at various places around the world. During his sermon George called upon the community to be more understanding of each other's personal perspectives before they reacted emotionally to each other. It occurred to me that this sermon would be very appropriate in the United States and Canada as well, as such things were common human issues we all had to deal with. "How did such emotional behavior develop?" I thought. "What would it take for people to start listening more to each other and to respect each other's different perspectives?"

By now the communion had started. I noticed a somewhat older man together with a woman, whom I guessed was his wife. They were both distinctly taller than the rest of the community. Two younger men and women, around my age and accompanied by some children, followed them. They were all well-dressed, and clearly better groomed than the rest of the people in the church. They had strong southern European facial features in comparison with the Indian face of most of the farmers. "That must be the landlord," I thought.

When the service ended people started to converse with each other before gradually leaving the church. George approached me and wanted to introduce me to some people.

On his way out, the landlord noticed us and confidently walked over. "I am Garcia Villa Nova Castillo," he said as he firmly shook my hand. "And this is my wife, Anna."

"We would be honored if you could join our family for a lunch barbecue," Anna invited.

"Oh, we haven't made our plans yet for the afternoon," George stammered.

"Well then, that is great," Garcia said with a sense of authority. "We would not want to interrupt any plans. So can we expect you in half an hour?" he asked demandingly.

"We will be there," I answered. This was a unique opportunity to meet the landlord and his family and get an understanding of their perspective on the world. I had felt George was trying to get out of it for some reason, and I did not want to lose this unique chance.

"Good!" Garcia smiled, "we'll see you in half an hour."

When the church was empty George and I walked over to his house. He was upset with me for accepting the landlord's invitation.

"Why did you accept that invitation?" he snapped.

"Well, I want to understand who the landlord is and how he perceives the world."

"That is what I am afraid of," George replied.

"What is wrong with that?" I asked, confused.

"You have no idea how these people think!" he said. "I have worked for years to get to some kind of truce with them, and I don't want to shatter that fragile cooperation."

"And what makes you think attending this barbecue would endanger that?"

"Your desire to understand his relationship with the farmers! You hold strong opinions about things and ask sharp questions. Garcia might not appreciate that and blame me for it later."

"I had no idea," I apologized. "What can I do to prevent your relationship from being damaged?"

"Do not, under any circumstances, talk about politics or the division between rich and poor in the world," George said demandingly. "They still support Pinochet and strongly feel they are better than the farmers that work for them. If it was up to them, Pinochet would get back in power."

"What was it like in this country under Pinochet?" I asked, changing the subject. I knew that in the seventies and eighties, human rights had been violated under the dictatorial rule of General Pinochet, who came to power—with the financial help of the United States administration—by overthrowing the socialist, democratically-elected Chilean government of President Allende, and I was curious to find out if George had witnessed any of this firsthand.

George shrugged his shoulders. "I don't really want to talk about it," he said. "Let me just say it was a tough time and there was a lot of fear among the farmers."

Since I did not want to pressure George on this clearly uncomfortable subject, I focused back on our lunch meeting with the landlord.

"So what *can* I talk about?" I asked.

"Talk about things the rich are interested in," he answered. "Like your business, hunting, sports, wine and so on."

"Well, that shouldn't be all too difficult for me. I will just consider this to be a business lunch."

George's face lit up in relief. After he changed out of his priestly robes we left for the landlord's hacienda.

On our way over George explained there were no streets on the left side of the main street because it was all the landlord's private property. We entered the estate through an old Spanish stone and iron gate. The driveway must have been a few hundred yards long, and was paved with cobblestones. "Just like the old streets in Europe," I thought. The candle-like conifer trees on both sides of the entrance lane created the illusion of pillars. Brightly-colored flowers bloomed in the sunlight between the green columns.

The driveway turned right and we drove through another gate, entering the courtyard of the hacienda where several cars were parked. I noticed a Mercedes, a Jaguar, a Land Rover and two smaller cars. On the right of the courtyard were the barn and stables. In front of us was another building with a large gate, and on the left the entrance door to the hacienda's living quarters. This colonial palace was constructed out of natural stone, and had an antique character and historical charm. It was absolutely gorgeous.

The entire family was there to welcome us. There was Garcia, the landlord, and his wife Anna, their daughter, Fabiola, with her husband and three children, and their son Cesar, with his wife and four children. The youngest of all the children was just 6 months; the oldest, 11 years. During the meal I learned that Fabiola and her family lived in the left wing of the hacienda while Cesar inhabited the right wing with his wife and kids. Garcia and Anna occupied the central portions of this Spanish estate.

They led us through the hacienda to the garden where a beautiful large wooden table was set on a stone tiled patio. While walking through the large hallways I noticed a variety of beautiful floors of marble, mosaic tiles and wood in the rooms we passed. The furniture was antique, and the hacienda was decorated with art, statutes and paintings, giving it a real historic feel.

The servants, dressed in black and white uniforms, were all very busy preparing the food. Garcia insisted on taking care of the meat on the barbecue himself.

"So where do you live?" he asked, interested, while one of the servants offered me a glass of red wine.

"In Calgary, Canada," I said and sipped from the wine. It was excellent, with a strong taste of fruit and berries.

"The wine is excellent," I complimented.

"The best!" Garcia said. "Our Chilean wine is way better than Argentinean wine," he boasted, "and slowly the world is finding out. This bottle comes from the vineyard of a good friend of mine."

We talked a little bit about my family and life in Canada. When the meat was ready, Garcia ordered us in his friendly, charming but directive manner to the table. I sat down across from him. George, who sat next to me, was sitting opposite Anna. Fabiola, Cesar and their respective families had all gathered around the other end of the table.

The servants came around with a variety of salads. I had to try the avocados and the artichokes, which were grown on Garcia's land. For the main course there was a choice between rice and potatoes with a selection of cooked vegetables, and of course different kinds of meat prepared by the host himself. The food was delicious, yet I wondered how it felt for the servants to serve such a variety and abundance of food while they barely had enough to exist on. During the party the evening before, we only had salted chips and coke! How would it feel to work in such a palace-like hacienda, and then go home to a small little concrete house shared with a number of children and relatives?

"What brings you to San Cristobal?" Garcia asked.

I explained to him about my business in Latin America, the travel it required, how I had not seen George for more than fourteen years and how this was a great way to kill a weekend on my way over to Peru. I did not share with him the mystery that had colored this trip.

"So who have you been doing business with in Santiago?" he asked.

I did not want to share any names. Experience had taught me that a lot of rich business people in Latin countries knew each other. Sometimes they were friends, but at other times they were vicious enemies. In the latter case they would go to the end of the world to prevent success of their perceived opponents.

"A number of hotel developers and owners," I replied, and continued with a question of my own so Garcia could not dig further into the subject. "Would you be interested in investing in hotels?"

"No," he laughed, "but I was wondering if you would know someone who would be interested in buying that mountain from me?" He pointed to the big mountain to the east of San Cristobal.

"Why do you want to sell the mountain?" I asked.

He explained to me that the entire valley and the surrounding mountains had been in his family since they had settled there.

Cynically, I thought, "He probably meant *conquered* it."

Through different generations they had tried to make money from a variety of crops and trees on the mountain flanks. Finally he had found success with citrus trees, which were now maturing.

"The problem is," he said, "they are too labor intensive. And I already have enough people to take care of." He gestured towards the farming community.

"What do you mean?" I inquired. I could feel George's eyes burning into my side.

Undisturbed by my question, Garcia answered, "Well, it is a big responsibility to take care of so many families. Without me they would end up in the slums, drink themselves to death, or get involved in drugs. We have expanded some of our farmland here in the valley. I have taken the workers from the mountain to work on these new fields and have no one left to take care of the citrus trees. Without expanding my work force, which I don't want to do, the mountain will dilute in value. Therefore, I am trying to sell it."

Glad to have gotten an insight into how Garcia looked at the world and his relationship to the rest of the people in the village, I decided to drop the topic and save George from a nervous breakdown. Jokingly I said, "Well, I am afraid it is not exactly a good hotel location, so I am pretty sure none of my contacts would be interested in it."

"So, how did you like the beef?" Garcia then asked proudly. "Is it as good as in Canada?"

I complimented him on his beef but also told him about the world-famous Alberta beef of which our ranchers were equally proud.

"But personally, I don't eat a lot of beef," I continued. "Most of the meat we eat at home is from deer and elk, which I hunt."

Once I brought that subject up we were good for a long conversation that lasted through a delicious chocolate desert. They could not believe I hunted with a bow and arrow. Enthusiastically he told me his brother had a ranch up in the mountains, which was great for hunting red deer. He asked the servants for the phone and wanted to call his brother to schedule a hunting trip for me the following day.

"I am sorry," I said. "I would love to take you up on your offer, but my plane for Lima is leaving tonight."

"Oh, just change your trip," he said in his charming, demanding way.

"I am afraid I cannot do that," I replied. "I have potential business clients who are expecting me tomorrow morning."

"I understand," he said, slightly disappointed.

"Actually, if you want to catch your plane in time, we should go," George interrupted.

They all said goodbye to me like I had been a friend of the family for years. "What nice and hospitable people," I thought, "yet

82

how can they live in such luxury, when poverty is staring them right in the face, and sleep well at night?!"

When George and I drove down the driveway he smiled and said, "That went over really smoothly. This was the first time I have been invited to a meal with them. What great food!"

We both laughed, but I could not shake the confusion that had arisen in me from the two contrasting experiences of the last twenty-four hours. The pleasant birthday party in a small, primitive house with chips and coke, coupled with Ethel's zest for life and her maturity, and the extreme riches of the landlord and his perspective as caretaker of the community, as well as his hospitality and friendliness as host.

This feeling of confusion illustrated to me how complicated it would be to bring change and more balance into the world. How do you convince such a landlord that there must be another way? How do you motivate such a person to explore different ways of living and working, which most likely would dilute his personal wealth but greatly improve the general life circumstances of the farmers in San Cristobal? I had no idea of how or where to start.

I shared with George my feelings of confusion due to the experience of all those extremes. He smiled understandingly and said, "Try and work in this environment for ten years."

I admired his courage and perseverance.

We got back to his house, where I quickly packed. It was time to get to the airport.

When we left San Cristobal once again, the same kids were playing on the streets, their innocent faces full of joy. Like before I triggered reactions of finger-pointing and laughter.

Both George and I were quiet on our drive to the airport, deep in thought. I had to think about the children of San Cristobal, their future and their choice between a life in the village working for Garcia or a life in the slums. I wondered how long it would take before their adult life experiences would softly kill that innocent sparkle of joy in their eyes.

A Story of Sharing

We arrived a little early at the airport. I checked in, and we decided to have a last drink together in one of the airport cafeterias before my departure.

"It is amazing how synchronistic all my experiences have been during the last week," I said once we were sitting down and each had a cold beverage. "It really started with Tom's question last Sunday."

"What did he ask?"

"He asked why people had to pay for food," I replied, "In other words, he was questioning why hunger was still such a problem in our civilized society. While I did not expect to be confronted with such a display of poverty and riches during my visit here, I somehow had hoped it would provide me with some understanding, some justification for why things are this way. But it didn't, it didn't at all. Do I understand how things developed to this point? Yes. Did I meet any people who were intentionally evil? No. Do I have some ideas as to how things could be improved? Yes. Do I have any idea how to sell those ideas to those who are in power? Absolutely not! The perspectives of people as to why such poverty has developed and how to deal with it are so different. Poverty is a social problem that in one way or another affects everyone in our society, and it seems impossible to work out a solution for it as long as people are more focused on obtaining and protecting personal individual possessions rather than living according to a moral social code."

"There is a lot of truth in what you are saying," George agreed, "and your son has certainly formulated a profound and fundamental question. Let me tell you a story about the experience of a friend of mine, Marc, who is a missionary in South Africa.

"One day, Marc had been hiking with two colleagues for hours through a very dry and desolate part of the country. They had underestimated the duration of their trip. They were short on food and their water had just run out when they came across a small group of Bushmen. The Bushmen are one of the few indigenous people from around the world who have been able to hold on to their traditional ways of living. They greeted Marc and his company and immediately invited them to sit down to eat and drink with them. They shared everything they had. After the meal, they provided the travelers with half of their water, before they smiled, turned around and continued on their journey.

"Astonished by the selfless act of sharing, one of Marc's European colleagues, who had only recently arrived at the mission, asked if the Bushmen would have enough water for their own journey now. Marc explained to him it would be an immoral act for the Bushman to find a person in need of food and water and not share whatever they had, even if that meant endangering their own survival. Their need and respect of social community, like most other indigenous tribes, is stronger than that for individual possession and survival."

"Wow!" I gasped. "If most of the old cultures were like that, I wonder when we lost that sense of morality?"

"And how do we get it back?" George added.

It was time for me to go. George and I embraced and I left for Lima.

Arrival in Peru

The flight to Lima was uneventful. However, I did notice the airplane was almost empty, and that I was the only gringo on board. It was late at night, so I slept for most of the trip. We landed in Lima shortly after midnight. This was my first time in Peru.

When I walked out of the plane onto the tarmac I was struck with a strange feeling of anxiety, one which alerted all my senses. Oddly enough, I had no idea what had triggered it. People in military uniforms guided us into the airport building. In a dimly lit hall we waited in one long line to pass through customs.

In order to enter Peru for business, you had to have a special visa. Given my time constraints in planning this trip, I did not have such a visa, and had to enter the country as a tourist. Tourists did not require a special visa. But the idea that they might question me about the purpose of my visit made me nervous. After all, this was a totalitarian country, which at the time was still under Fujimori's rule. While President Fujimori had saved the country on the brink of collapse in the years following his election in 1990, human rights violations were common under his dictatorial regime.

To my relief, no questions were asked when it was my turn. After getting the required stamps, I entered a country with a dictatorial regime, strong military presence, and a questionable justice system. "No wonder I have such feelings of anxiety," I thought. "When the security of human rights and justice falls away, you are bound to become very alert and worried. I wonder if I have picked up on the general feeling of the population in this country?"

While waiting for my luggage, I could see a large door in a glass wall at the other end of the arrival hall. Outside was a section set off with metal-framed panels, behind which a crowd of people was waiting. Several policemen with machine guns were standing inside of a secured area in between the crowd and the airport.

Taxis were allowed into the protected section through a barrier. One of the passengers waiting next to me warned me not to take a taxi outside of the protected area. He informed me the taxis that were allowed in the zone were airport-licensed taxis only.

"Oh, someone is picking me up," I said.

"That is always the safest here," he answered.

I had no idea what he meant or what the danger was, but I could not exactly say I was feeling comfortable when I looked at the scene outside of the airport building. Somewhere out in the crowd, Pedro should be waiting for me. I got my luggage and walked outside. The temperature was comfortable but it was very windy. I had no idea what Pedro looked like and frantically searched for a sign with my name on it. It was noisy. People were shouting, cars taking off and blowing their horns, and I decided very quickly that I was not going to leave the protected zone without having found Pedro first. I walked closer to the metal panels in order to look further into the mass of people. Finally I noticed my name on a little board held by a somewhat shorter man of my own age. He was waiting calmly, and had clearly decided to stay out of the pushing and shoving closer to the fence.

"Pedro?" I called.

"Paul?" He replied and a smile appeared on his rounded face.

I nodded.

"Go to the barrier; I will meet you there," he shouted over the noise of the crowd.

I did as he said, and followed Pedro through the crowd towards the parking lot. He did not exactly offer the protection of a big bodyguard, which I had hoped for. But as I was walking through the people, I noticed that all of them, except for those men who offered me taxi rides, stayed focused on the airport area and made room for me to pass through.

Once we got to the car Pedro properly introduced himself. We got in and he drove me to my hotel.

"Someone warned me at the airport to only take airport taxis," I said. "Why is that?"

"Unfortunately it happens from time to time that tourists are picked up by a taxi outside of the protected zone in front of the airport and are driven outside of Lima and robbed," he responded, slightly embarrassed. "Poverty leads people to desperate actions," he mumbled.

"I am surprised," he said, changing the subject, "that you came at such short notice and during these difficult times."

"What do you mean by 'difficult times?'" I asked.

"Don't you know?"

"No," I said. "This is my first time in Peru and I have not exactly followed the economic and political situation here. I know the country is ruled by Fujimori and that there is a strong military presence here. On the news I heard that Fujimori recently got re-elected and that some democratic watchdog organizations were questioning the election process. But that is about it. I was hoping you could bring me up to speed on what the situation in the country is like."

"You have come at the worst of times," Pedro said, concerned. "There are protests and riots all over Lima on a daily basis. The police and military are absolutely everywhere, and a national strike is planned for later this week. However, I have made our travel arrangements in such a way that we do not have to depend on the airlines or other public transportation. We will fly tomorrow to Ayacucho, but from there we will do all of our travel with one of the company vans. We must stick to our schedule so that we can get you out of here before the end of Thursday—before the national strike."

I started to wonder if there was more behind my feeling of discomfort at the airport. Why had I not paid better attention to the news about Peru during recent days? Why had I chosen to come exactly now? Oh, of course, there was the invitation to travel to

Ayacucho written on the piece of paper that I had found in my hotel bedroom in Salta. Still, I had no idea by whom it was written and for whom it was meant to be. It was because I had found it in such an obvious place, *under* a desk, the type of place where I always look for my personal messages, that I thought this message must have been for me. Of course there was the incident with the old woman before I entered the Salta hotel and Mario's experience, both of which had confirmed to me that this note was meant for me. But who in their right mind would have acted on such vaguely-connected coincidences? What had I gotten myself into? From the sounds of it, this country was on the brink of some serious internal trouble, and now I was running the risk of getting stuck right in the middle of it.

In an attempt to distract my mind and focus on something more positive, I started to ask Pedro questions about his personal life and the company for which he was working.

As my travels with him in the following days confirmed, Pedro was a very humble and smart man. He was self-confident, had a relentless thirst for knowledge and a caring heart. That last aspect was ever-present when he talked about his family, his country and his company, and his dedication, loyalty and love for all of them.

He had a wife, and his two kids were about the same age as mine. For the last seven years he had worked for Primus Hotels. The company had gone through several serious changes and a significant expansion due to the acquisition of multiple hotels around the country. Currently they had performance problems in the hotels I was going to visit, and were considering franchising them or putting them under the management of our hotel group in the hope of attracting more international guests and improving the financial return of the properties.

It was just after 1:00 a.m. when we arrived at the first hotel. I found it surprising that the receptionist did not speak any English at all. This was an obvious hurdle for a quality business hotel, located in the middle of a banking district, which was trying to attract international guests. I checked in, thanked Pedro for picking me up at the airport in the middle of the night and went to my room. The room was large and finished according to North American modern standards. If the hotel was doing as badly as Pedro said, it certainly was not due to the product. So I was curious to meet with the general manager and to experience the hotel's services. If the check-in experience was any indication of what I could expect, then it should not be too difficult to improve the performance of this property with the management and training services my company offered.

E-mail would have to wait for tonight. It was late, and I was too tired. Besides, I had to get up early in the morning. My meeting with the owners was scheduled for 8:30.

An Arrogant Aristocrat

The music of my alarm clock woke me up in the morning. I had set it fifteen minutes later than the time for which I had asked reception to give me a wake-up call. I was glad I had taken that precaution, because reception clearly had forgotten all about me. "Another sign of the service level at this hotel," I thought, slightly annoyed. I decided to skip breakfast, quickly download my e-mail, and go to the meeting.

When I walked in the meeting room at 8:20, Pedro was already waiting for me.

"Did you sleep well?" he asked, genuinely concerned.

"I slept very well. The room is very nice," I said, and decided not to mention the undelivered wake-up call in case he took it too personally. I was glad of my decision when relief flooded his face.

"I am sure the board members will arrive any minute," he said apologetically.

"I am sure they will," I comforted him. "I know I am ten minutes early."

A few minutes later a big man with a distinctly English accent walked in and introduced himself as Allen. Then a slim, Spanish-looking man and a lady with a friendly look in her eyes followed him. Pedro introduced them as Luis and Adela. The three of them were the main shareholders and thus the company's major decision-makers.

"So what is your opinion of this hotel?" Allen started off.

"It's too early to say," I deflected the question. "I have to see more of it and experience it a little bit longer." It was too soon to ruffle any feathers. I first wanted to find out more about what was going on in this company and what the leadership was like before telling them the things that were not working.

"Let me explain to you why we have invited you to this meeting and what our interest is in exploring the possibility of working together with your company," Adela started off in a polite and formal manner. She explained how they had expanded their hotel portfolio with two hotels during the last two years in an attempt to become a country-wide hotel chain. Although they had intended to maintain the management of the acquired hotels, within the first six months after the acquisitions, the general managers had left the company.

"In an attempt to provide some security for the staff and create an environment that offers future growth opportunities, we promoted one of the department heads from each hotel to general manager," Adela continued.

"I told them from the beginning it was a bad idea and would not work," Allen interrupted bossily. "How can you keep control over these people if they are managed by one of their own?"

"Because of Allen's concerns," Adela continued, "we decided after three months to swap the managers amongst the hotels. We did this in an attempt to address Allen's control issue and to maintain an environment in which employees continued to see growth opportunities."

"The effort to address the control issue was well-intended," Allen interrupted bluntly again, "but like I told them, promoting the department heads was a mistake from the beginning. We needed experienced business executives who knew how to keep these employees in line and who could make sure they were not overspending anywhere. And that is what we have now!"

"So you have new managers in the hotels?" I asked.

"Yes, for after those incompetent promoted department heads were not able to increase profits for the following six months, I told them things were not working, and we brought in some serious and well-trained executives," Allen bragged arrogantly.

"When did that happen?" I asked.

"About nine months ago," Adela said a little timidly.

"And how have things been going since?"

"Well, these guys don't have it easy," Allen replied. "They hardly get any cooperation from the employees. I told them they should fire some to set an example, but they are telling me trained employees are scarce in those small towns. Here in Lima the general manager has been changing employees already. I am sure we will soon see the effect of this."

"Things have not really improved," Adela added in a polite tone, "so that is why we invited you. We would like you to visit the hotels and make an assessment as to what needs to be done to turn them around."

"I am sure," Allen added in his direct and commanding tone, "that our current general managers will perform excellently when supported by your training and control systems. After your visit we would like to get a report from you. Based on that, we will then make our decision. Obviously we want profits to increase! We invested in this business to make *money*, and it currently is not making enough!"

"I understand Pedro has arranged for a visit to all the hotels," I responded politely but firmly, "and I will assess all the hotels during my visit. I will provide you a conclusive report based on a service assessment, interviews with the general manager and the staff, an analysis of the hotels' competitive market and supply and demand trends."

"There is no need for employee interviews," Allen said abruptly. "The general managers know all there is to know."

"The employees can provide me with important insights into the work atmosphere of the hotels," I replied calmly. "If we are going to be responsible for the operations in the hotels, I need to know what currently goes on in those properties."

"I think it is good for you to interview the employees and make your own assessment of the general managers," Adela jumped in. "We do not want to keep any managers in place if you, with your experience, don't find them to be qualified for the job. We need to make sure we get it right this time."

I noticed Allen's eyes were shooting fire at Adela during her last comments, but he apparently decided to stay silent for the moment and let me have the employee interviews. During the rest of the meeting we provided each other with information about our respective companies and had a general discussion about the hotel industry in Peru and the impact the country's current political crisis was having.

It was obvious that both Adela and Allen had serious differences between them. I expected this was reflected in a continuous power struggle, which was likely harming the company's strategic and operational consistency. Luis tended to be more agreeable with Allen's control-driven perspective on things, but he had stayed silent most of the time to avoid conflict with Adela, whom I learned was his older sister. I had the impression that Allen was only interested in making money, no matter how, as opposed to Adela, who aimed to build a long-term stable business that cared for its employees, and would play an important role in developing the Peruvian hospitality industry.

I liked Adela's caring, nurturing attitude, but certainly after my recent experience in San Cristobal, had a hard time understanding how people like Allen could sleep comfortably at night with all this poverty around them. He had made it sound like all employees were crooks and thieves, who were simply waiting to make their move. I couldn't wait to get to Ayacucho and see for myself what things were like.

As I thought about going to Ayacucho, a nervousness developed inside of me. Tomorrow was the twenty-first. Would I meet someone in Ayacucho who would provide me with further insight into the question I had been pondering ever since I found that piece of paper in Salta? Or would all of this turn out to be a creation of my overactive imagination? The time of truth was getting close, and the closer it got…the more my anxiety rose.

After the meeting Pedro showed me around in the hotel and I detected more service issues. During a short interview with the general manager of the hotel, it came to light that she had no previous hotel experience. She was an engineer and friend of Allen, who had recently lost her job as a director of a state-owned energy company. Her management style was that of a true dictator, and she was proud of it. I did not need any further interviews with any of the employees, as I had seen enough. This hotel was in serious trouble due to its management. Given her connection with Allen, I had no idea how I was going to present this. But I did not want to give that any thought just yet. I only wanted to get out and start our journey to Ayacucho.

When I told Pedro I was ready to go, he informed me we could take an earlier flight that would get us to Ayacucho shortly after four if we left immediately. Excited, I told him to make the arrangements and went to my room to pack.

A Glimpse of True Power

Ayacucho!

Two hours later, during takeoff, I looked through the airplane window down on the vast slums around Lima. "I wonder if Allen has ever walked through there and talked to those people?" I thought.

We left the ocean behind us as the plane turned east and headed for the Andes. I was curious as to what this famous mountain chain would be like. On some of my previous travels I had flown over it on my way to Chile, but I had never had a chance to experience it. I loved the mountains. There was something mysterious and powerful about them. They were an expression of the Divine in all its beauty, a place to find stillness and to surrender to that feeling of timeless peace within raw, and sometimes harsh, creative energy. The mountains were my church, my place to connect with the One and be humbled by Its beauty and power. That's why seven years ago I had moved to the foothills of the Rocky Mountains near Calgary.

To my disappointment, after fifteen minutes of flying the view to the ground was blocked by a thin layer of clouds below us. Both Pedro and I were silent, absorbed by our own thoughts. Still, I was excited. With each minute passing and the engines drumming I was getting closer to Ayacucho. The mystery was finally unraveling. Would

I really meet someone there who would provide me with more insight into the questions? I was about to find out.

Suddenly I could see mountains rising up out of the clouds in their longing to catch the diminishing warmth of the lowering sun. The Andes! They were treating me to an abundance of color shades: brown, red, gray and green. Distinctly different from the Rocky Mountains with their jagged rocky peaks, snow-covered tops and blankets of forests on their flanks, the Peruvian Andes appeared much older, more rounded and seemed quite a bit dryer. But like the Rockies, they expressed great power. Most of the vegetation was spread out and not very tall. Some areas were entirely without plant life, consisting solely of different kinds of reddish and brown rock.

Then we crossed the tall mountain peaks indicating the South American Continental Divide. A lot of the valleys on the east side were cultivated in plateaus, like giant stairs along the mountain flanks. During the remainder of our flight I could see these finely cultivated plateaus almost everywhere. "What a fabulous display of human ingenuity," I thought. A feeling of deep admiration for the creators of these giant stairs welled up inside of me. Their vision and labor had turned the mountains into cultivatable fields providing food for millions of people across the centuries.

The plane started to descend, so we had to be close to Ayacucho.

"We're almost there," Pedro said in confirmation of my thoughts.

After a smooth landing the plane came to a standstill on the cracked concrete runway of the Ayacucho City airport. When we walked out of the plane the dry afternoon heat welcomed us to the land known as 'the corner of the dead.' We debarked onto the tarmac and were led into a small airport building.

The airport was only an old hall with a worn luggage belt. The walls were bare and had a yellowish, sandy color. In front of one of the walls was a unique piece of artwork of a kind I had never seen before. It was a large, built-to-scale, three-dimensional landscape of a religious procession. It included hills and mountains, little houses, a church, lots of people in ceremonial dress, animals, trees, vegetation and Christian religious symbols. It was created out of clay and painted in vibrant colors. This absolutely marvelous piece of work was a depiction of the Holy Week celebrations before Easter, according to Pedro. Throughout Latin America, the Holy Week is a very special Christian celebration.

A well-dressed man greeted us and was introduced to me as Eduardo, the general manager of the Ayacucho hotel. While we were all waiting for our luggage to arrive, the airport had transformed into something like a little market place packed full of people. All around us people were greeting and hugging each other. Taxi drivers were hustling to get clients, and hotel salespeople were offering cheap accommodation. I noticed that all this happened under the watchful eye of armed guards.

Our luggage arrived. I picked up my bag from the belt and draped my jacket over it. The general manager offered to carry my bag. As I never felt it was appropriate to have my luggage carried by someone else unless it was the bellboy who made his living that way, I politely turned his offer down. Upon leaving the building I noticed on the side of the airport exit a woman dressed in vivid blue with a brown hat. Her baby, draped in a shawl of vibrant rainbow colors, was resting against her breast. She was begging for money. After my experience in Salta, I was determined to give something to this woman and walked up to her. While holding out her hand, she looked at me and there I saw them again. The eyes! The same dark, deep mysterious eyes like the old woman in Salta and the young Ethel in San Cristobal. I was paralyzed and felt myself drowning once again in those mirrors of the soul. However, the baby's cry returned me to my wits.

I turned around, got my wallet out of my jacket on top of my bag and took out some money. When I turned back to give it to her, she was gone. Vanished! In total disbelief I frantically looked around to see if I could detect any trace of her, to no avail. How could she have disappeared right from under my nose? I had only turned my back on her for some thirty seconds or so!

Pedro and Eduardo walked up to me, concerned.

"What do you need?" Pedro asked.

"Are you looking for something? Did you lose something?" Eduardo added.

"No, no," I explained. "I just wanted to give something to the begging mother with her baby, and she suddenly disappeared. I don't know where she went. Did either of you see her walk off?"

A confused expression appeared on both Pedro and Eduardo's face. They looked at each other, then back at me like they wanted to say something but were short of words.

Finally, Pedro managed to stammer, "We are sorry, Paul, but we did not see a mother with a child at all. I think we were discussing the recent protests in the city and the upcoming national strike too intensely to notice her."

"Are you saying you did not see the woman I walked up to a few minutes ago? She was all dressed in blue with a brown hat, and her baby was strapped in a shawl around her neck. You must have seen her!" I responded in disbelief.

"I am sorry, Paul," Pedro politely replied. "We did see you walk off, but we did not see any woman with a baby. We thought you had dropped something and were trying to find it."

I didn't know what to say. "Am I starting to hallucinate?" I thought, embarrassed. "Could the altitude cause this? What must these guys think of me?"

But deep inside, I *knew* she had been there. I had seen her. I had looked into her eyes, and the baby had cried.

"Well, she must have walked away before both of you looked over here," I declared. "Let's go to the hotel."

As we drove to the hotel I replayed the airport event in my head. I knew I had seen this woman. She had disappeared as miraculously as the old woman in Salta and at Santiago airport. The mystery was certainly continuing here. "Hopefully, I will get some answers tomorrow," I thought.

Like Salta, Ayacucho was a Spanish colonial city with red clay tiled roofs and romantic architecture. An old city, it clearly had lacked the required capital to maintain its buildings and streets during the last half century. Its streets of row houses were small, leaving just enough room for two cars to pass each other. On both sides were small walkways, and throughout the town the asphalt pavement was cracked, chipped and occasionally scarred with big potholes. The houses were painted mostly in white, terracotta, green, blue and yellow. Once in a while a fresh painted facade would jump out, but most of the homes had seen their last coat of paint a long time ago, leaving them with a dirty, dull appearance. A bunch of telephone and electricity cables ran along the facade of the houses.

There were lots of people, but cars seemed scarce. Most of the vehicles I saw were at least twenty years old, and in a condition that we would consider unsafe in North America. The older women in town were dressed in colorful traditional Andean clothing with either brown or black hats. A lot of them were carrying packs on their backs in their vibrantly-colored, woven shawls. The younger people and the men were mostly dressed in commercial jeans, T-shirts and jackets.

The hotel was right in the center of town. We passed by the central market square with its arched Hispanic walkways topped with balconies. There was an old stone church, and in the center of the square was a little park with flower beds, benches and some trees surrounding a statue of Simon Bolivar—South America's greatest general and freedom fighter who had liberated the continent from the Spaniards in the early 19th century. The market square was well maintained, and seemed to be the jewel of the city.

The hotel was one block beyond the square. Upon arrival we entered the spacious lobby of an old colonial hotel. As the bellboy unloaded our luggage, the receptionist greeted us warmly and offered us some coca tea, made from the same plant of which cocaine is produced. A bit surprised by the offering of the unusual local drink, I threw a questioning look towards Pedro.

"It helps to prevent altitude sickness," Pedro explained. "If you drink it as tea, there are no other side effects. It certainly doesn't make you high!" he laughed. "However, you might want to be careful, because I have heard that it does leave traces of cocaine in your hair, and you might test positive to cocaine use when you travel back to America."

Since my flights from Latin America to Canada always took me through the United States, I decided to play it safe and declined the tea. We checked in, and went to our rooms to quickly refresh ourselves.

My room was spacious but very old. I estimated that the last renovations must have been completed more than thirty years ago. I liked the antique character of the furniture, but the bed with its solid slat bottom and worn linen was anything but comfortable. The view from my window over the city with its vibrant red rooftops, surrounded by the Andes' dry old mountaintops, was magnificent. I checked if I could log onto the internet, but quickly noticed this was not an option. The telephone cord had a fixed connection in the wall, and no other plugs were available. E-mail would have to wait for two days.

When we met again some fifteen minutes later Eduardo gave us a professional tour of the property. The hotel, with its Spanish colonial architecture, certainly had potential. It was spacious and had large rooms. The problem was that it required a significant investment to renovate basics like the beds, bathrooms, floors and curtains. I just wasn't sure that such investment would be justifiable based on the potential numbers of hotel guests this city could attract.

One of the stops on our tour was the hotel's rooftop. The vistas of the setting sun above the Andes were incredible. In every direction I was treated to a spectacle of colors and shades that were dancing over the rounded mountains.

"I really would like to travel into those mountains," I said dreamily.

"Don't worry," Pedro replied. "On Wednesday we'll drive through just such a landscape for a full day on our way to Ica."

"I am going to enjoy that," I smiled.

"It is going to be an adventure for both of us," Pedro promised. "I have not crossed the Andes by car either. We will drive over one of the highest mountain passes in the country.

"But what do you want to do tonight?" he asked, changing the subject.

"I don't know. What did you have in mind?" I questioned in return.

"Whatever you would like to do," he insisted. "Eduardo has volunteered to take us for dinner. However, it's his son's birthday, and he would have to cancel his family's birthday dinner."

"Eduardo," I said, "family is very important to me, and I would not like to miss the birthday dinner of my son either, so I think you should celebrate at home tonight. We can have lunch tomorrow."

I explained to Pedro that I always enjoyed meeting with locals and eating in typical local restaurants.

"Let me make a phone call," he responded. "I might be able to arrange something I believe you will enjoy."

We returned to our rooms and agreed that Pedro would phone me with the details as soon as he had made arrangements. I unpacked my bags and had just laid down on my bed when the phone rang. "We are going for dinner at my friend's house," Pedro said. "He teaches history at the university. We have to leave in ten minutes."

"Sounds great," I replied. "What should I wear?"

"Something casual. Jeans are fine." Pedro answered.

Corner of the Dead

A little later we were driving the hotel van in an easterly direction through the streets of Ayacucho. The further we got away from the center, the worse the condition of the roads got. Eventually the asphalt pavement changed into gravel and took us up the flank of a hill to some more recently built concrete houses on the edge of town. They didn't sport the nice colonial architecture as those in the center of town, but did have a fabulous view of the city with its lights twinkling in the night sky set against a backdrop of dark protective mountains. All the houses up here were detached, and most of them bigger than the ones in the town streets. They also all had their own small private garden.

Pedro pulled up at a yellow house and said, "This is where Victor lives."

An older, suntanned man opened the door. He had deep lines in his forehead below his graying hair. His dark piercing eyes revealed great intelligence and deep wisdom. He looked to be in good shape, and like most Peruvians, was quite a bit smaller than me.

"Pedro, my friend, I am so glad to see you again, " he welcomed in a deep, warm voice and with a smile on his face.

Pedro introduced me to Victor before we entered the modest house. In the dining room we were introduced to Carlos and Isabel. Both must have been in their late twenties or early thirties, and had a certain serenity and maturity to them. Their eyes revealed a mixture of painful memories and visionary dreams.

We sat around the table, and while Pedro explained the purpose of my visit to Peru, we enjoyed a modest meal of corn soup followed by pork chili.

Since Victor was a history teacher at the Ayacucho University, I decided to question him about the origin of the town's name.

"Victor," I started, "I have been told Ayacucho means 'corner of the dead' in the Quechua language. How did it get its name?"

"You have been informed well," Victor answered. "Most travelers who visit this region don't know that. It dates back to the days when the Incas took control over the region. The province of Ayacucho has been populated for at least twenty thousand years, and archeologists have found the earliest human remains in all of South America here. Before the arrival of the Incas, the Waris dominated the region. They had a sophisticated civilization and build a city of forty thousand people.

"When the Incas conquered the region during the late 1400's and early 1500's, they faced fierce opposition and launched a genocidal campaign. This blood bath got Ayacucho its Quechua name, and it has been almost like a curse on the region ever since."

"What do you mean?" I asked, intrigued.

"Well, ever since the blood bath, the region has suffered much in the way of death due to poverty, violence and war. It is almost like all of South America's injustice, human rights violations and suffering have been amplified in Ayacucho. Several violent battles, which were key turning points in the continent's history, were fought here. For people to really understand the origin of violence in this area today, it is essential to understand our history."

"Are you implying there is still a lot of violence in the region, even today?" I questioned, surprised.

"Absolutely!" Victor confirmed adamantly. "People long for peace, but with such historic scars of poverty and violence, it almost seems hopeless to rise above that. Hopefully people like Isabel and Carlos will be able to make a difference."

"So what violence is the region plagued by nowadays, and what are you trying to do about it?" I asked Isabel in an attempt to involve the others in the conversation, but it was Victor who answered again.

"Let me first explain how we got to this point, because today's problems find their roots in yesterday's world. It all started with the Incas' drive for power and control. It may have been well-intended, for they created a highly organized civilization. People had to work hard, but nobody suffered from hunger, and there was a sense of justice. The Incas respected traditional tribal values and a sense of community. Through wise dictatorial rule they organized the labor force around public and agricultural projects like terracing the mountain flanks to create more cultivated land, which is something we still benefit from today. However, their rule did not last very long. During the end of the 1530's the Spanish conquistadors defeated the Incas and established the City of Ayacucho. The Spanish did not apply the same wisdom in their government as the Incas. They looted, plundered, raped and murdered. This abuse and violence led to extreme poverty, and caused Indian farming communities to break down. Migration and rebellions were common. By the beginning of the 17th century, the Ayacucho genocide inflicted by the Incas was dwarfed by Spanish brutality. The Inca population, approximately eight million before the Spanish conquest, shrunk to a little over one million in merely seventy years time.

"During the next hundred years Ayacucho's culture and commerce flourished. A lot of colonial houses and churches were built during this time, and the university was opened in 1677. However, all this wealth was created at the expense of the poor rural Indians, and their situation worsened all the time. The Andean terraces were not maintained and started to break down, resulting in decreasing crop yields and more poverty. During the last years of the Spanish colonization Ayacucho's importance was overshadowed by Lima's increasing popularity amongst the rich and powerful.

"More violence came to the region in 1824. This was when the combined republican forces of Colombia and Peru, under the leadership of Simon Bolivar, defeated the last Spanish army in South America in the ultimate battle that lead to the independence of Peru. This historic battle took place on the pampas of Ayacucho. At last there was hope! Unfortunately, the creation of the republic did not improve the situation of the Indians in the Andes. Ayacucho further declined as all power and commerce became concentrated in Lima, and the local Indians still had to give up parts of their crop to the Republic."

"So is it this poverty that leads to the violence today?" I interrupted Victor's history lesson.

"Ultimately it is," he said, "but it first got much worse due to the globalization of trade before an organized rebel movement grew from it."

Victor's statement immediately caught my interest since it related to one of the questions I was trying to solve: "Is a global society a social globe?" If I had understood Victor correctly, then a global society was actually creating anything but a social globe. It was forming a rather inhumane, unsociable globe, which left poverty in the wake of international trade. I had always been taught the opposite—namely, that globalization brought wealth to countries. I wanted to understand better what Victor meant with his last observation.

"How did the globalization of trade lead to more poverty?" I asked. "Doesn't globalization generally improve economies and create employment?"

"It does indeed for Western countries," he answered. "They are reaping great benefits from it, like the imperialists did from the colonies."

"Certainly you cannot compare the economic drive for globalization with imperialism!" I protested.

"By way of illustration, let me explain the results of globalization as they affected the peasants of Ayacucho," Victor started, unaffected by my slight agitation. "During the late 19th century and early 20th century, Peru established global trade. Large sugar plantations sprouted up along the coast, and English and American investments shaped the course of economic life in and around Lima. The resulting industries created predominantly cheaply-produced goods for export to Western countries, and were in desperate need of cheap labor. The solution was a forced labor draft that allowed these companies to bring Indian workers from the Andes to the coastal regions. With all the focus of economic development on Lima and the coastal regions, the situation of the poor farming communities, which now had also lost some of their strongest workers, became even worse. Then the expansion of global trade during the 20th century shifted industries from Peru to other countries that had an even lower production cost! The now-obsolete workers, who had been forced decades earlier to move from their farmlands in the Andes, desperately tried to survive in the slums they created around Lima. So can you see how globalization only creates a temporary benefit for countries like ours? Once the corporations that lead this drive for increased wealth find cheaper ways of production in other countries, they move on, and leave in their wake an impoverished people. People here who once knew how to provide for themselves had lost that skill entirely over two generations, their knowledge reduced to only that which was necessary to perform their tasks for the multinational companies. Unfortunately for them, the skills they possessed were no longer needed."

"I never realized this," I shamefully admitted. It did not feel good to look at the globalization picture from this perspective because it ultimately made me, as a consumer of those cheap products, guilty.

Victor noticed my discomfort and continued. "The appalling situation of poverty in the Ayacucho area ultimately gave rise to the creation of Sendero Luminoso, also known as the 'Shining Path,' in 1980. The Shining Path was a revolutionary group that vowed to bring changes by creating a country-wide uprising of the poor farming communities. Like a lot of revolutionary movements, this one found its origin among the educated middle and upper class in the Ayacucho University. However, it would not have seen the light of day if a poverty-stricken population had not originally backed it up. The war they started lasted till the early 1990's, and killed approximately forty thousand people, of which ten thousand were right here in Ayacucho.

"In an attempt to eradicate the rebel movement, government forces and police resorted to cruel practices that violated fundamental human rights. Everyone in this town of 120,000 inhabitants has been affected in some way by the resulting violence."

"So are you now dealing with the aftereffects of that rebel war, or has new violence occurred?" I questioned.

"Both, since today's violence is the result of more than a decade of civil war." Victor explained. "I am working with Isabel and Carlos, two of my old students, on a community project to curb the city's youth violence. I wonder how long it is going to take to heal the town's wounds from its violent past," he mused.

"I did not know youth violence was an issue here," Pedro said, entering the conversation, "and I don't understand how it relates to the war with the Shining Path?"

"Ayacucho is currently being plagued by violent youth gangs. It is not that these are really bad kids; their behavior is the result from the war, poverty and oppression," Victor explained. "People's behavior gets shaped by their experiences. You need to realize that during the 1980's more than five thousand children disappeared in Ayacucho. Some two thousand were executed, or their dead bodies simply turned up. The kids had been captured by government forces and tortured in an attempt to get the names of the rebels. Under torture the children gave the officials any name they wanted to hear. If they were ever released, it was only to see their moms, dads, brothers, or sisters disappear. Even today, the police force has been known to use abuse and torture practices to fight the gangs.

"So these children have learned that those who have guns wield the power. As a result they have organized themselves into gangs. Their experience has taught them that violence will lead to power, and that's what they are trying to achieve. It is their way to create a sense of family that values and protects them. In their desperate search for happiness they find love, respect and safety in their gangs."

"What do you believe the solution to this problem is?" I asked.

"The personal violence that both Isabel and Carlos have experienced during the most active years of Sendero Luminoso allows them to connect with these teenagers. Once they are able to establish a relationship based on trust and respect, they focus on these children's unique abilities and skills, to gradually show them an alternative way to a happy life and societal integration."

"May I ask, what kind of violence have you experienced?" I carefully questioned Isabel and Carlos.

In a calm, controlled manner, Carlos started. "It was 1988. I was seventeen and lived in a small village in the mountains some fifteen kilometers from Ayacucho. Sendero had been active in the region for a while, and had attacked our neighboring village just a week earlier. One day, government military forces raided our village in the early morning. They rounded all of us up at the center square and explained they were searching for hiding Sendero fighters. They accused the village mayor of supporting the rebels, and executed him right in front of us. Then they picked a number of teenage boys and girls out of the crowd. In the process they kicked and hit them. I was the last one they brutally pulled out and pushed into the back of a truck. Before we drove off, I could see a group of soldiers take a number of young woman and girls and lead them to some different farmhouses.

"We were brought to a military base in Ayacucho and interrogated for our involvement with Sendero. I had never been involved with them, and tried to explain that I was needed at home since my dad had died when I was ten, and I needed to work our land in order to provide for my mother and my three younger sisters. Yet I was beaten and raped with the barrel of a gun. While I had told them the honest truth, under torture I ultimately confessed to what they wanted to hear. They convicted me and put me in jail. I spent eight years behind bars for something I did not do! In fact, I didn't even know anyone involved with the rebels, and all our villagers were afraid of Sendero.

"I was lucky in that the sister of my mom was married to a rich businessman in Lima. In 1995 the government granted amnesty to all military personnel involved in atrocities. In addition, they also started a process of investigating wrongful convictions in 1996. My mother's brother-in-law used his influence to get me on the list of innocent prisoners. I was one of the first ones to be pardoned. Unfortunately this process stopped in 1999, and there are still hundreds of innocent people in jail. I have been very lucky to get out. A lot of young teenagers like me were picked up for interrogation and never returned."

There was a long painful silence when Carlos finished his story. I simply did not know what to say. From the look on Pedro's face I could tell he was as shocked as I was.

After having allowed some time to let Carlos' unjust treatment sink in, Isabel commenced her story with a soft voice and a melancholy, painful gaze in her eyes. "I was twelve when I joined Sendero Luminoso," she said.

I sat nailed to my chair. I had no idea the experiences of violence and injustice were so close in front of me. This man and woman were younger than I was, and had a life experience far beyond the imagination of rich country citizens in our 'civilized' world with its global economy.

"That was 1984," she continued. "My mother was a peaceful activist and confronted the military and police with their human rights violations. She raised attention to the disappearance of the Ayacucho children and was even successful at getting some of them back. On January 10th, 1984, at noon, a paramilitary execution squad gunned her down right in front of my eyes in the middle of the street. The rest of my family received death threats and decided to move to Lima, but I ran away and joined the rebels. A fourteen-year-old boy from our street had disappeared the week before. His body was found the day before they executed my mother. I concluded that if things like that could happen, my life was not safe anyway. So I decided to fight this evil. I wanted to create a better world, one where people would find justice and not starve from hunger. A more balanced world, where community values were important and people cared for each other. I wanted to fight for the poorest and the oppressed."

She paused for a while in thought and then hesitantly said, "And I wanted to avenge the death of my mother. Sendero just happened to offer that opportunity. I was too young to understand their entire philosophy and vision, but they allowed me to fight the evil people. That was enough for me at the time!

"Still, it was not an easy life. We would walk for long distances, sometimes in the middle of the night. Some days we had no food at all. In the beginning we would attack only military and strategic targets. I fought fiercely in battle each time, reawakening the memories of my mother's assassination. I have always thought she protected me and prevented the bullets from hitting me. By the time I was fifteen I was the leader of a rebel party. Our targets expanded to include aide workers, teachers, community leaders, nuns and priests. Sometimes we were ordered to attack peasant villages when it was believed they had betrayed us.

"But by the time I was seventeen and my need for revenge had somewhat subsided, I started to question what we were doing. I had a sense we had become as cruel as those whom I wanted to fight in the first place, but by then Sendero had become my family. These were my friends and comrades who would fight with me side by side and give their life for me. We cried together, mourned together, celebrated victory together and laughed together. The love of my life was a brave guerrilla. He was my right hand in leading the column. Then, in 1999, Fujimori's government armed the farmers, who organized peasant patrols to protect their villages against us."

She paused again and gazed, eyes filled with painful tears, into the burning candle in the middle of the table. Nobody even thought about disturbing the silence. Her soft voice, now vibrating with sorrow, continued, "One winter morning we raided another village. It was a target because its people had refused food to another Sendero group and had threatened to shoot them. Felix, my boyfriend, got shot that morning. A poor peasant who defended himself and his family against us killed him. Felix died in my arms just before sunrise. Then I realized we had become as evil as those I wanted to fight, and that those whom I wanted to protect and fight for had killed the man *I* loved in protection of what *they* loved.

"After that raid I left Sendero. I know now that the Shining Path was the wrong path. I did not have bad intentions when I joined them; like most of my fellow comrades, I did not follow this course to kill people, although there was a revenge element in my case. We only wanted to create a better world."

Totally captured by the depth and tragedy of Isabel's and Carlos' stories, Pedro and I stared speechless into the candle flame.

"Because they endured the same pain, they can connect with today's teenagers at a deeper level." Victor broke the emotional atmosphere. "They have been there, walked the path of violence, endured the torture and ultimately found a way to peaceful happiness. Teenagers identify with them, and when Isabel or Carlos praise their skills, it means a lot to them. Once respect and trust is established, Isabel and Carlos challenge the teenagers' path and, based on their life experience, offer them alternative, non-violent directions. It is a slow process, but one cannot expect fast progress and change in a city with such deep wounds."

Pedro looked at me and clearly did not know what to say.

"Isabel," I asked, "based on your experience with Sendero Luminoso, what is your opinion about violence as a means to change?"

"As you can imagine, I have given that question a lot of thought since leaving the rebels. As part of my quest for knowledge and understanding I met Victor. During the 90's he ran evening and weekend classes for adults who had not completed school. Apart from farmers, there were a lot of ex-prisoners and rebels among his students. That's how Carlos and I met," she said while she lovingly covered his hand with hers.

"In my search to find justification for violence, I studied the Bible and Tolstoy, to get a religious perspective on the subject; Gandhi, to understand the pacifist rational, the concept of peaceful disobedience and how it led to his success in India; Che Guevara, to understand the view of the ultimate guerilla fighter; and the Tao Te Ching, to understand the natural universal forces of life. I am not sure if I have a correct answer to your question at this point. I am not even sure if there *is* a right answer. It might well be possible that my answer will further evolve and change over the coming years, but I will share with you my current perspective.

"The Bible is quite clear about violence and totally rejects it. We should not kill, and when someone harms us, we should turn the other cheek, forgive and love them. Tolstoy's work analyzes that particular subject of the Bible in depth and makes an absolutely solid case for pacifism. However, as indicated by Tolstoy, it is a difficult path, violated by the Church itself throughout history whenever it suited its quest for power, wealth and expansion. Ironically, while killing is forbidden in the Ten Commandments, throughout history numerous wars were fought by so-called Christians in the name of God. People kill and get killed in wars!" Isabel said, raising her voice somewhat in frustration.

"Gandhi was inspired by Tolstoy's work," she continued thoughtfully. "He applied total pacifism and was successful in convincing the masses to follow his peaceful disobedience approach, leading ultimately to the independence of India. However, fighting did occur and people did get killed in the process, although not by the hands of Gandhi or those he led. Nevertheless, I do question if its practical success can be copied to a country like Peru.

"In Gandhi's situation, Gandhi was opposing British rule. Britain was an important world leader at that time and an example of civilization in the world. As a result, Gandhi's peaceful resistance received much attention in the British press, which allowed the British people to witness firsthand how their government was respecting human rights. When you have a dictatorial, corrupt government that does not honor human rights and does not pretend to care about them, peaceful disobedience would continuously be met with violence until all the activists were dead. I do not believe that Gandhi's way would have worked with the Chinese government of the time, or the Russian government under Stalin. He was successful because through the media the citizens of England, a rich, developed country whose image was on the line, were watching.

"I did have a problem with total pacifism as described by the Bible, Tolstoy and Gandhi, as I could not imagine being able to love those who had murdered my mother or tortured my friends. I might be able to forgive them for their ignorance and related actions, but such evil needed to be stopped. By not doing something against it, it would continue to spread and exist.

"I related strongly to what Che Guevara wrote, but believe that towards the end of his life his experience was similar to mine. I, and many guerilla fighters like me, only intended to do good and fight for the poor. However, the use of violence, the sense of empowerment and the lack of support where we expected it corrupted our judgement and ultimately our actions. As a result we became the evil we tried to destroy." Here Isabel paused for a while, thinking about her own words.

"I do not claim to understand the Tao Te Ching, but know it is based on the universal laws reflected in nature. In line with that principle I started to observe the universal forces and energies in nature in an attempt to find an answer that might be a middle road between total pacifism and violence as a way towards liberation. Everything in nature fights when its existence is threatened. That could be the existence of its own life, its offspring's or its group's, like in the case of a wolf pack or a gorilla family. So it seems to me that violence born out of a fight for survival is a natural phenomenon, and therefore also natural to human beings.

"What I could not find in nature is the useless waste of lives as a result of violence in order to maintain power and control. This led me to conclude that violence is justified *if* it protects life and is directed against those that threaten life. This means that self-defense or assistance in defense is always justified. When a larger force is threatening life, like the military and police force in Peru during the eighties, the defense should concentrate on the aggressors' leaders, its generals and commanders. However, it should not be directed at random against its soldiers, as a lot of them do not really have bad intentions. Most of them just follow orders. They are also the mothers and fathers of children. If you kill them, you become the evil to fight in the eyes of their children. Under no circumstances should violence ever be directed at civilians, or be driven by motives of revenge or the principle of an eye for an eye.

"I hope this answers your question," Isabel concluded. "I might not always have been very clear, but please understand that given my experience, I found this a very difficult subject to deal with, although an important one as well."

"Your analysis and position makes sense to me," I reassured her. "What do you think of the saying that 'power corrupts?'"

"I do not think it is power that corrupts," she said categorically, "but rather the *fear* of losing power. Gandhi, for example was a very powerful man, be it as a result of his actions rather than his ambitions, but it did not corrupt him. I do believe that the founders of Sendero Luminoso had honorable intentions when they created the movement. It was when they were confronted by opposing positions and recognized there was competition from church leaders, mayors and aid organizations for the hearts and minds of the people, that fear set in. The fear of losing power. I believe this is what led to a drive for absolute power. The result was corruption and the wrong choice of targets.

"It was fear that caused us to become the evil we wanted to destroy. There is a time for leaders to rise to power, and there is a time for them to let go of it as the world moves on and people, communities and societies reach their next point in their evolutionary process. Unfortunately few understand this, and a lot of leaders get corrupted because they do not want to let go of their power and attempt to obtain absolute power."

"That is very well said," Victor added in support.

It was well past midnight now. While I enjoyed the company and wanted to stay much longer, Pedro and I had to go. We had to work in the morning and today was March 21st. I wanted to be well awake, full of energy and alert for mysterious clues.

"I really appreciate that you shared your stories and insights with me. I am glad I met you both. It doesn't happen very often that I meet people with such first-hand experience with oppression and violence," I said to Isabel and Carlos. "It has been eye-opening for me to listen to what happened in your lives and realize that when all this was taking place I got married, my life was a party and I was mostly concerned with building a career and making money. In a way, I am ashamed! Ashamed to be part of a rich world that profits from this poverty and allows such injustice to take place. Other than making contributions to charitable organizations, I wish I knew what I could do to make a difference. To be of help."

"There is something you can do," Isabel replied, softly. "Tell our stories, make people in your country aware of what goes on in the world. The more people know and hear about this, the more chance there will be for solutions and a way out of this misery."

"I will do that," I promised her. "Unfortunately we need to go now. It was an honor to meet all of you, and I thank you for lifting the veil on Ayacucho's dark past for me."

Pedro and I stood up, embraced our hosts and left. Digesting the stories of the evening we drove back to the hotel in silence.

"Let's meet together for breakfast at eight," Pedro suggested when we arrived at the hotel.

"I will see you then," I replied and went to my room.

Waiting in bed for sleep to come, I tried to imagine what my life would have been like if I was born here instead of in Belgium.

How would I have dealt with such daily oppression right under my nose? What would I have done if my mother had gotten assassinated in front of me in a country where you cannot trust justice and its enforcing body? I probably would have joined Sendero Luminoso as well and ultimately would have reached the same conclusions as Isabel.

The Shining Path guerilla movement was born during the early eighties. This was a time of global trade, the existence of the United Nations and an awareness of human rights. It was the unseen, disregarded recurrence of extreme poverty and oppression that gave life to Sendero. Without it, it would not have had a purpose. While the blatant abuse of human rights seemed to have decreased a bit, poverty was still prevalent throughout Latin America. How many more Shining Path movements would have to rise up before we, in the First World countries, would become interested in this and address poverty as the root cause of all this violence, abuse and terror? With those questions shooting through my head I eventually fell asleep.

The Power of Listening

The nurturing light of the rising sun danced on my eyelids in the morning and woke me from my sleep. The curtains were in such bad shape I had not bothered to close them the night before. Besides it had been quite enjoyable to gaze at the millions of stars while I was deep in thought. Now it was close to seven o'clock.

"Good morning, sunshine!" I laughed. "What a magical way to wake up on what is supposed to be a mysterious day," I thought.

I took a shower and went downstairs to the lobby. It was 7:40 a.m., so I had another twenty minutes until my breakfast meeting with Pedro. I decided to go for a short walk around the block and enjoy the awakening of this Andes mountain-city.

Remnants of the coolness of night could still be felt, but the loving light of the sun was already warming everything up. People were walking on the curbs, men and women on their way to work. Small groups of kids were chattering and laughing on their way to school. Merchants were in the process of opening their stores, and street vendors were displaying their goods curbside. The small number of cars on Ayacucho's streets during the morning rush hour and the freshness of the mountain air were striking.

"How nice," I thought, "to live in a city with so few cars. People walk everywhere and in the process get their daily exercise without having to allocate time and money for the gym."

After enjoying the hustle and bustle of the waking city, I thought about Isabel's and Carlos' stories. "What would the mornings have been like here in the eighties?" I wondered. "How did fear affect people? Did they wake up questioning who was going to die before the sun would set, or who disappeared while they were sleeping? Or had they become so numb to the ongoing violence that they just didn't care anymore? Were they still able to enjoy the beauty of the rising sun?"

I tried to detect any remaining traces of fear, anger or sadness on the people's faces around me, but was unable to discover any of it. On the surface, it was impossible to tell what these people had endured.

"How many times do we really scratch the surface and try to find out what someone could potentially offer us or how we could be of help to them? Are we scared about discovering what we could find underneath the surface?" I questioned as I walked back to the hotel.

The bellboy directed me to the breakfast room where Pedro was waiting for me.

"Good morning, Paul," Pedro smiled cheerfully. "Did you sleep well?"

"I actually did," I answered. "And I was greeted by the morning sun when I woke up. I just went for a little walk. It's a beautiful day!"

We sat down and ordered breakfast. While we waited for our food Pedro took me through the agenda for the day. First we would meet briefly with Eduardo to get an understanding of the main financial and operational challenges of the property from his perspective as general manager. We then would meet with the restaurant manager, the bar manager, the maintenance manager and the head of housekeeping. To conclude the morning we would lunch with Eduardo. During the afternoon we would visit some of the town's competing hotels, although Pedro assured me that based on the quality of this hotel, there was really no competition in Ayacucho at all.

"After we have done our work, I will show you some of the marketable tourist attractions in the region," Pedro concluded.

In the meantime our food had arrived. I had noticed a mismatch of plates and cutlery when it was served, but could not complain about the quality of the dish I had selected.

After breakfast, I picked my briefcase up from my room and we headed for Eduardo's office.

Eduardo greeted us energetically when we entered.

"How was your son's birthday party?" I asked.

"Oh, very good. Thank you, sir, for letting me attend it last night!" he politely replied in a subordinate way.

"You don't have to thank me for that, Eduardo," I responded. "First, I am not your boss so you were entirely free to do what you chose to do, and second, even if you were to work for me, you would find out quickly that I consider family of primary importance."

We talked a little bit about his family, and I learned he had a wife and three kids of approximately the same age as mine. His mother lived with them and took care of the children after school because he and his wife both worked.

Once I had him talking it was quite easy to find out anything I wanted to know. He had worked in the hotel business all his life in various capacities. He had been assistant general manager in the hotel in Ica a few years before Primus hotels had acquired it. When he applied for one of the general manager positions with the Primus group, he had hoped to return to the Ica property as general manager but was, to his disappointment, sent to Ayacucho. Until this recent move, his wife and kids had lived in Lima. Given the violence and history of Ayacucho he did not feel this was the right place to raise his children.

Eduardo eagerly shared with me what he saw as the key problems with the hotel. He praised his employees and executive staff for the work they did with the little means available. Headquarters' lack of financial commitment and the related shortage of tools and materials resulted in a dilution of their quality of service and a decaying building. Establishing a trusting relationship with his employees, something he believed to be fundamental for the team's success, had been difficult for him, as his predecessor had been an internally promoted homegrown general manager. Also, throughout the hotel's history, positions of power had been held by people of Spanish descent from

Lima, and he had no idea how to overcome the employee's adverse attitude towards that. As a result, he was at a loss as to how to turn the performance of the hotel around. The financial results of the property were disastrous. The only good news was that tourism was slowly increasing again, now that people from outside of Ayacucho had forgotten about the years of terror.

Eduardo was a good man and I believed him to be a capable leader as well. It was wrong to put him here in Ayacucho because it indeed reconfirmed to the staff that the people in power had to come from Lima. It also failed to make good use of the experience he had with the operation in Ica. In addition, Eduardo was still young, and could benefit from some leadership coaching, which was much easier to provide in Ica due to its proximity to Lima.

"Eduardo, I thank you for your openness and honesty in assessing the situation," I said. Then I turned to Pedro and continued, "I think it is time for our next interview."

We walked to the bar and met with Garcia, the bar manager.

"How are you doing, sir? Can I offer you something to drink?" an overly polite and nervous man in his late forties asked me.

"I am fine. It is a beautiful morning!" I cheerfully replied. "How are you doing today?"

"Me?" Garcia stammered.

"Yes. How are you doing today, Garcia?"

"Oh, just fine, sir. Thank you, sir," he responded politely again.

"Garcia," I said, "I would appreciate it if you could get me a glass of water, some coffee or water for yourself and Pedro and sit down with us."

"Right away, sir!" he replied and away he went.

The bar had bright windows along the street side. I had noticed a door to the street in between the bar and the restaurant, but throughout the time I had been in the hotel it had been closed. The bar was spacious, had dark wooden furniture and beamed with character. As far as I could see, there was no reason for this bar not to function properly, as long as people could access it directly from the street.

A few minutes later Garcia came back with my water and coffee for Pedro and himself.

He sat down with us and asked politely, "How can I be of service to you, sir?"

"Garcia," I started, "I am representing an international hotel group and am investigating the possibilities for improving the operations of the Primus hotels. If, based on my research, I conclude that the performance of the Primus hotel properties could be increased, then we might get involved with the management of the hotels. We tend to optimize the results of hotels by helping the employees to perform at their best. We help them by providing training and the tools they need to deliver good customer service." I wondered how many times Garcia had heard this before without seeing any real change. "Now, while I might have some ideas on how to improve the performance of this bar, I do not know Ayacucho and the social habits of your citizens at all. Actually, I have little knowledge of Peru altogether. So my ideas might be all wrong.

"During my career, I have learned that the people who work in a certain job most of the time know best how to improve the performance of their business unit. That is why I want to talk to you. I would like to know from you, what you would do to improve the financial results of this bar if you were the owner of this establishment? Oh, and Garcia, please call me Paul."

"You want *me* to tell you what is wrong with this place? What needs to be changed in order to make it profitable?" he stammered with his eyes wide open.

"That is exactly right," I responded.

Garcia glanced over to Pedro, who sat quietly next to me and carefully listened.

Hesitantly he started, "Well, I think all is fine. We are the best hotel bar in the city. Right, Mr. Pedro?"

I could see Pedro's presence made him uncomfortable to answer my question.

"Garcia," I tried, "everything you tell me is totally confidential. All the recommendations in my report to your head office will be my recommendations, and I will make no reference to what I learned from hotel employees."

Still uncomfortable, Garcia quickly glanced at Pedro again. This time Pedro noticed and said reassuringly, "That is right. Everything you say is totally confidential. It just will help Paul to prepare a better report. Nobody at the head office will find out about what has been said during these interviews. I personally promise you that, and if you want, I will leave you with Paul alone."

"No, no, Mr. Pedro, I believe you," Garcia said, apologetic and more at ease.

I had noticed since our arrival that Pedro had a good relationship with quite a few of the employees. They respected and trusted him.

"So how does this bar compare to the most successful bars in the city?" I asked Garcia.

"Oh, sir..." Garcia started.

"Just call me Paul," I interrupted in a friendly tone.

"Okay, Mr. Paul," Garcia replied. "I don't think you can compare this bar with all other bars in the city; after all, we are part of a hotel."

"But if this was your bar, Garcia, would you not want it to be the best performing bar in the city?"

"Yes, of course, sir, uh, Mr. Paul. But it is not possible because people do not have to enter through a hotel lobby in all the other bars."

"So you are saying that in order to compete with the other bars in town, you need a direct access from the street into the pub."

"Exactly!" Garcia nodded.

"So what about that door to the street?" I questioned, pointing at the closed door between the restaurant and bar. "Why is it closed?"

"Oh, that door has been closed for more than twenty years now, Mr. Paul. It was originally closed to improve the security of the hotel during the years of Sendero Luminosso. We suggested opening it again when Primus acquired the hotel, but headquarters instructed us to keep it closed."

"Well, suppose it would be opened," I said. "What else would you do to improve the business of this place?"

Understanding that I was really seeking his honest opinion, Garcia started to explain all the things that were wrong, and provided suggestions for change and improvement. A number of issues I had already noticed but Garcia added some items I would not have thought about since they related to the specific social customs of the city. When he was finally done, I thanked him for his sincerity and for providing me such valuable information.

"Do you have any questions for me?" I asked Garcia.

He asked me about the company I worked for, my views on the tourism potential for Ayacucho and drinking customs in Canada. I answered all his questions as best as I could.

When we finished and were ready to move to our next interview he shook my hand and grabbed me by the shoulder.

"Thank you, Mr. Paul," he said while looking me deep into the eyes. "Thank you so very much."

"You don't have to thank me, Garcia," I replied. "I haven't done anything yet, and as I told you, until we decide to do business with Primus, none of these changes you requested will be implemented. So I don't know if any of it is ever going to happen."

"I know, I know," he replied, "but thank you for listening to me. No one has ever before asked me for my opinion on the business. Thank you for asking me, Mr. Paul!" He smiled with respect and gratitude in his eyes.

"You're welcome, Garcia," I said. "I only did what any good manager or consultant should have done."

Unfortunately a lot of managers and consultants didn't do so because they had too much of a need to demonstrate their own knowledge and skill. As a result they forgot to involve those employees on the front line who had first-hand, specific knowledge, and most of the times could provide simple and effective solutions.

Pedro and I had similar conversations with the restaurant and the maintenance managers. The last person on our list was Felicita, the head housekeeper.

After learning what I needed to know from Felicita, I asked her if she had any questions for me. She looked at me, deep in thought. It felt like her eyes were going to burn into my skin and it started to make me feel a little uncomfortable. Then she suddenly gasped, "You are the gringo! You are the one! You are present; you inspire and you genuinely care! I did not believe in the prophecy because I have never met a gringo with those traits. But you're the one! You are the gringo! I have to take you into the mountains; Anna Maria needs to talk to you," she said with a sense of excitement and urgency.

The sudden turn in the conversation left me speechless. I was expecting something to happen today, but once again the events took me by surprise. I knew I had to go with her and see this whole thing through. I looked at Pedro and noticed he had a bewildered and totally confused look on his face; I was going to have to explain the mystery to him.

"Felicita," I said, "I will go with you to Anna Maria. Can Pedro come too?"

"I guess he can. If Anna Maria does not want him there, she will send him out anyway," she answered matter-of-factly.

"Where are we going?" Pedro asked, still confused. "You know someone here?"

"Pedro, I will explain everything to you over lunch. It's a long story."

"Felicita, is it okay if we leave after lunch, at two o'clock?" I asked.

"I normally don't finish my work until four," she hesitated.

"I will talk to your manager and tell him I would like you to act as a guide during our sightseeing tour," I offered.

"If you can arrange that, then two is fine for me. Make sure you have comfortable shoes. We will have to hike for approximately forty-five minutes," she replied, "and beware; we will not be back before dark."

"Paul, it can be dangerous in the mountains, certainly after dark," Pedro warned. "You heard about the gangs yesterday, and there are still some small rogue cells from the Shining Path in operation as well. You don't hear a lot from them, but they do exist."

"Pedro, I have to do this, whatever it takes! However, if you are concerned, you can stay here," I said, focused and determined.

"No, no, I will come with you," he stammered. "But where are we going?"

"I have no idea." I smiled and I could see in Pedro's bewildered eyes that he was really concerned. "As I said, I will tell you everything I know during lunch. But now let's go to Eduardo and tell him our lunch plans have changed."

After making meeting arrangements with Felicita, Pedro and I headed for the general manager's office.

I started the meeting with Eduardo by complimenting him on his personnel and provided him with my general perception about the hotel's situation and potential opportunities. However I was careful not to share any details of the conversations I had had with the employees.

"Eduardo, I hope you will not take this personally, but unfortunately something has come up and I have to change our lunch plans. It has nothing to do with you or the hotel, but there is some urgent business I need to discuss over lunch with Pedro."

"No problem. I fully understand," Eduardo replied. "Would you like to use my office?"

"No, thank you," I answered. "I love the sunshine. In Canada it is winter at this time, so I was planning to take Pedro to the market place and get a small meal at one of the local restaurants while enjoying this nice summer weather. In any case, I appreciate your offer."

"No problem!" Eduardo smiled.

After Eduardo gave permission for Felicita to act as our guide for the afternoon, Pedro and I went to our rooms and changed into something more casual. I was glad I had brought my sneakers on this trip. They would be much more comfortable for such a hike than my business shoes. At around one p.m. Pedro and I left the hotel and walked in the direction of the market square. We found a little restaurant, ordered some food and sat down at a little table outside under the arched walkways that surround the center square.

"Now tell me," Pedro said impatiently, "what is going on?"

"What I am going to tell you will sound unbelievable. You might even think it is all a product of my overactive imagination and who knows, it might be, but I have to see this through to the end now." I tried to prepare Pedro in the hope that this story was not going to discredit my professional relationship with him.

"Just tell me what is going on!" he said impatiently.

"It all started a week ago in Salta, Argentina," I commenced the story, telling him everything that had happened since I had met the old woman. Pedro did not interrupt me once. He listened attentively. Throughout the story I could see his face change from disbelief, to amazement to absolute intrigue. "...and so today it is March 21st, and according to the mystery, I have to meet someone in Ayacucho who will help me to solve the question, 'Are human beings being human?'" I concluded almost an hour later.

We were quiet for a while. I tried to figure out from Pedro's face how much damage was done by my sharing this crazy story.

Then all of a sudden he said, "Fascinating; a real Incan mystery. I have seen how Felicita looked at you. She did refer to an old prophecy, and somehow recognized you in that. I've heard traditional Incas still practice some powerful magic, and although I have always been very skeptical about these things, the events that happened to you seem beyond coincidence. I would love to come with you. I am actually curious to find out who Anna Maria is."

Relieved, I felt the tension in my body fade away. "I am so glad you don't think I'm crazy!" I gasped and leaned back on my chair.

"I didn't say you are not," he smiled, "but I realized if I had experienced the same series of events, I would have been as crazy as you are!"

We both laughed, and I was glad to be in the company of someone as open and understanding as Pedro.

"Let's go," Pedro commanded energetically as he stood up. "Felicita must already be waiting for us."

A Hike in the Andes

Half an hour later we were leaving town in a northeasterly direction. Pedro was driving the hotel van, and Felicita had insisted I sit in the front passenger seat. She was leaning in between us to provide directions. After we left the city the road wound down into a river valley. Alongside the pavement were empty pop cans, plastic bottles, paper wrappers, chip bags and other junk; it was almost like driving through a garbage dump. Pigs, chickens, street dogs and cats were running everywhere trying to find their next meal among the trash piles. Lots of people were walking along the road with their cows and loaded donkeys. Those that did not have any pack animals were carrying piles of wood or other goods on their backs, shoulders or heads.

Gradually the roadside junk diminished, and by the time we reached an old stone bridge over a river, there was hardly any more litter. The river valley was lush and green, a stark contrast to the dryness of the surrounding rising hills. The road across the river started to climb, and took us higher and higher into the dry and rocky mountain landscape. The bare stone mountain slopes were scarred by vertical crevices persistently carved out by water searching its way to the sea. Cacti, small trees and shrubs could be found in areas where minimum life-supporting conditions existed. In this intriguing desert-like mountain landscape, the testimony of human ingenuity, perseverance and creativity was reflected in the lush green terraced mountain flanks that always announced the approach to a primitive human settlement. These agricultural villages and surrounding fields were a demonstration of the human capacity to survive in the harshest of landscapes.

Out here, away from the city, the country was clean, untarnished by garbage or trash. People were mostly self-sufficient, and plastic or tin packaging simply did not exist. After some forty minutes, Felicita directed Pedro to turn left onto a gravel road. Big rocks sticking up on the trail alternated with deep potholes, making our drive treacherous and slowing down our speed significantly. At times I wondered if the van would be able to hold it together. We were following a single track winding up along the side of a river gorge that took us higher and higher into the mountains. Below us ran a small little creek through a wide stony riverbed. I wondered what would happen if another car would approach us from the opposite direction.

After approximately half an hour the road came to an end at the foot of a huge rock mass. A small waterfall trickled down from the rocks into the canyon we had been following.

"We'll leave the car here," Felicita said. "We'll have to hike the rest of the way."

A small trail led us in between big rocks higher up into the mountains. In single file we hiked at a good pace. I followed in the footsteps of Felicita, who had taken the lead. Pedro followed behind. The thin air was giving Pedro difficulties, and once in a while we had to stop so he could catch his breath. Felicita, who had been born in Ayacucho, was accustomed to the high altitude, low oxygen air, and I figured it was not affecting me because I lived in the foothills near Calgary at four thousand feet.

The path ran alongside the creek and we had to cross the riverbed several times. The steep, stony landscape did not leave many options to find a way up. After a strenuous climb between large rock boulders the landscape suddenly opened up onto a mountain plateau. Up here the stream meandered more leisurely along the slow sloping highlands and was surrounded by terraced fields. Patches of trees grew along the side of the fields and creek. Nestled in the saddle of two mountains, the plateau offered protection from the elements. In the distance I detected some huts sheltered against a rising triangular cliff, the highest point of this spectacular highland. To the right side of the houses I could see more rounded mountaintops in the distance.

"Who would have imagined a village here in such a high remote location?" I thought.

The trail to the village led us along the terraces with their walls of stacked rocks. Seven stone and clay houses were built around three sides of the village square—a rectangular bare piece of land. The front side of the square was open and provided a clear view of the fields. Children were playing and a few women sat on the ground in front of one of the huts. I had seen three men working on one of the highest terraces as we made our way to the village, and a small herd of llamas was grazing on the hillside.

The children spotted us first and came running towards us. They all gathered around Felicita, who clearly knew them and handed out some candy, which I assumed she had specially brought for them. As we entered the village square, the women, who were de-boning a small slaughtered animal, got up and approached us, barefooted. There were five of them, all wearing big colorful skirts with large grayish blood-stained aprons. They wore white blouses and colorful woolen vests, their long black hair hanging in braids from underneath their brown- or black-rimmed hats. I estimated the two youngest to be in their late twenties or early thirties. The other three were older and must have been well past fifty.

While they greeted Felicita in a friendly manner, they glanced at me rather cool and reserved. There seemed to be some anxiety over my presence. They conversed with Felicity in a mix of Spanish and Quechua. As a result I did not understand everything that was being said.

After a short conversation, they nodded towards Pedro and me. The two youngest women continued whispering and from time to time looked shyly in my direction, and timidly smiled. In a prolonged explanation with the three older women I heard Felicita mention several times the name of Anna Maria. By the time she had finished, the expression and hospitality of the women had changed. They all came over to embrace me and tell me how glad they were I had come.

Entering the Light

"I'll check if Anna Maria can see you," Felicita said, and disappeared in a little house on the foot of a small trail leading up the cliff. The house, built of stacked stones and clay, had a thatched roof and a small door. There were no windows and smoke was rising up from the chimney on the far right corner of the hut. Pedro and I waited outside while the other women went back to their task of food preparation. I noticed some goats grazing just behind the houses, and concluded the women had slaughtered a goat and were preparing the meat.

The view up here was stunning. To the north I saw in between the houses a large valley with more majestic mountains on the other side. To the south, the open side of the main square faced the terraced fields where the men were working and the animals grazing. Next to the trail that led to the top of the cliff spring water trickled out of the rocks into a small pond surrounded by big flat stones. There was no electricity, no plumbing, no gas and no stores. There was also no noise, no garbage, no pollution and no junk food. These people were completely self-sufficient, living in harmony in the beauty of Mother Nature. I assumed they traded goods and crops with neighboring villages, and maybe once a year made the long hike to Ayacucho. I wondered if it was possible to complete this trip in one day. After some fifteen minutes Felicita finally stepped out of the modest hut.

"Anna Maria was just feeding her baby," she said. "She is ready to receive you now."

"She has a baby?" I asked, surprised.

"Yes, woman have kids here as well, you know," Felicita snapped.

"Of course, I know," I replied apologetically. "For some reason I thought Anna Maria would be the elder of the village."

"Well, as you'll find out, you don't have to be old to be wise," Felicita laughed. "She did ask that you come alone." She lifted her shoulders up in an apologetic move towards Pedro.

I walked up to the little house, knocked on the open door, bent down and entered a one-room hut with a strong smell of smoke. Once inside, my eyes needed some time to adjust to the relative darkness. A little fire in the corner, surrounded by some cooking pots, provided the only light. A variety of tools, harnesses and llama hides were hanging from the roof beams. The floor was composed of hardened, almost polished dirt. Next to the fire Anna Maria was sitting on a llama skin, her baby sleeping in a poncho against her breast.

I looked Anna Maria in the eyes and shivers ran up my spine. Not only were these the already familiar eyes, which I had seen for the first time in Salta, but this was the woman I had seen at Ayacucho airport the previous day.

"You were at the airport yesterday when I arrived!" I gasped, totally forgetting to greet her and properly introduce myself. "I wanted to give you some money, but you suddenly disappeared. How did you do that? Where did you go? How long does it take you to get to the airport? Do you go there often to beg for money?" The questions flooded out of my mouth.

"Gringo! Welcome. Sit down!" She interrupted in a warm, deep voice while her eyes radiated with love. She gestured to a hide next to the fire.

Getting my wits back, I said, "Thank you. I apologize for all the questions; please understand that all of this is very strange for me."

Anna Maria did not answer. It was quiet in the hut, uncomfortably so. The only sound was the occasional spark of the fire. I could hear the women outside talking and the goats bleating. Anna Maria was gazing at the fire, so I decided to do the same. As time passed, the outside noise seemed to fade away. I could still hear the sounds, but it was like they were coming from very far away.

"You have been guided here by the Universe." She suddenly broke the silence. "I understand you have a lot of questions. I can assist you in your search for answers, but ultimately you will have to discover the truth for yourself."

Another question popped into my head, but from the way she was talking I realized that I was not to interrupt.

"You were chosen because you're a gringo who listens and withholds judgment. Not many are like that. Most people's drive for acquisition and protection of their personal interests leads them to judge everything as 'good' or 'bad' in that limiting context. They judge people and events without considering alternative perspectives to their own. As a result they fail to see the lessons in the reality that presents itself to them, and in their ignorance frequently hurt other animal, plant and human brothers and sisters with their selfish actions. Your journey to Ayacucho—the walk through the 'corner of the dead'—was a test to see if you were worthy to meet Her and strong enough to walk the path. She needed to know if your love and curiosity for new discoveries were stronger than your fears. I am only here to guide you in your quest for answers and to prepare you to meet with Her. Are you willing to walk the path that is being offered to you?"

The question took me by surprise. I had a choice! I could walk away from this entire mystery! Originally I had thought Ayacucho was the ultimate destination on this journey. However, based on what Anna Maria had just told me, Ayacucho was only just the beginning of something much bigger. A life's journey! How was all this going to change my life? It made me nervous, but at the same time I knew I could not turn back anymore. Not now, when I was so close to lifting the veil. If I did, I would question for the rest of my life what would have happened if I had chosen to continue. I decided to put my anxiety aside and completely embrace what was being presented to me.

"Yes, I do!" I pledged.

"Then follow me," she instructed as she got up and walked through the door. "The time has come! We need to hurry now!"

Outside Felicita and Pedro were sitting down with the rest of the women. It must have been late afternoon already since the setting sun was low above the mountains. With her baby in the shawl around her neck, Anna Maria started climbing the trail to the top of the cliff at a strong pace. I wondered if she would be able to keep this up all the way to the top. But she did not relent, and by the time we arrived at the top of the cliff the sun was about to set and retrieve its golden light from the majestic mountains it had nurtured all day. I was well out of breath as we stood in front of a stone circle.

"We're just in time," Anna Maria said. "This setting sun marks the midpoint, the moment of balance, between an equal time of darkness and an equal time of light. It marks the equilibrium of the duality that drives our earthly existence. It is the fall equinox, for from this point forward in the cycle of life, darkness will dominate light and the Earth will rest, reflect and recover until a new balance is reached in the spring, after which point the Mother will give birth again and new things will grow once more."

I marveled at the absolutely stunning 360° view. Long shadows danced amid red golden light over the Andes which, after absorbing the life-giving warmth of the sun all day, would soon prepare themselves for the night. A light breeze and the fading heat of the sun were stroking my face now. The vast beauty and power of this landscape, and its utter stillness, made me feel very small and humble.

"Sit down in the center of the circle and face the setting sun," Anna Maria instructed.

I did as I was told.

"Now look into the setting sun and let its light flow all throughout you. Once its light fills you, close your eyes and keep them closed until I tell you to open them again."

Slightly confused as to what was expected from me I started to stare into the setting sun. When I could not observe anything else but the blinding of my eyes, I decided to imagine how the energy of our galaxy's life-giving star was flowing into me through my eyes. To my surprise I became aware of a golden, shining energy flowing into me. When this sensation filled me to the tips of my fingers and toes, I closed my eyes. Astonishingly, with my eyes closed, I could still see the sun clearly at the point known in many cultures as the 'third eye.' Never before had I seen anything with my eyes shut, for I did not even dream! This experience was new for me.

I concentrated on the sun in my head and all else around me faded away. Suddenly, I felt an energy vortex circling in front of my third eye. Instinctively I knew that Anna Maria was initiating this. She did not touch me, but with my eyes closed I could feel her finger spiraling in front of my third eye. A little bit later I felt the energy of both her hands gliding over my entire body. While she continued her energy massage, the power of the sun increased in my head and the vibrating light in my body intensified in brightness. Softly and rhythmically, she started to sing in a strange tone, words I could not understand.

"Concentrate on your breathing. Feel life-giving air enter and leave your body. Feel how its force energizes your entire being," she guided while pausing her humming.

In the past I had questioned the value of instructions like this and marked them as impossible or at best very difficult. Now I just did them, and to my surprise found them easy and invigorating.

A little later Anna Maria softly said, "Now, when you breathe in, I want you to squeeze your buttocks and pull the energy of the Earth below you into your body. Experience the power of our great Mother."

Without judgment, without expectation, and totally open for new discoveries, I followed her guidance. After a while a warm sensation of tingling energy started running up my spine. Once again I became aware of Anna Maria's hands, which were now working around my back and the top of my head. As the heat increased and flowed further up my spine, she seemed to concentrate more and more on the top of my head. Suddenly, she pushed her thumb hard onto the crown of my head. An intense pain penetrated my skull and made me nauseous. Everything started to turn in my head. I was glad to be sitting down, as I most certainly would have lost my balance if I were standing.

"Keep on breathing and pull in Mother Earth's energy," she commanded with a sense of urgency in her voice.

I focused on the heat running up my spine and tried to ignore the feelings of sickness. When she pulled her thumb away, I started to shake and intense, hot energy ran up my spine all the way to the top of my head.

"Now let go of it by breathing it all out through the crown of your head. Send it all the way up into the stars to the center of our galaxy," Anna Maria said softly.

I did, and for a split second a beam of white energy connected the earth and the sky right through my back. Then everything became white. It felt like I had left my body and the world around me had completely disappeared. A timeless state of total bliss immersed me. I just was! Surrounded by white light! Actually, I was part of it, and yet in some inexplicable way I still maintained my own identity and abilities of observation. It was the most serene feeling of peace and love I had ever experienced. I was part of it, part of the light, part of this blissful peace, totally at one with it...and yet I had my own identity.

This magical moment was so overpowering that I did not want to return to my ordinary state of being. The mountains, the air, the wind, Anna Maria, everything had disappeared. I was light! Loving, peaceful, wonderful light! From a distance, I could suddenly feel a slap on my face, then another one, and another one. I could feel my body pulling me back. Next I could hear Anna Maria's humming again and my connection with the light became thinner and thinner until it suddenly broke and, at lightning speed, I got sucked back to our earthly existence.

"Aaauw," I shouted when the next slap hit my face.

"Ha, Gringo, you are back! Hi, hi, hi." I heard Anna Maria laugh.

When I opened my eyes everything around me seemed to vibrate and glow. Anna Maria was dancing. When she stopped she reached with open arms to the now star-speckled night sky and closed her eyes. The almost full moon had risen, covering the mountains in a blanket of magical silver light. Herbs and small flowers were scattered all around me in the circle. And my perception of everything had changed. Everything was even more beautiful, more magical, than it had appeared to me ever before.

When Anna Maria opened her eyes, she walked over to me, took my face in her hands and said with a smile on her face, "You have seen the Source, the Source of all that is. Now, let's get back and I will try and help you find some answers to your questions."

Asking the Right Questions

We did not speak during the walk back. The moon's light guided us on our path through the treacherous terrain. As I glanced upward I thanked her for illuminating our trail. Never before had I given thanks to the sun, the moon, the animals or plants. But something inside of me had changed. I had become aware of the living energy that permeated all that is.

Anna Maria's baby made some gurgling noises. Up until now, the little boy had been quietly resting against his mother's chest. When we got back to the village, nobody was in sight, and Anna Maria's son started to cry a little bit. Anna Maria invited me to drink at the spring. We both refreshed ourselves with the cool mountain water and then entered her home.

Anna Maria laid her son on a nice woolly hide in the middle of the floor and put some logs onto the fire. We sat down on some rugs and she lovingly watched her child who now seemed totally happy again with his newfound freedom.

Then she looked at me and smiled. "You did well up there. I wasn't sure you would succeed. I am glad you found the light." She nodded silently and gazed into the fire.

"That was the most amazing, intense feeling of love and peace I have ever experienced. I don't know how to describe it with words, just that it was absolutely out of this world," I said, and noticed my voice sounded calmer, deeper and more relaxed than before.

"You have opened yourself to meet the One. You have been re-united with the Source and experienced the true power of the human soul. It is this power, this energy, that enlightened wise men like

Buddha, Jesus and other powerful medicine men and women learned to access at will and use to heal life on Earth. I have helped you discover the way. It is now up to you to practice this meditation on a regular basis and learn to access it on your own.

"Don't be discouraged if you only see the beam of light and fail to enter it. It can take years before you can access the Source all by yourself. Don't force it. Once you're ready for it, you will find your way to it all by yourself. However, it is of vital importance that in your heart, you carry strong passionate reasons for living before you try to enter the Light on your own. Without it you might not make it back. I know you wanted to stay with the One tonight, and I had to intervene to get you back."

"But I have reasons to live for now, and still, when I was in the Light, I did indeed want to stay there and just be Light," I admitted.

"So what passionate causes do you live for now?" Anna Maria questioned.

"Well, I love my wife dearly, and I have my children whom I love very much and want to raise well," I responded nostalgically.

"What else do you live for? What is your purpose in life?" she asked, apparently not satisfied with my answer.

"I don't know; isn't what I said enough?" I protested.

"You tell me—was it?"

"Uh... well ...I guess it wasn't since I did not want to come back. While in the Light I knew my loved ones also had access to the Source and would find love one way or another even without me around. I am somewhat embarrassed that I did not want to return for them, but somehow, I knew it wasn't necessary. The Light was so powerful, so amazingly beautiful," I admitted hesitantly.

"Don't be ashamed; your feelings are totally normal. Experiencing the Source is a profound, life-altering experience. But as I said earlier, before trying this on your own, you must discover your purpose in life. What legacy do you want to leave behind, and why? See, up until now you've seen your life only in relation to the people around you. It is essential for you to become aware of your higher

141

purpose. Why are you here? Once you can answer that, you'll find your true life's passion, the internal flame that will keep you going when all else fades away. When that flame is awakened, you will be able to leave the Light at will because you'll always be closely in touch with the Light inside of you," Anna Maria explained.

"I think I understand what you are saying," I said. We were both silent and absorbed by the fire for a while.

"How long were we on the top of the cliff?" I asked.

"Now that's a typical, senseless, gringo question," she replied shaking her head. "Why is that important?"

"I don't know…I was just curious since I lost all sense of time up there!" I stammered in reply.

"And that is exactly why you succeeded! Through meditation and prayer people can silence their mind and momentarily transcend the experience of time and dualism. At that point their spirit experiences its full potential and sometimes unites with the Divine. Don't ever keep track of time when you meditate because this will prevent you from freeing your spirit from this earthly existence. Most gringos are trapped by time, and as a result fail to reach their true potential."

"How do you mean?" I asked curiously.

"Time keeps a lot of human beings imprisoned in a limiting, dualistic, black-and-white perspective of the world. Ultimately it is people's misunderstanding of time that is the underlying root cause of their continuous judgmental attitude and their categorization of things, people and events as either 'good' or 'evil.'"

"That's exactly where I am stuck!" I exclaimed. "I can't find a conclusive definition of human values."

"That's because you are asking the wrong questions," she replied categorically.

"How do you mean? Shouldn't I find out what human values are in order to determine if human beings are living accordingly?"

"Throughout history, a lot of wise men and women have attempted to solve that question and suggested answers for it. None of them has been able to formulate a conclusive, universally acceptable answer. The bloodshed and conflicts, resulting out of differing values around the world, are a testimony to that. And the enforcement of dogmatic value systems has destroyed lots of lives."

"So how am I supposed to solve the riddles that have been posed to me?" I anxiously asked.

"As I said, by changing your questions," she repeated patiently.

"So, *what* should I ask?"

"Let me suggest a few questions to help you understand how to change your thought patterns. You need to dig more for the basics if you want to understand if human beings are being human. Rather than trying to determine what human values are, you should ask what values are? Why are people developing values? Why do they have a need for values? What do people want to achieve with the application of a set of values? In other words, make your questions transcendent of the duality on which all life is based."

"But will I eventually not get back to the same duality since all life is based on that?" I asked cleverly.

"If you want to understand duality and find out how to transcend it in daily life, don't ask what is good or bad; instead, try to understand duality. The true essence of duality is time. Therefore you should be asking, what is time? What causes time to be? Finding the answers to these questions will change your perspective of duality and help you understand that dualism doesn't mean you have to judge everything as either good or bad."

"I was hoping to find some answers here," I said, a little disappointed. "However, it seems the further I progress on this journey, the more questions I get, and no answers."

"That's because you are too eager to find answers," she said empathetically. "Generally people don't spend enough time thinking about the right *questions*. Once you learn how to ask the right things, you will find it easier to discover truth. For example, when you analyze the question 'Is a global society a social globe?' and want to provide a wise answer to that, you first need to formulate two other questions:

'What made it possible to create a global society?' and 'What is required to create a social globe?'

"If people would learn to ask more questions—and think about them before formulating them—they would be much happier in their relationships as well. Unfortunately, in the current egocentric world, most people have their eyes only on their personal rights and possessions. For example, when a mother forbids her daughter to go to a dance with some friends, the young girl will likely accuse her mother of being mean rather than trying to find out, through constructive questioning, her mother's underlying concern. Conflict and misunderstanding could be avoided if people would focus more on understanding each other rather than fighting for their perceived rights."

"I'm starting to see your point," I said. "And I guess you do not plan to provide answers to the questions I am currently dealing with," I tried.

"That is right," she smiled. Caringly she continued, "This is your journey! You need to discover your answers. I can only help by guiding you onto the right path."

"Is there any other advice you have for me?" I asked, dreading the end to our conversation.

"When you think about the issues at hand, break them down into their simplest components. It is much easier to understand the needs of a family and the behavioral drives of its members than to analyze how the needs of a nation drive the actions of its citizens. You will find the same essential dynamics in both scenarios, only the issues of the nation are, due to their size, more difficult to comprehend. Therefore it is much easier to analyze the dynamics of the small scale family unit and to extrapolate your findings to a larger segment of society."

"That does seem logical," I said.

"My last two pieces of advice to you are to observe and learn from nature, and be aware of the cycles in everything you do," she continued.

"What do you mean by cycles?" I asked.

"The universal cycle of life, which repeats itself in all that exists," she explained.

I remembered the conversation with the professors in Chile. Luciana had talked about the continuously repeating cycle of birth, growth, decline and death from which new life gets born again.

"I understand the cycle," I said. "So what should I learn from observing nature, other than how nature functions?"

"All existence is permeated by the same universal laws. Nature is the manifestation of the One in all its splendor and beauty. From a tree we can learn that when its branches are flexible they will not break easily. However, if they grow stiff and old, the limbs become more brittle. We are not different from the tree, and therefore it's better to keep our minds young and flexible rather than stiff and rigid. From water we can learn that its persistent flow to the sea cannot be stopped; it even carves through the strongest rock. At best you can guide it and try to direct its path. Evolution, change, the cycle is like water: You cannot stop it. At best you can guide it and provide direction to it."

"I have the opportunity to spend a lot of time in the mountains in Canada," I said. "I understand how to learn from nature, and in the future I will observe the Universal Laws more carefully."

"The Divine teachings are being displayed all around us. We only need to take time to observe and learn. Unfortunately, most people are so detached from nature they do not even understand their connection with it. They see themselves as separate from the Mother rather than as an integral part of Her. Some very strange behaviors have developed from this perspective, like the idea of sin in Christianity. The love between a man and a woman is the most sacred thing in this world and their union, through sexual intercourse, leads to the birth of new life. It's the ultimate divine act of creation. The magnificence of this miracle can be seen everywhere in nature, from the plants to the animals, including humans. It's unhealthy and limiting to use a set of narrow dogmatic principles to judge such a celebration of life and love as a sin. Such blatant misconceptions lead to very unnatural, and sometimes destructive, behavior."

"I completely understand what you are saying!" I responded. "I will start paying more attention to what Mother Nature and the Universe are teaching us each day."

"Let's go and see if we can find your friends and get you some food," Anna Maria said, changing the topic as she picked up her son.

A Test of Faith

I followed Anna Maria outside. She walked over to the largest house on the other side of the square, knocked on the door and said something in Quechua. After someone answered we entered the house. Three women and two men from the village, as well as Pedro and Felicita, were sitting on the floor around the fire. They were laughing and eating soup out of clay bowls. Four children were playing in the opposite corner. The house was packed.

Anna Maria said something to one of the woman who gave her two bowls. She filled them with the soup from above the fire and handed one to me.

"Eat this now," she said. "It will warm you up and provide you energy for the trip back."

I thanked her, sat down next to Pedro and tasted the soup. It was a delicious goat broth with different vegetables and large pieces of meat and potatoes. Several of our hosts were involved in conversation about the day-to-day life in the village and constantly got everyone laughing. To the delight of the crowd one man told us a story of how one of the llamas had pushed him in the pond when he was washing his face. It was a unique experience to share a meal with such real people who lived in complete harmony with their surroundings and were able to find joy in the small things of life.

It must have been close to midnight when we left. Following Anna Maria's advice about the futility of time, I intentionally did not look at my watch. I only wanted to enjoy this moment here, high up in the Andes, in the company of these people. They had invited us to stay the night. However, Pedro had reminded me that we had to leave early in the morning in order to cross the Andes and make it to our next destination, Ica, in one day.

When we walked through the terraced fields back in the direction of the car, I was glad for the guiding light of the moon. Without it, I don't think we would have made it down through the rocky descent ahead of us. Just before starting the climb down I looked back at the sleeping village bathed in silver light at the foot of the cliff. On top of the cliff, against the horizon, I detected a dark silhouette of a woman with her arms stretched out towards the moon. "Felicita," I whispered, "look up there!"

"That is Anna Maria," she said. "She probably climbed up there to offer a bowl of soup to the Spirits. She might stay there for most of the night."

"She is a remarkable woman," I said in admiration.

"She most certainly is," Felicita confirmed.

I sent Anna Maria my thanks and recalled her words on our departure. She had walked with us a few hundred yards on the trail. After saying goodbye to Pedro and Felicita, she had taken my hands and said, "Go now. Get to Salvador before the full moon on Friday night. Find your friend. Be attentive and open. Learn from your experience. You'll have the opportunity to attain a lot of wisdom during this final part of your preparation. Be ready to recognize and accept it."

During the silence that followed she had looked me deep in the eyes. I had marveled at the beauty and peace of her soul and the depths of wisdom embedded in this mother. She had embraced me and at that moment, the light of our hearts had touched and merged. I had felt the pureness of her soul, and her energy and light had flowed throughout my body. When we broke that magical connection she had said, "You're a good man. Go now. Have courage on your journey. I'll be with you and guide you to the Truth." Then she had turned around and returned to the village.

The experience had left me speechless. It was only when she was walking back to the village that I shouted, "Thank you. Thank you, Anna Maria."

I turned away, left the plateau behind me and started the downhill journey through the rocks. There was something mysterious about hiking in the Andes under the silver light of the moon. We were all quietly enjoying the silence of the night when suddenly, just before the final creek crossing, two dark figures stepped in front of us from behind the rocks. In panic I looked behind me and noticed another four men. Searching desperately for an escape, I detected approximately a dozen men on each side of the gorge. With rifles aimed at us, the men closed in. They were dressed in black, or mostly dark, clothing. Black shawls covered their faces, and the light of the moon was blocked from their eyes by the rims of their hats.

Felicita was rudely told to shut up when she started to explain that we were just ordinary civilians.

"What did I get myself into?" I thought. Once again I questioned why I had so foolishly followed the mysterious clues that had now gotten me into some serious trouble. Then I remembered my experience in the Light, and decided to trust the path and not judge or question what was going on at this point. I would go with the flow as advised by my Argentinean friend, Mario, and see where it would lead me.

Their leader, or the man whom I assumed was their chief, stepped forward. "Where are you going?" a rough voice asked.

"To Ayacucho, back home." Felicita answered, trembling.

"Where do you come from and why are you traveling at night?" the leader questioned in the same unfriendly tone.

When Felicita started to explain, a figure came running out of the darkness straight towards the leader. The slipped-down face cover revealed the face of a young woman. She whispered something in the chief's ear, which made him relax his body language and drop the point of his rifle down towards the ground. He shouted something to his men, and all the guns around us disappeared. I breathed a sigh of relief.

Next he walked straight up to me, totally ignoring Felicita and Pedro. I still wasn't quite sure what was going on, but tried to focus on my experience with the Light and banned any emotion of fear.

When he stood right before me, he shook my hand and said, "It is an honor to meet you in person, Gringo. My apologies; I did not realize it was you. These hills are dangerous at night. I wish you strength and success on your mission."

I stood still, absolutely perplexed.

He turned around, made a one-armed signal, and all the men vanished into the darkness of the night. Before he disappeared he said something to Felicita, and then we were suddenly all alone again in this mysterious rocky landscape.

"What did he say to you?" I asked curiously.

"He told me they were a farmer's patrol and did not mean us any harm. He assured me we would not see them anymore on the remainder of our journey. However, they would make sure we would safely reach Ayacucho," she explained.

"I really thought this was the end!" said Pedro, shaken by the whole ordeal. "I prayed and said goodbye to my wife and kids."

"Well, we're lucky we ran into the good guys," Felicita said relieved.

"What do you mean?" I asked.

"The war with Sendero Luminoso has technically not ended yet," she started to explain. "While the rebels have lost their power and are not a real threat to the government anymore, rogue cells still exist out here. These groups don't carry the same political ideals anymore; they just plunder, rape and kill. So the farmers still run their own night patrols to protect their families and animals. I am glad we ran into a peasant patrol, and not a rebel group."

I had had no idea of how dangerous this hike would actually be. Fortunately, our journey continued without incident, and we made it back to Ayacucho by one thirty in the morning. For safety reasons we decided to bring Felicita home before returning to the hotel. We all got out of the car in front of her house to say goodbye.

"Gringo, I am so glad I have been able to help you," Felicita said somewhat formally. "I will be proud for the rest of my life. Now I can tell my children and grandchildren how I played my role in the journey of the Gringo. Thank you!" She smiled and kissed me.

"Felicita, it is me who needs to thank you," I replied. "I would not have continued this magical journey if you had not recognized me and courageously brought me to Anna Maria. When you see Anna Maria again, please tell her I will always be in her debt."

"I will," she said, "but know that she will answer that you owe her nothing and that she will pray for you to recognize that."

We laughed and embraced each other before she entered her home. When Pedro and I got back to the hotel and went to our rooms he said, "Make sure you get some sleep. In the morning I will wake you at six. We need to leave the hotel by seven if we want to get across the Andes in time. After our adventure tonight, I want to make sure we leave the mountains behind us before darkness falls."

We both smiled and entered our rooms. Once in bed, I recalled my experience with the Light again and quickly fell into a deep peaceful sleep.

Educating for Sustainability

Loud knocks on my door woke me up in the morning. It was still dusk.

"I am up," I answered Pedro. "I will be downstairs in half an hour."

Despite the short night's sleep I was well rested. I showered quickly, packed and went to the lobby. Pedro and I had a quick breakfast, and by the time the sun was rising we had left Ayacucho behind us. Today we would cross the Andes over the highest pass on our way to the coast.

Just like the previous day, the side of the road was full of litter, and at regular intervals we would pass groups of people on foot together with their pack animals. After driving for about half an hour, the road trash started to disappear gradually.

"Pedro," I asked curiously, "why did we see so much garbage along the roadside when we just left Ayacucho, and now there's hardly any left?"

"Look at all these people," he said. "They are walking. Have you seen any other car so far?"

Confused about his answer, I admitted I had not seen another vehicle.

"What kind of garbage did you see all along the road?" he continued questioning.

"I don't know, just trash," I replied uncertainly.

"Did you see broken televisions, or old furniture or pieces of metal?" he probed.

"No."

"So, what did you see?" he prodded.

"Well, most of it was cardboard boxes, plastic and glass bottles, lots of pop cans, wrappers, plastic bags and some dead cats," I recollected.

"Apart from the dead cats, what kind of trash is this? What's it used for?" Pedro continued questioningly.

"I don't know. Why is that important?" I asked, a little agitated since I had no clue as to what his questioning was leading up to.

"Well, if you understand what kind of garbage you have seen alongside the road, you will also discover how it got there and why there is hardly any here," Pedro patiently explained. "As you will see when we drive for another half hour, there won't be any trash at all anymore."

I realized Pedro was only trying to help me solve the question on my own. The fact that he did not immediately give me the answer I was looking for was no reason for me to get agitated. That was my traditional gringo attitude surfacing! "Time is money and I want to get answers now! How arrogant we can be," I thought, "and how much real learning we miss due to such attitudes!" Pedro was making me think about the problem. Rather than getting annoyed by it, I needed to welcome his guidance.

"Okay," I said, much more engaged in the problem now. "Wrappers, pop cans, bottles, cardboard—I guess you could say all of that is packaging material."

"That is right," Pedro smiled, clearly glad I had started actively analyzing the problem.

"Most people here are walking," I continued my analysis. "It must take them a few hours to cover the distance we have driven in half an hour. So basically they throw away the packaging material from the goods they eat and drink during their hike. Since most of their goods have been consumed by the time they get here, they have nothing to throw away anymore, which explains why there is hardly any trash around here."

"Exactly," Pedro cheered.

"So are we going to see this phenomenon around each village we will pass?" I asked.

"No, you will only see this around the cities throughout Peru," Pedro answered.

"Why only around the cities?" I queried.

"Why do you think?" Pedro smiled, hinting he wanted me to further analyze the subject.

I thought about the small village of Anna Maria the previous night. It was as clean as a whistle. There wasn't any garbage, not even a single piece of trash on the trail to the village. But then there was no packaging either, no electricity, no factory and no store.

"All right, let me try this," I started. "There is no packaging around the villages in the Andes because there, people are self-sufficient and have no packaged food, drinks or other materials. They produce most of their own food, trade some and drink spring water. From the proceeds of their sales they buy tools and clothing on the rare occasion when they go to the city. Their poverty makes them very creative, so they don't waste anything and find alternative uses for things once they wear out. For instance, they will make toys from tin cans or bandages from old clothes."

"Very good," Pedro complimented.

"But why do people litter the roads around the city?" I questioned, unsatisfied. "If most people in Peru live so close to the land, don't they realize they're polluting their own environment?"

"Well, there are a few reasons for that," Pedro answered. "First, those that live in the city are so detached from nature that they don't think about the consequences of littering. They don't respect Mother Nature, and fail to see their relation to Her and how all this garbage will prevent Her at some point from providing for them. Second, those who live and farm in the country have no idea what littering is! They simply do not have the education to understand that plastic does not dissolve and pollutes the soil. You have to realize these people have thrown vegetable and other organic items away for generations. When they are in need of a peeled stick, they remove the bark from a branch and throw it away. They have learned that Mother Nature absorbs that which they do not need anymore. It requires education to make them realize these chemically-produced goods harm the land that provides them with their food and water."

I had never realized this. In the West we take so many things for granted, like education. I never considered the problems that occur when highly sophisticated products and materials get into the hands of an uneducated population. If this litter problem exists in the same way in the rest of the developing and third world countries, then the progress we have made in the West with regards to pollution is just a drop in the bucket. We all live in one world with a completely interconnected ecosystem, so we had better start thinking about garbage strategies that extend beyond our own backyard! After all, is it not we, the shareholders of these big corporations, who benefit from the sales profits in these countries and therefore are directly responsible for the pollution in these poorly-educated regions of the world?

In the meantime we had entered the vastness of the Andes Mountains. Indeed there was no garbage at all along the road anymore. We passed through a few small villages and were climbing higher and higher. The few souls we saw from time to time were farmers on their way from their homes to their fields.

Trade and the Creation of Value

We drove alongside a deep gorge with a small mountain stream coursing through the rocky riverbed a few hundred feet below us. I was admiring the shapes of the rocks and the trees that had managed to survive in this stony landscape when the opposite side of the gorge caught my attention. It was covered over its entire height with a thick layer of shiny yellowish sediment that ended in the streambed below and caused large amounts of bubbly foam on the water.

"What's that?" I asked Pedro, intrigued.

"Chemical waste from a mine," he said with a tone of sadness.

"What kind of a mine?" I asked in disgust at this sign of blatant disrespect for Mother Nature. The villagers downstream from here were most certainly irrigating their fields with this water, so how could anyone act so irresponsibly?

"Some kind of mineral mine," Pedro answered. "There are mines all over the Andes, most of them controlled by Canadian and American mining companies."

"So don't they follow the government's environmental regulations?" I questioned.

"Yes, they do. But that's exactly the problem: There's hardly *any* government regulation!" he stressed. "Peru, like most of the other developing countries, is desperate to attract industrial investment since it creates employment and helps the economy. As you heard at Victor's house, the government has to combat unemployment and poverty because it's such a fertile breeding ground for violence. In order to attract these foreign companies the government tries to make it as

156

lucrative as possible for them to set up shop here. One way of doing that is to have few or no environmental regulations. Cheap labor and very limited environmental rules increase the profit margins for these companies and compensate for the political risks they face in countries like ours. The mines provide a great export industry for Peru and allow us to obtain foreign funds to buy products our country needs to import."

"And for the multinational corporations, it provides a way to produce cheaper goods for their customers in the first world countries," I concluded with sadness. Ultimately this meant I, the gringo consumer, the shareholder, was somehow responsible for this grotesque pile of chemical waste. "What are we ultimately trying to achieve with this globalization?" I thought, acutely aware of my active role in it all. During this trip I had found in the wake of global trade only large scale environmental pollution and poverty. Most certainly, this could not be what multinational corporations—which in essence are *us*, as consumers, shareholders and employees—intended to achieve! For years, we have been telling ourselves that globalization is the solution to poverty and allows developing countries to develop a healthcare and education system. So what has been going wrong? Was one of our underlying assumptions fundamentally wrong? Is a global society a social globe? Now that I was witnessing the results of socially irresponsible behavior, I really wanted to understand why it was not.

"Pedro," I confided, "I did not get any of the answers from Anna Maria in regards to the riddles I need to solve."

Since we had left the village last night, Pedro had not once asked about what had happened. He seemed to respect the mystery surrounding the events, and would probably never have talked about it had I not chosen to bring it up now.

"I only got some hints as to how to discover the answers to the questions," I continued. "She told me to break the question down into different components, and that I would find the answers as long as I asked the right questions."

Pedro listened carefully but still held back from engaging in the conversation.

"With everything I've seen and heard during the last forty-eight hours, I really want to dissect the riddle about a global society being a social globe. Since we are going to be driving all day through these beautiful mountains, would you mind exploring the subject with me?" I asked.

"Am I allowed to do that?" he questioned. "I mean, did Anna Maria give permission for that?"

"Well, not explicitly. She only provided guidance as to how to progress with the analysis. I know I can, and should, seek advice from anyone whom I deem appropriate. By discussing it with you I hoped to be able to combine our knowledge, perspectives and insights. Hopefully both of us will get a bit wiser from it."

"It is a very interesting question," Pedro said with a sparkle in his eyes. "I would be honored to explore the subject with you. So where do we start?"

"Anna Maria suggested to ask what made it possible to create a global society and what is required to create a social globe. I think we should add a third question. What motivation led to a global society?"

"Okay. Let's maybe first explore your last question, and then tackle the questions which Anna Maria recommended," Pedro proposed.

"I suggest that the driving motivation behind a global society is trade," I said.

"I would agree it has something to do with that, but what element of trade drives globalization? After all, people can trade locally just as well," Pedro contributed.

"Good point," I complimented. "I guess it is the search for raw materials, cheaper production costs, new products and more customers. In other words, our striving for an expansion of wealth has led to a global society."

"Yes, I believe I could agree with that," Pedro concurred.

"But it sounds like striving for wealth is an intrinsic element of trade."

"Don't you think it is?" I questioned.

"It really brings us to an even more basic question: what is trade? If you look at trade today, clearly its purpose is to make money. But has it always been that way? Maybe for some reason trade evolved into something it was not supposed to be."

"That is an interesting approach," I replied. "Let's explore the origin of trade."

"As far as I understand it, trade first appeared among the hunters and gatherers. For instance, someone who had two fish and no meat decided to trade one of his fish for some meat with another person. First the two argued about what a fair exchange of value would be, and when they came to an agreement a trade took place. If the one person was a better fisherman and the other a better hunter, trading provided each of them with the ability to concentrate on their best skills and still provide a differentiation of food and goods for their families. Through living life in community with others and based upon an exchange of equal and fair values, each person improved their chances for survival. The specialization of skills resulting from the exchange of fair values allowed communities to grow bigger and to develop different trades, like tool making and eventually farming," Pedro concluded.

"It seems to me that within such a context of trade some people might make out somewhat better than others, depending on their relative skill level. However, it appears unlikely for someone to grow really rich while a number of other community members became poor," I observed, following Anna Maria's advice to analyze complex problems on a small scale. "After all, you could only trade that which you had produced, harvested or grown yourself. So that product must have had a relative value to the time and cost the trading partner needed to produce, harvest or grow something else. Value must have been measured by how something improved someone's chances for survival."

"Right," Pedro said. "And if someone started mining ore to make bronze spear points, that would not be of much value to you as a hunter if he poisoned your drinking water in the process."

"Exactly," I cheered. We were both feeding off of each other's energy, and I felt a great sense of pleasure in this team analysis.

"So how did we end up with a model of global trade where the pollution of this river below us is not included in the value representation of the products this mining company brings to the market?" Pedro asked.

"Good question," I admitted. "Maybe we need to look at the fundamental differences that exist between trade as we know it now and how it was when it originated? Hopefully we can find out what went wrong with this great concept of entrepreneurial activity and how greed, or the striving for wealth with no purpose other than that of accumulation, got into the picture?"

"All right," Pedro agreed. "First off, it seems that today not all production costs are accounted for by their respective companies. For instance, the pollution of this river is a cost to society and yet the corporation, which is responsible for initiating it, is not held accountable, despite the fact that it is a direct result of its production activities. In the same way, the health care cost related to obesity or lung cancer is clearly a social cost, and should be carried by the producers that cause these problems, namely the cigarette and fast food industries. Likewise, when an industry shuts down in one region to reopen in another, like the sugar industry did in the early twentieth century here in Peru, it creates a social cost because of the loss of jobs that arises in the country that the industry left. Again this cost is not accounted for in the company's books; it is left as a tax burden to be carried by the citizens of the affected country."

"I see what you are saying," I acknowledged. "A second major difference is the existence of money. Trade originated by bartering goods, but now we pay for things with money. Somehow I have a feeling that it was the introduction of money that got us on the wrong path in the first place."

"Of course! That's it!" Pedro shouted. "It was gold that created the imbalance in the world. By introducing gold as a way to pay for things, people disconnected their trading ability from that which they could personally produce. See, I believe that people originally achieved happiness when they were able to provide for the basic needs of their loved ones. As a result of their valuable contribution to their immediate family and community, they developed self-esteem and personal satisfaction, both of which contributed to a state of joy. When gold got into the picture, things changed. People were suddenly able to discover or conquer a gold mine, which strengthened their trading position exponentially. People got confused and started to think happiness was the result of the accumulation of gold and material possession, instead of the development of self-esteem through such valuable contributions to society as the providing of food, shelter and clothing. Even today, in the imagery of advertising, feelings of happiness or other positive emotions are linked to the purchase of a certain product. If you remember the happiness of the people in the village last night, then you know that nothing is further from the truth."

"I know," I agreed. "And I have seen other happy poor people in Chile. I think you are on to something with your analysis of the introduction of gold. It is exactly this accumulation of wealth and money that causes stress and unhappiness in North America. People are so concerned with what they have, don't have, or might lose that they forget to enjoy life. They are so inundated with worries that they can't see the beauty of the rising sun anymore."

"Trust me, the rich here in Peru have the same problems," Pedro added. "It's this goal of the accumulation of wealth that has created this global society. First, people of material-focused societies have explored the globe and conquered land, resources and precious materials like gold. Then, when human rights were introduced in the rich countries and conquering was not socially acceptable anymore, they came back, but only to buy the mines and resources they needed with the wealth they had obtained from their imperial rule in the previous centuries. And so the exploitation continues today."

161

"Wow, we have made good progress with this riddle. I believe we have a pretty good picture at this point as to how our global society developed. While the *misconceptions* that arose from the process of trading created the current imbalance in the world, trade, in its intended entrepreneurial form, is not a bad thing at all. Now let's explore what would need to change in order to allow this global society to become a social globe."

"I believe," Pedro started, "that in order to create a social globe there needs to be respect for all life. When that exists, people would not exploit another's life for their own personal material gain."

"I think that goes in the right direction, but the question is, how can that be achieved?" I asked.

We both were quiet for a while, exploring the far corners of our brain for some creative answers. Suddenly it all became clear to me.

"I think I have it!" I said excitedly. "If we want to maintain free entrepreneurial trade, which we agreed is valuable in its original concept, all companies should be subject to the same global environmental and social regulations. An independent international body, like a division of the United Nations, should create these international trading laws. These regulations should include accounting rules that incorporate the environmental pollution and social costs incurred by a company through the production or sale of its goods.

"There also should be a set of fair trade regulations, or a corporate equivalent of international human rights, to prevent corporations from exploiting other human beings. Last but not least, people in the developed and rich countries of the world need *education*. They need to be informed as to how they indirectly cause poverty and pollution in the world so that they can change their investment, purchasing and working habits. Most importantly, they need to be taught how to obtain happiness, and to learn that material accumulation is not the way to obtain it."

"That sounds like a great answer," Pedro cheered, "although I am a little confused by your last statement. Are you suggesting that people with material possessions cannot be happy?"

"No. What I meant is that it's the focus on material possession that is standing in the way of happiness. If someone acquires material wealth as a result of being the best they can be and living life to its full potential, they certainly can become rich and be happy at the same time. In that case their focus is on enjoying life by creating value for society and not on the acquisition of material possession. Their wealth is merely a result of their labor rather than the prime focus of their life."

"I understand now what you mean," Pedro said, pleased with my clarification. "It seems to me we solved the question." He smiled, satisfied.

I was elated to have an answer to the question, "Is a global society a social globe?" Not only did I know that the simple answer to this was "no," but I also had a fair idea as to how we got to this point and what we had to change in order to turn this world into a social globe.

In Search of Happiness

For more than five hours we had been driving through an absolutely stunning landscape. During all that time I had not seen one other vehicle.

The Andes Mountains in Peru were somewhat like a stone desert. It was much dryer here than I had imagined. In places small trees and cacti decorated the colorful palette of various rocks. At regular intervals stairs of green terraced fields could be detected from deep in the valleys to sometimes high along the mountainsides. Like oases in a desert they allowed people to survive in this harsh climate. I admired those who had built these terraces and the farmers who had climbed these mountains throughout the centuries to farm their fields on the roof of the world. "Such activity must keep you in awesome shape," I thought.

Passing through a number of little farming settlements with llamas and sheep grazing on the rocky mountain flanks made me realize how hardy and tough these animals must be to survive on the scarce vegetation here. At times the beasts would stand right on the road and force our car to a complete standstill. The llamas had colorful woolen pompons on their ears so that each village, which had its own unique color, could identify their animals.

It was a beautiful day, with a clear blue sky. Although the sun was burning, the higher we got the cooler it became. I had not considered our climb would impact the car at all. But as we climbed higher the speed of the car decreased; at such a high altitude its engine was lacking the oxygen necessary to burn the fuel efficiently. Pedro had taken precautions before we left, and apart from adequate food and water for the next two days, he had also brought two oxygen tanks with him.

I wondered what social impact such isolation from the outside world would have on local village life. After all, the distance that separated these people from civilization made them totally dependent on each other, a concept unknown in our individualized modern society. I asked Pedro to stop in the next village. I wanted to talk with the locals and get a sense of their community life.

Approximately fifteen minutes later we passed through what looked like a fairly recently-built village. On the side of the road three women were sitting under a canopy. They were dressed in the traditional Andean clothing: colorful dresses and woolen jackets with white shirts and dark-rimmed hats.

We stopped and walked up to the women. Their eyes were pale, their faces blank. When we indicated we wanted to ask some questions about their village life, they shyly, and I thought almost fearfully, turned away from us and totally ignored us. Their strange behavior was in stark contrast with the other encounters I had had with locals on this trip.

"Maybe they don't understand us?" I suggested to Pedro. "Maybe they don't speak Spanish."

We tried once more and talked somewhat slower but got no reaction. During this time an older woman in the next house had been watching us. I had no idea for how long, but she did not seem afraid to look us in the eyes. When she noticed our hesitant return to the car, she walked up to us.

"Pedro, wait," I said, and signaled in the woman's direction.

After she told us to wait by the car, she disappeared into one of the little streets of the village and a few minutes later returned, accompanied by three men.

One of them must have been close to his sixties and another around his fifties, both of them dressed in ponchos. They wore black hats and colorful scarves around their necks. The youngest one, whom I guessed to be in his early thirties, was dressed quite differently. He was wearing jeans, a T-shirt, an older brown leather jacket and a baseball cap. She pointed the men in our direction and walked back into the small street. The youngest man introduced himself as Sanchez, the mayor of the village. The two other men were his counselors.

"What do you need?" Sanchez asked.

I explained to the men I was from Canada and was interested to learn some things about their life in the Andes.

"Your life here is so different from life in the part of the world where I come from," I said. "I am curious how this distance from the city affects your community, and I wanted to ask you some questions in that regard."

Sanchez turned around and exchanged some words with his two counselors.

When they were done, he faced me with a gentle smile and said, "No problem, but I have to ask you a favor in return."

I was somewhat surprised but curious about what he was going to ask me.

"Today is the seventh anniversary of this village," he started. "We are currently preparing for our celebrations tonight at the village square, and I would like you to address all our villagers in recognition of this anniversary."

Totally blown away by the nature of his request, I stammered, "So what do you want me to say?"

"Something inspiring!" he answered decidedly. "You are a gringo, and you come from the North where people are rich and have made it in this world. Tell my people how hard work and good business will increase their wealth! Tell them we are on the right path in this village to building a better life!"

I had no idea what to say. But with a broad smile uncovering his missing front teeth, Sanchez offered his hand and said, "Deal?"

How could I refuse his enthusiasm? "Deal!" I said, and shook his hand.

"So what do you want to know?" he asked.

166

Sanchez answered, openly and without reservation, each of my questions. I learned the village was fairly young. It was founded as part of a government-subsidized plan to help people from the city slums return to the country and become farmers. Sanchez himself had lived in the slums, and was one of the founding members of the new village. He was proud the village had been able to attract people of different ages, most of whom had lived in the slums, but also others who had farmed in the Andes all their life. This last group had been crucial in teaching them how to live off the land.

A few of the villagers went to Ayacucho once a year to buy supplies and to sell their crops, but they were mostly self-sufficient. A number of the government programs had improved their situation, most specifically with relation to hygiene and education. Sanchez himself had learned to read since coming to the village, and he was clearly proud of that.

"But not all programs were effective," he said, amused. "We received so many sanitary toilet containers from the government that we started to use them as storage shelters for onions and other vegetables. While we might not use them for their intended purpose, we are still grateful for them," he laughed.

The villagers' biggest concerns were health care and their children's education. While things had improved, they were far from what he wanted to see. The closest hospital was a five hour drive, and no one in the village had a car. The only way to get there was by bus. In an attempt to connect them with the rest of the world, the government had provided one phone and fax machine for the village. They considered themselves lucky for this luxury since they knew a lot of villages higher up in the mountains further away from the main road did not have such an item.

When I asked if the community members helped each other if one of them had a bad crop and not enough food to survive on, I got a surprising answer.

"No! They would have to leave and go see if they can find work in the slums," Sanchez answered categorically.

"So they don't receive any help from the other community members?" I questioned in disbelief.

"Sometimes," Sanchez admitted, "but the way we see things in this village is that we only want to keep the productive farmers. If they cannot provide for themselves, they have to leave."

"Is that the way everywhere?" I asked.

"No," he said. "In a lot of the older villages people will help each other and share their crops. The fact that we don't do that has been difficult to accept for the older people who have joined our community because their ways are different. But from living in the city I learned that in the rich parts of the world, people only look after themselves. That way the good workers are separated from the bad ones based on their skills. In this village we want to become an example of farming success in the Andes, so we cannot afford to keep non-productive farmers."

When I told him I had no further questions, he asked us to follow him to the market square. Sanchez led the way through a small alley with large blocks of concrete and rocks spread along it. A small trail ran in between the debris.

"What are you going to talk about?" Pedro asked.

"I have no idea. I am trying to come up with something right now," I answered.

We turned two corners and arrived at a small market square where approximately seventy villagers had gathered. The square had a small wooden church with green grass in front of it and little houses built around it. In the center the Peruvian flag was raised. With the rolling mountaintops of the Andes sheltering the village, it was a charming, picturesque scene.

As soon as the villagers noticed our approach, all eyes fixed on me. I was at least a foot taller than most of them and the only person present with blond hair. Undeniably a gringo! Some of the younger women started giggling, and a few of the kids pointed their fingers towards me before they all started laughing. Some of the men smiled while others observed me in distrust.

Sanchez addressed the crowd, and a few minutes later, when he had finished, urged me to stand on a bench. More villagers had arrived from the surrounding streets, and they had all gathered around us.

"Speak," Sanchez instructed.

"Hi," I started uncomfortably, searching for the right words. "Let me first say that it is an honor for me to be here during the celebration of your village's anniversary. I live in Canada. Like the Andes Mountains are the vertebrae of South America, so the Rocky Mountains are the backbone of North America. Like you, I live in the mountains, in the Rocky Mountains near a city called Calgary." And suddenly the words came as I continued.

"That's probably where the comparison between our two worlds end. Where I live the mountains are covered with lush green forests, lots of game, fertile valleys and many mountain streams with plenty of fish. Compared to you, the people in my country are rich. After having traveled through this country for the last two days and meeting some really interesting men and women, I've come to believe that the people in my country have it easier due to the resources they have available to them. I have seen how you and other Peruvian farmers have been able to turn these dry, inhospitable mountains into terraces of green where you cultivate your crops. I have seen how you live in small communities and are completely self-sufficient. I have seen how you understand your surroundings and live in balance with Mother Nature. I have seen how little you possess, and how much joy you are able to have. And I am in awe! I admire your farming and survival skills, I admire your sense of community, I admire your closeness to Mother Nature and I admire your passion and joy for life. For some of you, the richness of America, Canada and the European countries might seem attractive. But it brings its own kind of problems.

"Lots of people in the rich countries are depressed. They live in fear and have forgotten how to be happy. They cannot enjoy the beauty of the rising sun, the music of the birds or the growth of a seed because they are too preoccupied with accumulating more possessions and protecting the wealth they already have obtained. Their strife for personal material gain, at times, leads them to be cruel and disrespectful of the environment and other fellow human beings. A little earlier, Sanchez shared with me his vision that this village become an exemplary farming community in Peru. You have good potential and the necessary strong leadership to accomplish that. If you do, the importance of it will extend far beyond your own world.

"The day will come when people in the cities and the rich countries will realize their misery and commence a search for happiness. Then they will come to you and ask you to teach them how to live in community, how to live in balance with Mother Earth, and how to be happy." I had all their attention now, and some of the elders were nodding in approval. "So help each other through difficult times, care for each other as friends, cultivate your land together and utilize the strengths of each individual to build a thriving community rich in happiness and joy. May the future of your village be happy and bright," I concluded.

The villagers cheered and applauded. A number of them stepped forward to shake my hand. Those that could not get close enough tried to touch my shoulder or back like I was some kind of a celebrity. Sanchez then asked all the villagers to gather in a half circle around me so Pedro could take a picture.

At this point we had to leave; the stop had taken a full hour, way longer than anticipated. A number of villagers came up to me to say goodbye. The last one was an old woman dressed completely in black. She was quite a bit shorter than me, and the rim of her hat prevented me from seeing her face. However, when she grabbed me by both my arms, she raised her face up towards me. There they were again. The eyes! Deep and mysterious like I had seen them before, but now with a little sparkle of joy in them. As she looked at me she laughed and said, "Gringo! Gringo!" Some kids danced around us and repeated her words: "Gringo! Gringo!" Then she turned around and walked away.

"That was certainly a different speech than what I expected," Sanchez said when he accompanied us back to our car. "But I observed the faces of the people and you did inspire them. They liked what you had to say. I could see it in their eyes. I am going to think about your words," he concluded sincerely.

When I had met Sanchez, I had been surprised that he, the youngest of the three men, was the mayor. However, I now had a better understanding as to why the villagers had elected him. He was smart, determined, had a vision, was open to new ideas and listened to alternatives. I believed in him, and would not be surprised if one day his village made news as an exemplary farming community in the Peruvian Andes.

Crossing the Andes

When we continued our drive, Pedro and I were equally elated by the village experience.

"I have lived all my life in Peru," he said, "and had to wait for you to come along to get to know my country brothers in the mountains. I am going to make such stops more often when I travel," he said resolutely. Then he continued, "Did you know that only two years ago a couple of journalists were killed when they tried to interview some villagers around here?"

I was stunned. "You're telling me that now?" I cried in disbelief.

"Well, given the events of last night," he said, "I decided to trust your intuition and follow you whatever happened. And see? I was right! If I would have been afraid and told you this before, we would not have had this special experience. Maybe we would have talked to them on the street, but we never would have entered the alley and discovered the market place."

"You're probably right," I admitted.

The road was still climbing higher, and the landscape was changing. There were no trees and cacti anymore, only rocks with different tones of gray, green, brown, red, black and white. Suddenly right behind a curve in the road, along some huge rocks, was a police check stop. We had been driving for more than an hour since our stop in the village, and had passed the last small group of houses about half an hour earlier. We hadn't seen a living being since.

When we stopped, two policemen dressed in black military uniforms walked up to the car. One officer remained at the police car with his automatic weapon pointed at us. They checked our identification and asked why we traveled through the mountain pass. I could see that Pedro was visibly nervous and afraid. The policemen then searched the trunk and our bags, returned our passports and opened the barricade.

"Have a nice day," they said when we left.

It had been weird to observe Pedro's fear of the police. He knew we had done nothing wrong.

"Why were you so nervous?" I asked.

"Strange things happen in these mountains," he answered. "Praise yourself lucky you live in a country where human rights are respected and enforced by the police. Certainly things have improved here in Peru during the last ten years, but a police uniform still does not provide any comfort to me."

"But surely most of your policemen must act ethically and enforce the law?" I questioned.

"Oh yes, I am sure that's generally the case," he admitted, "but we have a history of abuse and torture by police, and it only takes a handful to continue such practices to tarnish the reputation of them all and destroy the trust with the people."

"I understand," I acknowledged.

In the hour that followed, we remained in awe of the surreal landscape around us. As we gained altitude the car drove ever more slowly. When we reached the top of the pass, the car's maximum speed was only twenty miles per hour. A sign indicating we were at 4,746 meters, or just over 15,500 feet, marked the highest point of the road where it cut through a saddle between two mountaintops. We stopped to take some pictures.

Pedro needed oxygen from the bottle here. I was fine without the oxygen tank, although I could feel that the air was thin. Consequently I had to slow down my movements in order to avoid being out of breath every couple of steps. I decided, however, that I wanted to climb the mountaintop on the right side of the saddle, which was only a few hundred feet high. Pedro decided to stay at the car since the oxygen bottle was fairly heavy and he did not have a pack to carry it on his back.

The hike took me longer than anticipated. At one point I pushed myself to a faster pace, but it took no time at all before I got dizzy due to the lack of oxygen. Consequently I settled on a slow climb.

The effort was certainly worth it. I estimated the top must have been just above sixteen thousand feet. Here I was, all alone on top of the world. There was no noise, no tree, no bird and no living soul apart from Pedro down below at the car. There was only the sun, the wind, the sand, the rocks and the grass. It was so peaceful. In all directions as far as my eyes could see, I saw mountaintops. I felt incredibly small, miniscule and unimportant amidst these majestic giant peaks. "How did we ever get the idea that we humans are at the center of this world?" I wondered. "Without us, these mountains would be just as tall and beautiful, and most likely much healthier."

In admiration I stretched my arms out to the sun. All around me Mother Nature revealed Herself in all her beauty while being caressed by the nurturing, warm light of the sun. For a while I just stood there, drowning in the moment. Then I paid my respect to the elements and the Divine, which permeated this creation, and made my way back down to the car.

Once back on the road it seemed our descent from the pass went a lot faster than the climb since the lower we got, the faster we could drive. By the time it got dark we had left the majestic Andes behind us and reached the coastal road to Ica. At around eight o'clock that night we arrived at a small, hacienda-style hotel. According to Pedro, we were in the middle of a sand dune desert, and the hotel was built at a real oasis.

The Universe as Accomplice

The entrance hall of the hotel opened up onto a beautifully illuminated courtyard with a Spanish-style fountain, big trees, flower beds and man-size decorative terracotta pottery. The idyllic garden was surrounded on three sides with arched walkways, which gave access to the rooms. On the fourth side was the restaurant and bar.

I loved this hotel. It had so much potential as a romantic getaway.

We both checked in and went to our rooms. "The rooms most certainly require some serious investment," I thought as I entered my sleeping quarters. While the furniture was charming, old and made of solid wood, everything else in the room needed urgent care: the walls, the floors, the curtains, the bedcovers and the bathroom. I quickly checked to see if I could find a modem plug to download my e-mail, since I had not been able to connect with the virtual world of business during the last two days. Unfortunately, no luck! I turned the air conditioning off to enjoy some silence and allow the already-overcooled room to warm up again.

Then I called my wife and shared the adventure of the last forty-eight hours. My evening call home had become a habit during my last ten years of travel. However, due to the fact I had been in a remote village in the Andes the evening before, I had not had a chance to touch base with her earlier.

I considered myself lucky to have such an open-minded and supportive partner. Quite a few women would get really concerned if their husband told them such a bizarre story as mine. After I finished my exciting recollection of my Andean adventure, I had to deliver the bad news. "I am afraid though I cannot come home on Friday as I had planned," I said.

"Why not?" a disappointed voice inquired on the other end of the line.

"Anna Maria told me that I have to be in Salvador by Friday night," I explained.

"El Salvador?" she asked.

"No, Salvador de Bahia, a city on the coast in Brazil. Anna Maria told me to look for a friend there. I have been working on a deal in Salvador, so I am going to arrange a meeting with the investor for Friday or Saturday. That will justify the trip. The problem is I have no friend in Salvador."

"Of course you do!" my wife interrupted. "Did you not see the newsletter from Peter?"

"From who?" I responded, totally not knowing what she was talking about.

"From Peter, the Austrian priest. You know, your friend from your ski holidays. "

"I didn't see anything from him. I actually haven't heard from him in more than ten years," I answered.

"Oh! Well, maybe this arrived after you left. He had sent an informational letter about his missionary work in Brazil to your mom, and she forwarded it to us here," my wife explained.

"So where in Brazil does he live?" I asked, not catching on yet.

"Salvador! He is a missionary in the slums of Salvador, Brazil."

Once more I was dumbfounded. "There must be a larger intelligence behind the universe that guides all these synchronistic events," I thought.

"Well, I guess that means I have to look him up," I said, still in disbelief. "Is there an address or phone number on the newsletter?"

"Just hold on; I'll go check," my loved one supportively answered.

A few minutes later I had the address and phone number of a friend in Salvador.

"I will fly home on Saturday night, so I should arrive on Sunday," I said.

"Just do what you have to do," she replied understandingly. "It seems that something really special is going on. I love you."

"I love you too," I answered, and my heart longed for her. "Four more nights and I can hold her in my arms again," I thought.

I left my room and welcomed the warm evening air of this green heart of the desert. "What a shame they don't have a patio setup in this courtyard," I thought when I walked to the restaurant to meet Pedro. But I had no idea yet how fairytale-like this place really was.

When I entered the restaurant, a waitress showed me to the terrace where Pedro was waiting for me. The outdoor dining area overlooked the oasis, which was bathed in the silver light of the moon. Palm trees, accentuated by spotlights, acted like protective guards against the darkness surrounding this mysterious pool of life.

"This is magnificent," I said to Pedro, who only smiled in response.

We ordered some food and reflected on our encounter with the villagers in the Andes. Then Pedro presented the schedule for the following day. It would be another long journey. He planned to take two hours in the morning to look at the hotel and interview some of the staff and the general manager. At around eleven we would leave for Nasca so we could visit the last hotel.

Nasca was a one and a half hour drive to the south of Ica. Lima was to the north, which meant it would take another four and a half hours to drive from Nasca to the airport. We would have the regular hotel visit and interviews at Nasca, and take some time to visit the Nasca lines, some colossal ancient mysterious designs in the arid desert floor around Nasca. He planned to leave Nasca around four, and hoped to get us to the Lima airport by nine. I was scheduled to leave on a flight to Dallas shortly after midnight, but given the change in my travel plans, we would have to rearrange my flights in the morning. Hopefully I would be able to get to Salvador before the full moon the following evening.

After supper Pedro excused himself and explained he had some work to discuss with the sales manager.

"Don't worry about it," I said. "I am going for a walk around the oasis before returning to my room. I'll see you here at this table in the morning for breakfast. How is seven o'clock?"

"Seven is fine," Pedro replied. "Goodnight, Paul."

Life is Time

I finished my glass of red Chilean wine and walked down to the sandy oasis beach. Absorbing the silence of the night and the peaceful power of this place I strolled along the shore. After about three-quarters of an hour, I found myself in a fairly dark area. There were no spotlights on this end of the water, only the moonlight, which created a palette of silver and dark shadows. I sat down against a large palm tree by the water since I did not want to return to the hotel just yet. I wanted to enjoy this enchanting place as long as I could. The moon, on the opposite side of the oasis, was stroking the water with a white beam of light.

"What a special moment...it is like time is standing still. Timeless!" I thought. "What did Anna Maria say about time? What was that question I needed to answer? ...Oh yes, that's it. What is time? What causes time to be?"

"You do," a voice suddenly answered.

I looked around me but couldn't see anyone in the darkness. Someone could easily be hidden behind the trees. But had I really heard something? After all, I hadn't said anything out loud.

"What causes time to be?" I questioned again in my mind, and once more the answer came.

"You do!"

This was weird. Was I going crazy? It was like I was answering myself. Yet the answers came out of nowhere: I didn't even understand them! Fascinated by this experience, I decided to ask another question.

"How do you mean, *I* do?"

179

"Time *is* because of your existence, or you could also say, you exist because of time," the answer came.

This made no sense to me. I definitely had not said anything, and was now also convinced I hadn't really heard anything. The answer had just entered my brain directly—and it was an answer I did not understand!

"Who are you?" I tried, not really expecting a response.

"I am the oasis oracle," the voice said.

"And I am Santa Claus!" I automatically answered, full of irony.

"Well, you are not the first one who does not believe me," the voice replied. "But why would I lie to you? Besides, what is the alternative? That you are having this conversation with yourself?"

This was turning into a frightening experience. Now not only did I get answers, but the voice was talking to me and even asking me questions! Was I talking to myself? Was I truly becoming crazy?

But I was not having these thoughts! I was only hearing them in my head. Yet how could I verify that I was not having a conversation with myself?

"Come on, don't beat yourself up like that. Be a little bit more open-minded! Who knows what you might discover? I might help you resolve some real mysteries."

"That's it!" I thought. "If I can get answers from this so-called oracle on questions I don't know the answer to, then I will have proof that I'm not talking to myself." I was determined not to leave this place until I had confirmation that I was not crazy.

"Don't worry, you're not crazy," the answer came again. "Just ask me what you want to know and I will answer you. I am delighted someone is consulting me again. It has been years since anyone asked me a question."

"What is time?" I asked.

"Time is memory," the answer came.

"How do you mean?" I questioned.

"Well, let's analyze time. Does the past still exist?"

"Of course it exists," I answered. "This afternoon I gave a speech to a number of villagers in the Andes."

"Yes, but that moment is past. Are you still giving this speech now?"

"No," I said, confused and not understanding what this was leading to.

"Because it is in the past, it does not exist anymore," the oracle explained.

"I guess not," I answered slowly.

"What you have planned for tomorrow...does that exist?" The oracle continued its questioning line.

"No, I guess it doesn't yet, because it still has to happen."

"Right!" the voice said, excitedly. "It is only the present that exists. We call it 'present *time*' because it *moves*. It moves from the future, over the present, and into the past. Without this movement, without this change, the present would be eternity. So our first conclusion is that without change, there would be no time. Which brings me to the next question: What is required in order for you to be aware of change, to observe change?"

"I don't know," I hesitated. "Something needs to happen, to change, to move on in time," I tried.

"Yes, but how do you *know* something has changed. How do you know that as a kid you were not as tall as you are now?" the oracle asked.

"Because I remember," I said, a little bit agitated by the stupidity of the question.

"Exactly," the oracle cheered. "So if you would have no memory at all, would you be able to observe a change?"

"No, I guess I would not. Things could have changed, but because I would not remember their previous state, I would not be able to observe and remark on the change," I answered.

"Which brings us to our second conclusion," the oracle said. "Without memory no change could be observed because there would be no reference point. That means you would not be able to observe something as warm, because you would not have a reference point which would allow you to consider something else as cold. The same would apply to high and low, thick and thin, long and short, unity and separation, love and fear, and so on. In other words, you would just be."

"I still don't see how that answers my question about time," I said.

"Patience! Follow the line of thought and we will get to your answer in the end," the oracle pleaded. "If you don't have another point of reference, what would motivate you to change?

"I guess nothing, because I could not determine whether I would be in a state of comfort or discomfort," I answered.

"Exactly," the oracle said, "which finally brings us to another conclusion, which is that without memory, there would be no change. Now let's take this one step further. Would there be life without change?"

"No, there would not be, since nothing would evolve. A heart could not beat, because the beat itself is change. There would only be one eternal state of being," I answered.

"That's right," the oracle said. "So let's piece all this back towards the concept of time. Life gives birth to change, and change gives birth to time. But without memory, time could not be observed, change would not take place and therefore life would not exist. Therefore time only exists in memory, in the mind. It is a creation of your mind, and so is life. So as I told you from the beginning, it is *you* who causes time to be.

"Time is a memory measurement tool that helps you with the order and categorization of your reference points. Everything that changes has a mind, since otherwise it would not be motivated to change. That means, for example, that a hare has a mind simply because it is alive. In addition, it uses memory to find its way back to its hole, and because it has memory, it has a perception of time. Maybe that perception is not as finely measured as yours, but it knows that at a previous time it left the hole to which it returns."

I had followed the logic, although I found it very difficult to completely comprehend. I remembered my experience with the Light under the guidance of Anna Maria the night before. "So how is it possible that I experienced a state of timelessness last night when Anna Maria helped me to discover the Light?" I asked, intrigued. This oracle was smart, way smarter than I was! Now that I wasn't concerned about being crazy anymore, I started to focus more on the analysis.

"You must be referring to the Source," the oracle said, "the Mother who permeates everything that exists. The One who is timeless! She is unlimited energy, illuminating light, eternal peace. She created the mind in order to experience Herself. When She created the mind, memory allowed the mind to compare things, to change and to evolve. Memory gave birth to a world of infinite possibilities, to life and to time. But it also allowed the mind to judge and to attach itself to the past. And it's judgment that has reduced an infinite creation into a world of duality.

"When you still your mind through prayer or meditation, you can connect with the One and experience Her power and eternity. Tell me, how did you find your way back to consciousness? Most people who get so close and experience the timelessness of the Light don't have the motivation to come back."

"Anna Maria helped me to return," I answered. "You are right: I did not want to return. I did not want to change my state of being anymore. It was so incredibly beautiful."

"The One is powerful and difficult to escape. You were lucky you had help. If you ever attempt to find Her on your own, make sure that in your heart you have a strong sense of what you have to do here on earth. It will be your heart's passion that will motivate you to return. Remember the One is without mind. She is only heart, pure energy, and when you merge with Her only that which is in your heart will count."

"That is what Anna Maria told me as well," I said, and realized how much I was enjoying this conversation with the oracle. "You mentioned the mind sometimes attaches itself to the past. What did you mean by that?" I asked curiously.

"Because the mind knows things always change, it tends to categorize experiences that have created a state of happiness in the heart as 'good.' When such a state occurs, the heart tends to attach itself to it, which according to the law of change it cannot. Since the mind knows that, fear finds root in it. It is exactly that fear which prevents people from staying in contact with their spirit and causes a lot of unhappiness in the world. It even leads to actions that disrespect life and the beauty of creation. Somehow, most people in the rich countries have turned things upside down. They have lost their happiness exactly because they had so many good things happen to them in the past. They get so attached to each positive experience that they start to fear what might come, since it could, from their limited perspective, bring something 'bad.' As a result they tend to live in the past with their hearts and in the future with their heads, thus missing the magic of the present all together. Their spirit loses its connection with the Divine present and the opportunity to experience true happiness."

"I know exactly what you are saying," I admitted. "Actually, I have done that most of my life. So how should we live then? How should we start to capture that elusive happiness again?"

"More and more of you have started to refrain from judging and to just experience and learn from the reality that presents itself to you. That's how you'll find everlasting joy! Use your mind to learn from the past, and live with your heart in the present. Embrace everything that occurs as a gift, no matter how bad it looks from your limited point of view. Let intuition guide your actions, and use your mind to focus the power of the Source to what your heart wants to achieve. Don't be fearful or pity yourself; instead, consciously co-create the world your heart longs for, and have respect for the creation of the One."

"So why should we refrain from judging in order to consciously co-create, and how does judging lead to duality?" I asked in order to deepen my understanding.

"The Universe provides an infinite scope of experiences. Through judgment the mind categorizes all these experiences into a dual reality of either 'good' or 'bad.' Yet judging limits human potential because it requires fixed reference points. The problem is that the Mother is unlimited, and so is Her creation. When something is judged, it is seen in a context that is relative to another point, yet given the limitlessness of creation, reference points always change. What you considered a tall building two hundred years ago is dwarfed now by the buildings people construct today. Therefore there is no absolute good or bad. Everything is relative, which makes judging pointless.

"It is much healthier to just observe the reality that presents itself to you, and then decide what your actions should be in order to execute your vision. For example, a virus enters your body and makes you feel sick. If you judge that virus as something which is bad or evil, chances are you will feel victimized, get frustrated, angry or sad, and bring your energy level to an even lower level than it already is. If, however, you're able to just observe the fact that you're ill, you can conclude you don't like that feeling and decide on the best possible course of action to heal yourself and increase your energy. If people are attached to the past they'll have great difficulties in doing that because they will not be able to accept their illness in the present. Without that acceptance, they cannot effectively plot a corrective course of action."

"How does judging limit our potential?" I questioned.

"When judging occurs, the mind forms boundaries in order to define the points of comparison. Those boundaries are based on past experiences and therefore do not recognize new possibilities. This is limiting. Let me give an example. You can be hot or cold. That's just an experience, nothing more. When you start judging the cold or heat as too hot or too cold, you will experience a state of discomfort and your body will act accordingly. For instance, every person could walk over hot coals without getting burned if they refrained from judging those coals as too hot and associating them with burning their feet. Many have proven this without getting a single blister on their soles. However, if any one of these people who successfully did so questioned their ability and judged the coals as being too hot, they would have burned themselves."

"So what *should* we do?" I asked.

"Learn and enjoy life! It is because people judge the world around them that they fail to take responsibility for it and learn from it. It is much easier to complain about things and allocate blame to something or someone than to act accountably and consciously create the world you live in. If you can withhold your judgment, you'll be better able to analyze the reality around you, refrain from disrespectful responses, and decide your actions based on your life's purpose; that is what 'consciously creating the world you live in' means. Then when unexpected events and hurdles present themselves to you, rather than allowing your energy to be drained by a number of negative emotions, like anger, frustration or fear, you'll see the opportunities and unleash your creative power to the benefit of a harmonious universe. I tell you, if you can make such a shift, you will discover true joy and your growth will be exponential."

"And how do I discover my life's purpose?" I asked curiously.

"You will find it in your heart, which means you will have to connect to your heart. It will be something that you'll feel very passionate about. It will require your best skills to achieve it, and when you are working towards it the universe will be your accomplice. This will be reflected in the large number of synchronistic events you attract.

"When you follow your life's purpose you'll feel a deep sense of satisfaction, have a relentless energy and experience great joy. So reflect now and create a vision! A vision that unleashes your passion, for which your skills and education have prepared you and which will allow you to leave a satisfactory legacy. Then execute your vision and find joy on the journey!"

"You have taught me so much I will need some time to digest all of this," I informed the oracle. "I really should go to my room now and sleep, as I have a long day tomorrow. Are there any final recommendations you can give me?" I inquired.

"Just remember: Life is one big learning opportunity. It is a journey of limitless discovery. Failure only exists in a limited dual world. The explorer will learn from all experiences and will find his ultimate joy in infinite discoveries."

"Oracle, I thank you for your advice, and I admire your beauty and life-giving capacity in this desert. I honor you," I said as I stood up.

"I wish you well on your journey. May you find happiness and never cease to discover new things. Enjoy the magnificence of creation," the voice said before all went quiet in my head.

I walked back to the hotel, alone with my thoughts. The experience had been strange, but incredibly valuable. However, in order to avoid being marked as 'crazy' in this judgmental world, I decided to keep this experience all to myself.

By the time I returned to my room it was after midnight. I quickly got into bed and fell into a deep sleep.

At six-thirty in the morning I got my wake-up call. I took a shower, got dressed and met at seven with Pedro on the restaurant patio overlooking the oasis.

The sun was already rising, and the palm trees reached out to embrace its warmth. The light of day revealed huge rolling sand dunes around the oasis. They resembled the so-familiar Rocky Mountain foothills, but these hills were bare of any life. Their virgin white sand would not allow anything to take root. Only around the life-giving water of the oasis was everything lush and green.

After my experience of last night I knew this was not just a pool of water in the desert. Its mysterious appearance and life-giving capacity in this land of sand was but a sign of the secrets and wisdom it contained.

Humming of Joy

"Good morning," Pedro said, snapping me out of my trance.

"Good morning," I smiled. "This place is so beautiful. I had such a peaceful walk along the oasis shore last night. With the sun on it now, the life-giving power of the oasis is accentuated even more against the backdrop of all this dry sand."

"It is a unique place indeed," Pedro agreed.

We had breakfast and took a quick tour around the hotel. By eight o'clock I was interviewing employees. I followed the same approach I had taken in Ayacucho, and tried to find out what they would improve if this were their business. During the last two interviews, Pedro left to change my flight arrangements.

By ten o'clock I was finished, and Pedro had me booked on a flight to Buenos Aires that left fifteen minutes after midnight. A connection via Sao Paulo would eventually bring me to Salvador some thirteen hours later. That would be two o'clock on Friday afternoon—not exactly ideal, but I would be able get there in time. Now I just had to set up the meeting and contact Peter.

Two phone calls later I had arranged a meeting with the investor and talked to Peter, who was very excited about my upcoming visit. He would pick me up from the airport upon my arrival. In the office of the general manager I had been able to download my e-mail. This would allow me to get up-to-date with business during my flights to Salvador.

As planned, by eleven o'clock, Pedro and I were on the road to Nasca. The landscape from Ica to Nasca was one big desert. The terrain varied from rolling sand dunes to barren rocky hills and flat dry plains. We arrived at the Nasca hotel just before one o'clock, and had a pleasant lunch with the general manager. The hotel was quite nice, but I could not figure out what attracted people to this town in the middle of this immense sand and stone desert. After lunch, like in the previous hotels, the employees opened up to me and showed they really understood their business and knew how to improve it. At around three o'clock we left the hotel.

"Now I'll show you the Nasca lines," Pedro said.

We drove to a little airfield at the edge of town.

"I thought we were going to the Nasca lines?" I said when Pedro stopped the car.

"We are; the only way to see them is from the air! They're so big you can't see the pictures from the ground."

Pedro talked for a few minutes with a pilot and ten minutes later we were taking off in a one-engine Cessna. It was as old as the cars were in this country, and I wondered if it still would be allowed in the air in North America. At first I had been hesitant to get into the plane, but when I reflected on everything that had happened on this trip, I decided to embrace the opportunity and go with the flow.

After a few minutes of flying we crossed some stone brown barren mountains, after which an immense flat desert plain opened up. From the height of the plane I could clearly distinguish multiple straight lines in the harsh soil. The plane lowered its altitude somewhat, and I could see the drawing of a huge spider on the desert floor, a condor a little bit further on, and then an ape. There were more than twenty-five cave-like drawings, some more than one hundred yards in size, embedded in the soil below us. I was fascinated. "Who made these drawings in this vast desert and why?" I questioned.

Pedro told me the lines were a complete mystery. They were estimated to be fifteen hundred years old. Archeologists, astronomers, mathematicians and geologists had analyzed them and so far no one had provided a conclusive answer as to whom had made them and why. They were composed of straight lines that seemed to cross the entire desert and immense rectangular and sharp triangular shapes that looked like giant landing paths. At the foot of the mountains on the opposite side of the desert I could detect a clear picture of a hummingbird in the sand below us. "Why would ancient peoples go through so much effort to create such art in the desert soil at a size they would not be able to see themselves, since they were unable to fly over it? Who knows what we might discover once these secrets are unlocked?" I wondered, and thought about Mario's theory that nothing was impossible. I had to agree with him as I realized that too many mysterious things occurred in this world to deny the existence of magic and to ever consider something as 'impossible.'

After three quarters of an hour we got back and left for our drive to Lima. Some fifteen minutes later Pedro said, "We are in the middle of the Nasca Lines desert."

As he had told me, there was nothing to see.

Pedro stopped on the side of the road next to a high metal tourist tower.

"Let's climb the tower and see how much we can see from there," he said as we got out of the car. The tower provided an opportunity for tourists to have a look at two of the desert drawings: a tree and a pair of hands. But even from the fifty-foot-high tower you could barely distinguish the shapes in the desert floor; they were simply too big.

When we got back down I told Pedro I wanted to walk out into the desert on my own and absorb the mystery. Understanding my desire for solitude, he indicated he would wait in the car.

For some twenty minutes I walked away from the road. I crossed several of the lines but the only thing I could see from the ground were trenches with sloping sides that were several feet wide. When I was far enough from the highway I sat down on the hot desert sand and closed my eyes. I pictured the image of the hummingbird in my head and sent it my greetings. It had really captured my attention during our flight. Suddenly, I could hear a strong buzzing sound approaching, like that from a monster bee. I quickly opened my eyes and two feet in front of my face a hummingbird hung motionless in the hot desert air. "Where did this bird come from?" I wondered.

"From the river valley just across the mountains," the hummingbird answered.

I had not expected an answer to my question. After all, who would expect an answer from a bird? But since my talk with the oasis oracle, I knew this was possible. I wondered if Anna Maria's preparation and my meeting with the Light had anything to do with my sudden ability to converse with an oasis and a hummingbird.

"Why did you call me?" the hummingbird asked.

"I am sorry," I said. "It was not my intention to call you. I just wanted to greet you. Your picture in the desert is so nice, so full of energy."

"That is the energy of happiness you observed," the hummingbird replied.

"How can an image in the sand radiate such energy?" I questioned.

"Everything radiates energy; actually, everything *is* energy! Because the image is attuned to *me*, the bird of joy, it radiates happiness, one of the most powerful energy forms."

"If you are the bird of joy, can you tell me how human beings achieve happiness?" I asked.

"Most people, especially in the rich countries of the world, believe there is a link between value and happiness. They are right in that regard, however they are confused about the matter. Happiness results out of a sense of value. It is not the accumulation of value that brings joy, but rather the creation of value for others, the giving to others and to the world. People in your world are so focused on accumulating material possessions that as soon as something or someone threatens these possessions, or the growth thereof, they become afraid."

"Is that the reason so many people in America are depressed?" I asked.

"Exactly!" the hummingbird answered. "All these possessions lead most people to depression rather than joy. Throughout history people have done some very cruel and harmful things to others in order to protect their material possessions. Apart from supplying the basic physical human needs like food, clothing and shelter, materials do not lead to happiness. It is the feeling of being valuable to others that leads to joy. You can be the richest man in the world, but if you don't feel loved and cared for, if you don't feel appreciated by others, you will not be happy."

"I never looked at it that way," I admitted.

"Gringo, I have to go now. It is too hot here for my little body. I need to get to the river for a drink before I totally dry out. Enjoy the rest of that wonderful journey called life. Remember: Give to others, love and help those who cross your path and happiness will be your reward."

In a blink the hummingbird disappeared. I got up and walked back to the car. There was power here. I wondered what we would learn once this desert and its mysterious drawings released their secrets.

It was five o'clock when we started our drive back to Lima. Soon I would be on my way to my last stop on this trip: Salvador de Bahia, Brazil.

Trust

The drive to Lima was smooth and uneventful. As soon as it got dark I fell asleep and only awoke when we pulled into the airport parking lot.

"Did you sleep well?" a smiling Pedro asked me.

"I did indeed," I answered. "I am glad I had this nap. The last two nights were short, and given my flight schedule, I can't count on too much sleep during the next twenty-four hours either."

We parked the car and entered the airport, where I checked in. I was lucky and got an upgrade on the flight to Buenos Aires; hopefully that would allow me to catch some more sleep. The other legs of the connection I would travel in coach.

I had two hours to kill between check-in and departure, so Pedro and I decided to grab some food in the cafeteria. Once we found a table and ordered some food Pedro told me how much he had enjoyed traveling with me during the last few days.

"I have learned so much from you," he said. "It was amazing: You only spent twenty to thirty minutes with each of the executive staff in the hotels, and they all wanted to start working for you! Their body language told me you gained their trust and respect during the first few minutes. That is so unusual. Most of the time people here are afraid to voice their opinions and to ask questions. The things people shared with you, the advice they provided and the questions they asked, were a sign of great trust."

"I appreciate the compliment," I said, "but I didn't do anything special. I am sure you would have had the same response from them."

"No, that is not true. I probably never would have considered seeking advice from the employees and executive staff, and if I would have, I would not have asked the same questions," Pedro argued. "You taught me a lot about how to gain people's trust and respect, and unleash their potential!"

"Well, I'm not aware of having done anything special," I said. "I just did what I had to do."

"For the last two days, I have been thinking about what exactly you did that established this trust and respect in such a short time. When you were sleeping during our drive back, I finally found the answer."

"Then, please tell me, because I have no idea what you are talking about," I curiously replied. "As I said before, I just did what I had to do, and it's nothing special as far as I'm concerned."

"Well, maybe it was easier for me, as an observer, to discover those elements in your behavior that led to this open and appreciative connection with the employees," Pedro persisted while our food arrived. "Let me explain what I have learned from my observations.

"You entered those meetings with a completely open mind. You might have had some ideas as to how to improve certain parts of the business, but if you did, it never showed. As a result the employees did not see someone with an ego and viewed your questions for them as sincere. You recognized and conversed with them as equals, and people in this country certainly are not used to that. Ultimately, by behaving that way, you gave these people trust and respect, even when they had not earned it yet, and in return they gave trust and respect to you."

"Wow," I exclaimed. "That is a pretty in-depth analysis of human interaction! I have never reflected upon my own actions in so much detail! What you are basically saying is that it was my behavior that caused the open and honest response of the employees."

"Absolutely!" Pedro confirmed.

"But the thing you said about trust confused me somewhat," I said. "I've always thought trust had to be earned, and you're talking about giving trust."

"Up until today, I too saw trust as something that had to be earned. That is why I could not understand how you gained people's trust so fast during those interviews. But on our drive here, it struck me that trust is given instead of earned."

I thought about my conversation with the Lan Chile stewardess, who had abruptly asked me why I trusted her. While at the time I had found it a fascinating question, after that conversation I had never revisited the subject and tried to figure out what trust really was. I had a feeling Pedro was going to shed some light on the matter.

"Explain to me again what you just said, because you completely lost me," I said.

"Well, suppose you tried to gain my trust, and for whatever reason, I decided not to give it to you. If that were the case, you could try to earn it as long as you wanted but you would never get it. Therefore, trust is ultimately given!"

"Okay, I see that, but does that make such a big difference?" I asked.

"It most certainly does. It changed my focus from trying to understand how you earned their trust so fast to analyzing *why* people *gave* you their trust," Pedro explained. "That shift in focus led me to conclude that people give trust once they feel respected and trusted. See, people withhold trust because they are afraid. When you respect them as equals and give them your trust by being honest and open, in a way you make yourself vulnerable, you become human. It tells them you are not going to hurt them by defending your position, since you have no inflated ego to protect. So my conclusion is that the fastest way to get trust and respect is to give trust and respect. Consequently, this is also the fastest way to unleash people's full potential, since they will not display all their creativity and ideas as long as they feel in any way threatened."

"The logic in your analysis is very clear," I responded. "What you say makes a lot of sense. I have never analyzed my behavior like that, but when I reflect on it, that is exactly what I have done throughout my life in order to release people's potential, develop team creativity or open up a relationship. However, it does come with some risks, and you have to realize those and protect yourself to a certain degree."

"How do you mean?" Pedro asked.

"Well, like you said, by giving trust to people early on in order to unleash their creativity and openness, you do make yourself vulnerable. I did encounter times throughout my life when people have really abused my trust. The first few times this happened, I felt betrayed. I was angry and my energy level just plummeted. Over time I learned to start giving people my trust within a set of clearly defined boundaries. This allowed me to test their trust in a context in which I was prepared to accept some damage. If my trust got betrayed, I learned to accept that as a risk I took to open up a relationship or unleash people's potential. So I held myself accountable and tried to learn from the experience and sharpen my intuition. I found that when I stopped blaming the other person, I did not experience those terrible feelings of betrayal anymore either. I just took note that they were not trustworthy within the framework I had given them, and removed them from my life. Only when people respect the trust they get from me and return it to me, will I expand my trust. Over time I developed my intuition in this regard, and this prevents me most of the time from giving trust to people with whom I should not get involved. The odd times when I do make a mistake, I take responsibility for it and move on."

"That is an important expansion of my insight," Pedro admitted. "I will take that into account as I start to practice giving trust within my own life."

It was a few minutes after eleven and time for me to get to my gate. I said goodbye to Pedro and we embraced before I left. As I walked away I knew I had gained a friend for life in this magical country.

When I passed through customs, I remembered my arrival only a few nights ago. Who could have imagined the adventures that were awaiting me here, the things I learned and the way I had changed in such a short time?

"Now, I even talk to oracles and birds and say thanks to the moon and the sun," I thought. "What a magical world we live in. What kept me from discovering it earlier?"

Punctually, at fifteen minutes after midnight, my plane departed. I left Peru behind me, but would carry its country, its people, its magic and the Andes in my heart for the rest of my life.

Now I had to focus on getting some sleep. Tomorrow I would be in Salvador. What mysterious adventure and secret teachings would await me there?

The Mystery Revealed

Salvador de Bahia, Brazil

Exhausted, I fell asleep before the airplane reached its cruising altitude. A friendly stewardess woke me up when we had to prepare for landing in Buenos Aires almost four hours later. I changed flights, and an hour after my arrival I was on my way to Brazil. Once again I slept through the entire flight.

I woke up during the descent to Sao Paulo. While I loved the passionate atmosphere of this Brazilian city, the view from the sky was, as always, uninviting. Concrete skyscrapers rose up from the paved ground as far as I could see. As the airplane got lower, I could detect vast slums with cardboard houses and open sewage strewn in between the concrete communities. Too many people lived in this overcrowded city.

After changing flights one more time I was on my way to my final destination. The empty chair next to me provided an extra space to work. After the long naps on the previous flights I was rested enough to catch up on my e-mail. Two hours later, at ten past two, the plane touched down on the Salvador tarmac. What would the mystery reveal to me here?

The steel and glass modern airport of this provincial coastal city surprised me. I got my bags and searched for Peter in the crowded arrival hall. I hadn't seen him for more than ten years and had no idea how he had changed. Suddenly, I recognized his face at the side of the crowd. I waved and walked over to him.

A broad smile appeared on his face when he saw me. He had a nice dark tan, was wearing white loose clothing, and his long blond curly hair was a touch lighter than I remembered it. He still had the same peaceful, grounded and humble energy around him, almost like a new age Christ.

"Peter, how are you?" I said once we met.

"I am doing very well. It is good to see you again, Paul," he replied. "How are you? Did you have a good trip?"

"The flights were fine," I said. "It wasn't exactly an ideal connection from Lima to Salvador, but I managed to get quite a bit of sleep. Did you know that until two days ago, I had no idea you lived and worked in Salvador?"

"Have you been here before?" Peter asked.

"No, this is my first time!"

"So, what are your plans?"

"Well, I have this afternoon and evening free. My only meeting is tomorrow morning at eleven. My flight back home leaves later in the afternoon."

"All right. Let's first get a little bite to eat and then plan the rest of our day," Peter suggested.

"Sounds fine to me," I answered.

We walked to his small old car and got on our way. Leaving the airport we drove through a lush green lane surrounded on both sides by gigantic bamboo bushes forming an exotic arched tunnel. There were palm trees and beautiful tropical flowers just about everywhere. Most of the streets and houses were old and needed repairs.

Some ten minutes later we arrived at a large white tavern on the beach surrounded by a beautiful tropical garden and waving palm trees. When I got out of the car a warm wind blew through my hair. I enjoyed the smell of the sea and got the impression that Salvador was an absolute paradise.

The front door gave access to a large, long kitchen. Several women were busy cooking delicious-smelling food in big pots on gas furnaces. Once we passed through the kitchen we entered a large dining space.

"Do you want to get a table in here or outside on the patio?" Peter asked.

"Let's sit outside," I eagerly replied, "so I can enjoy the sound and smell of the ocean."

We found a gorgeous spot overlooking a white sandy beach. The space between the restaurant and the beach was dotted with exotic palm trees.

"This is a typical local restaurant, so you will not see any tourists here," Peter explained. "The limited menu changes every day, and the food is exquisite, yet cheap."

Over a typical Brazilian dish we caught up with each other. I told Peter about the family, our move to Canada, my hotel development job, my travels and the unraveling mystery of this trip.

He told me about his missionary work, the little community school he had started and the work he had done in the Salvador prison. Nine years ago he had arrived here, and he was not planning to leave his community any time soon.

"I was made for this," he said passionately. "Here I can really make a difference. I can see it in the eyes of the people around me!"

"I am curious to see where you live and what you do," I said.

"Well, why don't I first take you on a scenic tour around old Salvador and then we'll go to my home. I live in the community in which I work. This evening I am doing a funeral service for a seventeen-year-old boy who was murdered a few days ago. You're invited to join me for that. You can stay overnight and in the morning I'll bring you to your meeting."

"Sounds like a plan to me," I replied.

Peter paid for the meal and we left for the historic town of old Salvador, built on a hill. Most of its small streets were paved with old cobblestones, and the house facades were painted in vibrant colors of red, yellow, blue and white. Apparently the city was the first major port and capital of colonial Brazil during the 16th and 17th centuries. The historic economic prosperity of the place was reflected in large private houses and baroque churches.

It was obvious, however, that the days of wealth were long gone. All the streets and houses were in urgent need of repair. Most of the cars in the city were really old. This was clearly a market for vehicles that were not allowed on the streets anymore in first world countries. Nevertheless, this city had a lot of character. On top of the hill we stopped at a square in front of a church and went for a little walk.

"This is the best way to get a feel for the city," Peter explained.

The people of this place were spontaneous and friendly. A lot of young men and women who hung out on the streets sported vibrant, joyful smiles. There was clearly a stronger African influence here than in Sao Paulo, which was reflected in its music, art and dominant skin color. I just loved the pulsing atmosphere.

On our way to Peter's place we drove through more modern, but somewhat rundown, suburbs surrounding the old city of Salvador. Once we left those behind us, the highway cut through the slums. After a few minutes we left the main road and headed for one of the poorest areas of Salvador.

Entering the Slums

Just when we were about to enter a small, unpaved slum street two beautiful little girls with broad smiles waved at us. They wore some old shorts, small tops and slippers, and must have been eight or nine years old.

Peter stopped the car and they ran over to his open window. Cheerfully they greeted him and excitedly related their discovery of the day. They had found fourteen eggs that afternoon and were on their way to the beach to sell them. The youngest one of the two suddenly ran over to my side of the car. When she was right next to me she looked into my eyes and there they were. The eyes! Deep, dark, mysterious, and full of happiness and passion! Totally unspoiled, unconcerned about tomorrow, and drinking up life with lots of joy.

"Mr. Gringo!" she smiled and waved. Both of them then giggled and ran away in the direction of the beach.

"It has begun," I thought. "The eyes have announced their presence."

"Every day, they find something to sell," Peter said with an admiring smile on his face as he observed their playful run. "And they sell it too," he laughed.

"I am not surprised. Who could refuse such eyes?" I uttered.

"Don't underestimate their competition. There are a lot of kids like them, on the beach and throughout the city, selling all kinds of things," he replied.

"How do you mean? Don't they have to go to school?" I asked.

"In this part of the world, survival comes first, Paul," he explained. "Most of the children here have to work in order to get their next meal. The poverty is extreme. A lot of them turn their work into play, like those two girls. That is why I believe they're so successful. I actually know quite a few well-educated adults who could learn something from them."

Once the girls were out of sight we entered the slums. Never in my life had I seen people living in such abominable circumstances. Small houses, or shelter compartments, were stacked against and on top of each other. A diversity of materials, from clay to sticks, pieces of metal, brick, and even cardboard, were used to construct them. There was no structure to the community. Little streets and alleys curved in all directions. Whenever someone would find the tiniest empty space, another shack would be erected. Everyone in the slums seemed to be black. In contrast, all the rich people I had done business with in Brazil were white, mostly of Portuguese descent. After a few minutes we pulled up at a concrete building across from a little church.

"This is my home," Peter said. He opened a garage and drove the car inside. We took my bags out and entered his modest house. His living quarters were on the first floor. From the small balcony he showed me the view over the community. The shantytown was built in a valley similar in size to the one where I lived.

"How many people live here?" I asked while looking at the overcrowded anthill. It stood in stark contrast to our peaceful valley in Canada, which was shared with twenty-four other families.

"The entire community, which continues over the next hill, counts some twenty thousand people," Peter said. "Probably half of them live in this valley."

"What do they live on?" I asked.

"Most of them have no jobs, but if they are lucky, they might get a day job somewhere around the city. They scavenge, work on the streets, and sell anything you can think of. They wash windows, steal or do whatever is necessary to survive. We have three drug gangs operating here that recruit the youth. There have been weeks in which

I have had to perform one funeral service daily in order to bury youngsters who got murdered by rival drug gangs. On average some three or four get killed weekly. The service tonight is for a seventeen-year-old boy who got shot in a gang fight. You will probably meet some of the gang members since they usually attend the service. Welcome to the most violent slum in Brazil," Peter said.

I was shocked. Here I was witnessing the result of several generations of international trade without consciousness!

It has been our drive to discover new resources and reduce production costs that has fueled global trade. Our focus on productivity improvement had centralized production and labor into big cities, but an insatiable thirst for wealth had caused companies and entrepreneurs to change production locations to areas with cheaper labor in the blink of an eye, leaving thousands of people without any means of living.

This line of thinking led me to consider the role of slaves in history. Slaves had no individual freedom, but at least they had a value. They were traded. They had no rights, but they made a contribution to society. These people here were our economic slaves: While they were free citizens, they had nowhere to go, no way to voice their needs and no means to stand up for themselves. How free were they, really? From a global socio-economic point of view, we were treating them worse than we did slaves. These people were obsolete to our economy! Without value, they were left to scavenge from our garbage! There was no room for them in our world of trade and wealth accumulation. Like worn-out goods, they had fulfilled their need and lost their value! "The human race will only live up to its potential once we are able to integrate these people back into our society," I thought.

I knew I was a guilty participant in the creation of this poverty. All too often when I had made a business decision with negative consequences for other people I had excused myself with the line, "This is not personal; it's just business." It was the perfect way to pardon just about everything. It was a widely accepted practice, and until now it had provided me with a clear conscience. After all, I had acted in the interest of business, which was the ultimate, most widely accepted method for creating value in our world.

Or was it? This attitude, which had been repeated generation after generation, had ultimately led to this shameful sight in front of me. I was determined to change my life! I still believed in free enterprise, but I failed to accept why empathy and care could not be included in business practices. I started dreaming of a model of ethical business, that would take humanitarian and environmental issues into consideration, rather than the current model, which usually concentrated solely on the accumulation of material wealth.

"I am deeply ashamed," I finally said, breaking the long silence. "I realize this is the result of the greed of rich companies and countries, and I am a member of both."

"It all started with the colonization of these countries," Peter answered, "and it hasn't stopped since. I feel guilty too. That is why I take so much satisfaction in giving something back to these people. It is my little contribution to pay for our past robbery. You know what is really ironic?"

"What?" I asked curiously.

"The fact that the conquering of these regions was supported by the Catholic Church, the same institute that I am now part of and which pays me. Colonization allowed the Church to become large and powerful. Yet even today, in my opinion, the Church is not outspoken enough about the resulting injustice.

"Quite a number of these people who live in slums around the world work in sweatshops for large corporations. A lot of the people who run these corporations justify their international labor and trading practices in the interest of their companies and shareholders. Yet most of those executives, company employees and shareholders are all church-going people. Neither the Church, nor any other religion I know of, promotes as prime value the acquisition of money and justifies merciless trading practices to attain that goal. So people are smart about it: in order to justify their exploitative activities they artificially split their business life from the rest of their life. This illusion allows them to keep their conscience clean. Obviously in reality, there is only one life, and people should apply the values of their religion also in their business practice if they want to be true to themselves, their God and society. Sadly, only very few religious leaders call their members on this in fear of losing followers."

"That is painful," I confirmed. "I never looked at it this way before. It sadly shows how hypocritical our society is, and how little impact religious institutions have had on the spiritual development of the large population."

"Unfortunately, only a few people realize this," Peter agreed. "The problem is most people confuse their aspirations with their values. Yet values are your code of ethics: they are reflected in what you do, not just in what you talk about. The world would change considerably if, rather than *aspiring* to a set of values, people would start *living* them. "

What are Values?

B ack inside we made ourselves comfortable on the living room couches.

"What are values, actually?" I asked Peter, who seemed to have thought about this subject quite a bit.

"That is a good question," Peter smiled. "Most people don't get any further than arguing about each other's values, what is right and what is wrong, without ever understanding the nature and origin of values."

"Well, I recently got stuck trying to find out what human values are. It was Anna Maria, the Peruvian medicine woman whom I told you about, that suggested this question to me," I admitted.

"Values are principles that guide people's behavior. So by observing someone's actions you are able to determine what values they live by. Someone's values are always reflected in what they do," he answered matter-of-factly.

"So how do we define our values, and how can values be so different between individuals?" I questioned.

"My understanding so far is that there are a number of universal human needs. These are things that every person in the world craves, and these can be divided into three categories. First are our physical needs, all of which relate to a healthy physical body. They include things like food, shelter, clothing, health care, human touch and sex. Second, there are our mental needs of discovery, learning, creation and freedom which fuel our evolution. The third group involves the needs of our spirit, the perception of our place, value and purpose in the world. Among these you'll find the need for recognition, self-worth, respect, belonging and love. When all these needs are met, people achieve true happiness. Ultimately that's what we all strive for in our lives."

"So where do values come into the picture?" I asked.

"People have different means to fulfill their needs. They can either obtain their sexual satisfaction by rape or an intimate relationship. They can develop a sense of self-worth by creating something or destroying something or someone else. They can acquire land or goods by negotiation and fair trade or by conquering and repression. Values are *guidelines* people develop to satisfy their primal human needs. Children initially develop their values based on the stories they are told and the behavior that is modeled by the adults around them. However, if their experience teaches these youngsters that in applying those values, primal needs are not met, they might start to explore different moral paths until such time when they discover a code of action that satisfies their needs," Peter explained.

"So that is why people's individual values can be so different, because each person's experience in fulfilling their primal needs is unique. And cultural values can be totally different and can influence personal values through the stories that are being told," I interrupted, understanding what Peter had just taught me. "That is a profound insight. How did you come to this understanding?" I asked.

"From my work in the prisons," he answered. "I concluded that none of the people I worked with were really bad. They were only desperate to fulfill some of their primal needs. The stories amongst a lot of young men in the slums are about the courageous deeds of certain gang members. They understand the power of the gang and how its activity helps its members to obtain their physical needs. Gang life provides a way for them to develop self-confidence, get recognition and demand respect from others. These youths have nowhere to go in our society, and feel of value in a gang. It is their only way up. So unless we open up alternatives for fulfilling their unmet primal needs, we will not be able to eradicate these gangs.

"The same applies to a lot of the young hookers with whom I have worked. A number of them are only looking for love, which they have never received or learned to give, and in their ignorance think they have found it in the brief act of sex. At the very least they feel valued at that point, which is something most people in these communities crave but never get. Others have no other choice than to enter prostitution simply to meet their physical needs of food, shelter or drugs. Don't be surprised I include drugs on that list, because once someone is addicted it becomes a physical need."

"You make it sound like these people are not responsible for their crimes," I said, disturbed.

"They are responsible for the crime and should learn from it. It is part of my work to help them see that so they can make better choices in the future. However, it is not good enough for the rest of society to just allocate the blame, punish and move on. We do have a responsibility in providing a nurturing environment to all children in the world. We need to model how life-respecting values do lead to happiness, and this should be reflected in our stories and our actions."

"But how do stories influence society? As far as I know, other than reading fairytales for kids during bedtime, there is not a lot of storytelling going on in developed countries," I remarked.

"Of course there is. The biggest storyteller of our age is the media. Movies, books, the daily television news and newspapers all tell stories. And these stories seem to have a lot more impact on the values in our society today than any of the religious tales. Our Christian parables are just not real enough anymore to appeal to people," Peter answered.

"I'm not sure why you are concluding that the media stories have more impact?" I questioned.

"Look at the dominant value in our society: Money! Which religious story teaches that value? None!" he answered passionately and slightly frustrated. "But every night on television people get to see stories of financial success. They listen to advertisements that promise recognition, joy or happiness, if only they buy the promoted products.

The daily news will always include a financial update of the market, and when a tragedy is reported, within minutes the financial damage will be quoted. The large majority of the modern stories focus on the acquisition of money and portray it as the path towards happiness. If we want to create a world of fairness, respect for life and empathy, we have to change our stories, we have to change our news. We need to get away from celebrating and honoring financial accumulation."

"But isn't it exactly this financial gain that is needed to solve a lot of problems in the world?" I challenged.

"Absolutely! I am not saying financial gain is necessarily bad. It all depends on whether it is the *driver* or the *result* of certain actions. What I am alleging is that we should change the focus of our stories and teach people that it is *sharing* that leads to happiness, being of value to others and society. The drive for accumulation of money is only a reaction to a sense of insecurity. If people would believe in their own value and know they would not be left behind by the rest of the world, then they would have no need to keep all of their money. A change in stories and some extra education could lead to better use of earnings and a sharing of wealth.

"Even a reallocation of some funds would do wonders in the world. Just think about all the money that is spent for military purposes and law enforcement. Instead of fighting so many individual injustices in the world, it would be more efficient if people tried to eliminate the root cause of such injustices: Poverty! It's poverty that provides a fertile soil for the seeds of violence, drugs, gangs, child prostitution, human trafficking, terrorism, extremism and revolutions.

"However, it's also poverty that provides us the slave labor to produce cheap goods, and I suspect that's why so little happens in this area, why governments find it easier to fight all the symptoms of poverty with laws and enforcement rather than addressing poverty on the whole. After all, if we want to create more harmony in the world and provide better circumstances for the extremely poor, it will require sacrifice. This ultimately means the rich will become less rich, and that can only occur once people around the globe realize happiness does not result from gathering wealth, but from sharing it. As I said before, such understanding requires a change in our stories."

"So how do we determine which values are good and which ones are bad?" I asked.

"Well, most of the time each individual personally perceives their own values and actions as good. Believing in 'good' and 'bad' is a very dualistic, black and white perspective, and I have come to believe there are unlimited shades of gray in-between," Peter started.

"I have been told before not to judge," I admitted, "and to refrain from categorizing things as 'good' or 'bad.'"

"We are in no position to judge others. Even when we need to defend ourselves against others, we should not judge them! I believe an action is justified if it respects life—not just human life, but all life on earth—and is driven by love. Most of the time when an action is guided by fear, it leads to destruction, or harm to others, because it shuts down the understanding that we are all connected. If, however the action is driven by love it tends to nourish the soul. I believe that in today's egocentric world, where criminals, terrorists and even governments try to instill fear in people, a lot of human actions are driven by negative emotions. However, ultimately nobody other than the person performing the action knows the driving motivation behind their action."

"But certainly we can tell when an action is disrespectful of life," I said.

"Most of the time," Peter answered. "But remember it is likely that people who act destructively only do so because they have a distorted perspective of how to obtain their happiness. So there are a lot of gray areas. Some day you might have to kill someone to protect your own life or that of your children. When you do that for the love of your life or that of your child, I believe you can kill with empathy, without judgment. However, if you do it out of fear of death or of losing a child, you will be emotional and judgmental and most likely will have no respect for the life you take. However, this is enough for now!

I have to get ready for the service or we'll be late. Is it okay if we walk to the church?"

"I wouldn't mind some exercise at all," I replied. "I have been sitting down most of the day."

Peter showed me my room for the night, and while I was waiting for him to get ready, I unpacked my belongings and refreshed myself.

The Forgotten Souls of the World

Some twenty minutes later, at around five thirty, we left his house. After a five minute hike through some tiny curving alleys we arrived at a small path that led through some green vegetable gardens, bathed in the late afternoon sunlight.

"I did not exactly expect vegetables gardens here," I said.

"It is another way for these people to get by," Peter explained. "Unfortunately, the yield doesn't feed a lot of mouths. But at least it keeps them in contact with nature. It's a place where people can find some peace."

The beautiful green gardens stood in stark contrast to the surrounding shacks that provided shelter to all these forgotten souls. Towards the end of the open field the path took us up a hill, and pretty soon we were making our way through small slum alleys again. I realized how unusual it was to be able to walk here as a foreigner, as I absorbed this overwhelming end-of-the-world atmosphere. It was something I resolved never to forget. I needed to burn this experience into my heart to always motivate me to make a difference in this world, and to protect me from the seduction of our attractive capitalistic money game.

The church was on top of the hill and crowded by shacks that surrounded it on all sides. It was a small square building of thirty by thirty feet, with clay walls; on top of its roof was a modest wooden cross. A number of people were already seated in the first two rows, awaiting commencement of the service. The walls inside had the same clay finish as outside. Ten small benches built from wooden logs provided limited seating, and a cross, made from tree branches, was the only decoration on the front wall. There was no altar, just some open space and an old small table in front of the benches.

Peter told me he was going to greet the family of the deceased boy and walked over to the people in the left front row. I guessed that the older couple, next to the mother, were grandparents. All were engulfed in tears. A young, visibly pregnant girl, whom I learned later was his fourteen-year-old girlfriend, was sitting on the other side of the mother. They were surrounded by a number of brothers, sisters and friends. I sat down on the second right bench and tried to draw as little attention to myself as possible. It was a futile attempt in this world of dark-skinned, black-haired and poorly dressed people. I was wearing my running shoes, jeans and a T-shirt, but felt oddly out of place. Too rich! Too well-dressed! Too clean cut! I was ashamed, and found it difficult to look these people in the eye. How could we treat other human beings as totally obsolete? What gave us the right to have all the food, money, gold and oil without sharing it? What had become of the world I lived in?

The church filled up fast. Those who could not find a place to sit stood on the side or in the back. I noticed a group of young teenage boys standing against the wall and just knew these were the murdered boy's fellow gang members. Some ten minutes after our arrival Peter started the service.

My Portuguese was not good enough to understand everything, but like in funeral services in the North, respect was paid to the spirit of the young boy. Two of his friends shared some stories depicting the boy's brave, intelligent and joyful character. Peter also addressed the family in an attempt to help them to deal with their loss. At the end of the service, the attendants embraced their neighbors, and some even walked around and made an effort to hug almost everyone. Without distinction, people included me in their embrace as well. It was sincere, from their heart. They said thanks to each other for attending this service together. Equally they said thanks to me.

I was humbled to be part of this moment, to be accepted and hugged by them. The mother of the deceased boy made a point to seek me out and embraced me.

Modestly she said, "Thank you for attending the funeral of my son, Gringo. Thank you for paying him such honor."

I looked her in the eyes and thought I could detect a faint glimpse of the deep mysterious eyes that had been guiding me on this journey. But I wasn't sure. It seemed the spark in her eyes had died, and only a faint memory of it lingered behind. I wondered if this was caused by the loss of her son or by the years of struggle here at the edge of the world. The boy's pregnant girlfriend had followed his mother and was about to embrace me when she looked into my eyes. There they were again! Deep, dark penetrating eyes! Windows into a soul, hurt and in pain, but still vibrant and full of passion. I could feel her pain, her loss, her desperation and her fear of the world in which she was going to deliver her child. But I also could sense her passion for life, her connection with all that was beautiful and her hope for a better future.

"Thank you for being here," she said as she embraced me. "Thank you for giving us hope."

I offered my condolences to the two women but did not know what else to say. I wanted to apologize. I felt guilty! I knew that indirectly, my actions in this interdependent world had led to their life circumstances and ultimately to the death of this boy. I had never felt such an intense feeling of shame in my entire life, and yet, their hearts were beaming loving energy into me. They were sincerely grateful for my presence, and I seemed to embody great hope for them. But hope for what? What was it all these people seemed to expect from me? Just answering 'Is a global society a social globe?' and 'Are human beings being human?' was not going to change anything. Or was it? And if so, how?

I felt the ground crumbling under my feet. I had always known what I wanted to do with my life. I had a five-, a ten- and a twenty-year plan, which defined my career goals, family goals and monetary targets. Up until now, I had been very successful and always reached these goals. Quite a few times I had reached my targets one or two years in advance. But tonight, I had been touched by the forgotten souls of our world, and suddenly, all my plans, all my targets, had totally lost their importance.

How could I be concerned about the amount of money I was going to make two years from now if I already made three times the amount I spent in a month? How could I be concerned about being able to buy a new car when I knew full well my existing vehicle could still last another five years? How could I be concerned about saving up for my pension if people were dying today due to impoverished life circumstances? How could I still be motivated about creating more material wealth while I was acutely aware of the millions of people who needed help to survive?

The church emptied slowly. Peter and I were the last to leave. It was already dark, and a reddish full moon was rising above the valley. The bright light of the moon painted the cramped barrack community with silvery white strokes and dark black shades. Despite the unappealing life in this neighborhood, there was a beauty in this scene. I could feel its life-energy, vibrantly struggling to grow and shine like all the rest of creation.

Peter decided we should return to his house via a different route. The experience of tonight had deeply touched me, and I wanted to be alone with my thoughts. I did not feel like talking. It was like Peter knew, because he didn't even attempt to start a conversation. In silence we descended from the hill through the small, impoverished alleys. Every few blocks, small gangs of young black teenage boys would be hanging out. Each time we passed such a group I felt their penetrating eyes. They observed me from top to bottom and I felt their hatred and rage stinging in my heart. Sadly I understood the origin of their violent emotions. After we had passed some eight or nine groups, I wondered why they had not bothered us yet since I could clearly feel their urge to hurt and kill me.

"Peter, why am I still alive?" I asked. "From the way these young men are looking at me, I can tell they would want to kill me."

"You are probably right," he answered. "We are walking through some of the most violent alleys in this community, and you, with your clean jeans, nice runners, white skin and blond hair represent all gringos. In their eyes you are the embodiment of the injustice in this world. If I were not walking next to you, they would make you pay for their suffering and take everything from your body. From their perspective, that would not be stealing, as the white man is the thief in their eyes. They are just taking back what should belong to them in the first place.

"So what keeps them from doing that?" I questioned again.

"Me!" he answered calmly. "In this culture, priest and medicine men and women are considered holy, untouchable, and are treated with a lot of respect. As long as I am walking next to you, no harm will be done to you because you are under my protection."

Appreciative of the life I still had and the uniqueness of the experience, we walked on in silence.

Divine Encounter

An old wrinkled grandmother was sitting on a log with her back leaning against one of the shacks. As we were about to pass her she raised her arm and opened her hand in a begging motion. With sparkling eyes of hope, she captured me in her gaze. I slid my hand into my pocket to find some change.

"Don't let anyone in this neighborhood see that you have money on you," Peter warned.

With the Salta experience of the begging old woman fresh in my head, I answered, determined, "It is a risk I have to take, Peter. This time I cannot pass this grandmother without giving her something."

Decisively, I walked over to her and put the equivalent of five dollars into her begging hand.

Without looking at the money, a bright smile appeared on her face. She had the same deep, dark mysterious eyes like the old Salta woman. I felt myself being engulfed by the love that streamed from those windows of the soul. She covered my hands in between her two hands and said, "Thank you, Gringo. Thank you for coming, for your courage to continue on this journey. You have passed the test. It is time!"

Captured by her loving gaze I felt like falling into her eyes and entering the soul of humanity.

"Look there," she said softly as she pointed down the alley.

Approximately a hundred yards away from us I saw eighteen-year-old Ethel. The moon was lighting up her face and she was dressed in a beautiful white robe. She was wearing a crown and necklace of bright red flowers. Barefooted and with a radiant smile on her face, she walked gracefully towards us. Her young vitality, her zest for life and passionate love were beaming from her eyes. A white halo of radiant energy surrounded her.

I suddenly noticed that apart from Ethel, the street was entirely empty; even Peter had disappeared. For just a second my mind told me it was impossible for Ethel to have traveled all the way from Chile to be here. But this was too beautiful, too majestic, to question and analyze. I just wanted to let the moment happen and experience whatever was going to follow. Welcoming, I smiled back.

Suddenly, when Ethel was some sixty yards away from me, the white halo lit up and a fog-like cloud surrounded her body. When the fog cleared up and I could recognize her face again, I was astonished to see Anna Maria with her baby in her arms instead of Ethel. She was wearing a red dress with a crown and necklace of pure white flowers. But the eyes and the soul had remained the same, for Anna Maria was only a different embodiment of the same vital, life-creating, loving energy, a different phase in the development of spirit. With the same loving smile she kept approaching me, but now the beam of love had subtly changed, from energetic passion to deep caring. In awe I absorbed the serene beauty of this magical scene.

Right in front of me, some thirty yards away, the halo lit up again and the fog concealed Anna Maria's face. As it cleared up I recognized the old grandmother I had met in Salta wearing a black robe with white flowers around her waist. Again the eyes had stayed the same, although now the love they radiated was all-encompassing, unconditional and empathic. She was the love and spirit of the universe, and vibrantly radiated all its power.

The grandmother was carrying something in her hands. At first I could not make out what it was. Then, with a sudden shock, I recognized it was a heart. A beating heart! Surrounded by a golden aura, it expanded and contracted in rhythmic pulsation. With a beaming, loving smile the grandmother kept walking towards me until she stood right in front of me. Only the pulsating heart separated our bodies. My heart was racing, and I had to suppress my urge to step back; I was not going to allow my fear to ruin this experience. Bewildered, I searched for support. She smiled. I looked into her eyes and found comfort by letting myself drown in these windows of the universal soul.

Suddenly, still radiating with love and without saying a word, she stretched her arms out right into my chest and held the beating heart inside of my body. Instantly I felt the same unlimited feeling of peace and joy as I had experienced on top of the mountain in Ayacucho. I was in total ecstasy, embraced by joy and happiness as my heart merged in rhythmic synchronicity with the golden, glowing love she had inserted into my chest.

I saw the old woman say something, but her words reached me only after an unusual delay, like they had to travel over a large distance.

"Look around you!" I heard her say in a strange, hollow voice.

The next moment, the beating heart in my chest was torn apart. I collapsed and felt intense, excruciating pain. My soul was hurting badly. Stinging arrows with feelings of sorrow, hunger, worthlessness, powerlessness, apathy, defeat and pure hate were shot into my heart. I cried out from the agonizing pain, for I was feeling the suffering of the entire valley.

After what seemed like an eternity I could hear the same voice instruct me from a distance. "Look me in the eyes!"

I struggled to concentrate on the hazy eyes of the old woman right in front of me in the hope of finding some relief from the torture. As I connected with her eyes, they lit up, and vibrant love started to penetrate my bleeding heart and slowly but surely heal the pain. She kept pouring love into me until I felt the same joy and happiness as during my original elated state, when she had first held the beating heart inside of me. Once I was absorbed by the bright and peaceful light she pulled the heart back out of me.

As I looked with wide, open eyes at the beating heart in her hands, it disappeared into thin air. In disbelief I looked back into her eyes, only to find the same undeterred radiating love.

"I am Anahita! Mother of all!" she said. "Anahita was the first name you have ever given me. I am the embodiment of the Divine, the Source of all that is, the creating power of the universe. Since you gave me my first name you've called me by a lot of other names like Kali, Anat, Isis, Astarte, Ishtar, Minerva, Athena, The Morrigan, Freya, Maria and many more."

Speechless, still captured by her penetrating love, I listened attentively.

"Before I was Goddess there was only my eternal Divine being," she continued. "It was because I wanted to know myself in my infiniteness that I had a need to manifest myself, to experience myself. This required a reference point. So out of myself I created the mind, the God who could compare current experience with past experience and anticipate future experience due to the capacity of memory and thinking. As such, time was born and life existed. The mind recognized how different it was from the remaining Me, the spirit energy, which permeates all things, and how essential its existence is to the experience of life itself. Without the capacity of comparing that which is with that which is not, without dualism, there is no life, there is no experience, there is only being. Life is time, life is change, life is experience, life is difference, life is learning and life is evolving. For life to be each point requires an opposite point in the universe. In the absence of that, in the absence of life there is only a state of eternal being.

"All that grows has a mind and is part of my spirit. Therefore, all that is has a concept of time. For if it did not have a concept of time, it would not be able to learn, grow and evolve because it could not compare with that which has been, which it is not and which it does not want to be. And therefore all are my children—not only human beings, but everything that grows and evolves, including those elements that learn so slowly that, in your perception, their change and development seems to take millennia. You are brothers and sisters with the birds, the bees, the four-footed, the trees, the soil and the micro-organisms. For I am all there is, and you are connected to all that is. All there is, is part of you, as you are part of me. Therefore what you do to the Earth, or to another, you do to yourself, to your children and ultimately to Me.

"The mind is totally free and I provide my energy to whatever the mind creates in thought. For if I had not given the mind total freedom, I would not have been able to experience my infinite self, but only a part of me.

"This absolute freedom has been an illusive concept for humanity, with its analytical mind, to grasp. The mind has the capacity to compare experiences, decide what the spirit was happier with and learn from the process. This requires judging, but the concept of judging has been totally misunderstood by humans. Judging is the capacity to decide whether the created experience has led to the desired experience. The purpose of such judgment is to allow all to learn from the process. By doing so, we evolve.

"As everything always stands in comparison with that which has been before, and because time cannot stand still, everything before always changes. As a result everything is relative, and everything changes constantly. There are no absolutes. The only absolute is eternal being, which is what I was before I created the mind and which is what I still embody today.

"Throughout time, a number of you have understood this. The human race has produced people who were exquisite learners, people who understood how to experience life and were, through their spiritual connection with me, able to experience me and guide my energy with their minds. Amongst the most capable of my children were Jesus, Buddha, Mohammed and Lao Tse. But there have been many others, some famous like Gandhi, Mother Teresa and the Dalai Lama, but most totally unknown. These exemplary human beings have tried to teach others how to reunite with me. Unfortunately in their search to rediscover me and consciously guide my energy to create their desired experiences, most humans have interpreted the teachings of those great souls as absolutes. And as you already know, there are no absolutes. Everything is relative in comparison to something else.

"Mass religions were developed in an attempt to improve the overall experience of the human race and to establish a closer connection with me. People developed lists of right and wrong, and started to judge everything against an absolute standard. Religious institutions developed dogmas based on the paths of the enlightened souls whom they worshipped. What people failed to understand was that there are an infinite number of unique souls, experiences and manifestations of those souls. Therefore there are also an infinite number of paths to connect with me, the eternal spirit, and guide my energy to obtain desired outcomes. It has been humanity's futile attempt to seek the truth, the right path, to do good and destroy evil, that has led man astray and made it more difficult for him to connect with Me.

"Remember that I'm *all* that is! Therefore, what you consider to be good and evil are both parts of Me. Each one contains the seed for the other to occur. If that were not the case, there would be no life at all since there would be no opposite experience and no memory to feed time and change itself. For you to connect with me it is essential to experience life to its fullest. Open up your soul, listen to your heart and don't judge what happens to you. Rather, use your mind to learn from it and use my power to create your desired experience. Since all beings are permeated with my spirit, they all strive to obtain the same state of being, and the same emotional state of peace, happiness, exploration and learning. The more you try to create these circumstances for all living beings around you, the more you do for yourself, since what you are doing is being done to me. Unfortunately human beings have been so focused on judging others and events that they have failed to optimize their growth in this way. As a result, the spiritual nature of the human race has hardly evolved during the last two thousand years."

"Where does all this leave me with the question, 'Are human beings being human?'" I finally stammered, uncertain if I was allowed to speak.

"Well, where is your thinking currently at?" she returned the question, all the while continuing to beam love directly into me.

"I got stuck in trying to understand what human values are and what it means to be civilized and educated," I admitted.

"And what have you learned since meeting me in Ayacucho?" Anahita persisted in her questioning.

"I think I have learned that there is no such thing as 'human values.' Or at least there is not a fixed set of values that could be considered 'human' since everything is always relative within the context it takes place," I answered.

"That's right," Anahita confirmed. "So what does being civilized or educated mean, according to your understanding now?"

"Well, since everything always changes, the learning process is unending. Therefore, being educated can never be a fixed state. I believe we are educated when we acknowledge that learning and education are unlimited and will never end. An educated person is therefore someone who is always open to new things and continuously learns from new experiences."

"That reveals good progress in terms of the way you have been using the term in your society so far," she encouraged.

"Civilized means 'polite,' and 'caring for others.'" I continued. "I have come to think that this is the crucial element in deciding whether human beings are being human. When I look around me here and open myself up to the pain and misery of the world we have created, I recognize that a lot of us humans have forgotten what it is to be human. Somehow we got disconnected from You, the Source of all and your all-loving energy."

"What happens when you lose the connection with me?" Anahita interrupted.

"We become afraid," I answered, undeterred and still captivated by her gaze. Each time she asked me a question, it was like I found the answers in her mystic eyes. So I continued, "When we lose faith in life, faith in you and faith in the personal power which you have given to us, we become fearful of what might come. When fear drives our actions we use the power we have in a destructive way. Creation results only out of love. The ultimate act of creation is procreation, but that same sexual energy, that passion, is also the source of all other material creation. Without desire, there is no focused effort and no action will take place; no creation will occur. All action results from a desire! An *evolving* human being is driven by the desire to experience, procreate, co-create and learn. A disconnected, fearful human being is motivated by the desire to maintain the status quo, possess, protect, secure and survive."

"Are you saying then that faithful human beings don't have the urge to survive?" Anahita tested.

"If they do, their drive for survival is driven by a different kind of desire. For example, they might fight for survival because they love their current process of creation so much. In contrast, disconnected human beings simply fear death, and their actions are driven by the fear to avoid it rather than by their love for life."

"What is death, according to you now?" she questioned.

"A transition into another state of being. From my perspective it is a great adventure which, when the time comes, I will be eager to discover and learn from."

"So what do you conclude out of all this with regard to the question I gave you in Salta?" Anahita asked.

"I guess that human beings will always be human since time forces us to constantly experience new things. As a result we endlessly evolve. Some of us might learn and evolve faster than others, but that is perfectly fine since we all have free will. As you pointed out, contrasting experiences must and will always exist in the universe, and the outrageous imbalance apparent in our world at this point is simply a reflection of how slow our evolution has been over the last two thousand years.

"You also explained that every point in the universe always has its opposite point in space or time. This means that our current state of imbalance will inevitably move towards a state of balance, which in turn will give birth to a new imbalance. And so life will continue. If we humans want to accelerate our evolutionary pace, it is up to us to co-create the current, much-needed balance in the world. We can do that by being more caring and loving of those around us, since what we do to others and the Earth we do to ourselves. We also have to challenge the status quo in our search for quantum structural shifts in our economic and social structures so that we can create a sustainable and harmonious global society. We shouldn't judge those around us, and our actions should be guided by a loving, caring desire to create rather than by fear."

"That is a fairly decent answer," Anahita concluded, and I seemed to detect an extra sparkle of joy in her loving and mysterious eyes. "The cycle of the great wheel of time and evolution is moving to the next phase, and so the world will be changing rapidly. How that change will occur will depend on whether human beings choose to help activate the change and co-create with Me, or if, led by fear, they try to protect their status quo. You cannot stop or control the upcoming change any more than you can stop or control the flow of water to the sea, but you can help in directing it. You, Gringo, are the representative of the white man. You have to awaken those of your race so that changes can take place with their support and guidance. If you fail, humanity's role in the next phase will not only be much less important, but much smaller as well."

"But why me?" I stammered.

"Why not?" she questioned.

"I don't have a powerful position or a teaching position. I would think those gringos with such backgrounds would be better suited for this task."

"Technical skill sets and position will not help much in this. It is exactly because you're ordinary, because you don't feel better than anyone else, because you *have* been afraid and uncertain, that you can listen to the people around you. It is because you live from your heart, acknowledge the beauty of your world, don't judge the ugly side of the world as 'bad' and take responsibility for your actions that you, along with many others, have been chosen."

"You mean I am not alone?" I asked, somewhat relieved.

"No, you are not! I would not want such a burden to be carried by one person. A lot of you have been called, in all kinds of different ways, and many more will be called in the near future. Some have answered the calling already; others are still trying to overcome their fears and find their way to me. Hopefully together you will create enough momentum so that human beings will co-create the future together with me."

"How will I know what to do?" I asked.

"Just listen to your inner voice. You will know intuitively. If not, then find a comfortable spot close to me, like nature or some sacred ground, and talk to me. Whenever you open your mind, you will always hear me answer. And the more you are aware of our connection, the easier it will be for you to communicate directly with me. See me in all that is, and every time you make love, do it in my honor. Because as you now know, it is through the loving union of man and woman that the ultimate act of creation is demonstrated. It is through the unification of man and woman that, for a moment, I become whole again and new life can be formed.

"I am going to leave now. Is there anything else you want to ask before I go?" Anahita concluded as she took two steps back.

"Why did you put that heart inside of me when you arrived?" I asked.

"For you to succeed, it was essential for your heart to feel both eternal peace and all the sorrow in the world. You had to live through that. Also, I had to make sure your heart was entirely open before introducing myself and discussing all of this with you. Now I know that at least you have a chance of making a difference," she explained.

"Thank you very much, Anahita," I said gratefully. "Life as I have known it has been changed entirely. You have taught me a lot, and I will cherish this experience all of my life."

"I know!" she said warmly while she reached out and touched my hands. Instantly bright, eternal, peaceful light engulfed me once again. Joy and happiness danced in my heart. I could not see Anahita anymore, for she had merged with me in a peaceful, ecstatic union. Then all of a sudden the light faded away and I found myself looking in the eyes of the old grandmother again.

"Thank you very much, Gringo," she said warmly and smiled. "May Anahita be with you!" Her wise eyes broke our contact as she looked down at the money I had given to her. She let go of my hands and started to hum pleasantly.

I looked over my shoulder and saw Peter smiling at me. "Well, let's hope you will not get robbed by the time we get home," he teased.

"Have you seen everything that just happened here?" I asked, still affected by what had just occurred.

"Of course. I have seen you giving some money against my advice!" he responded.

"No, that is not what I meant. Have you seen the young woman who changed into the mother and child and ultimately became the old woman, Anahita, who talked the whole time with me?" I asked.

"I have only seen you give money to that old grandmother there," he said, "and all of what you call that "whole time" was merely half a minute. However, I do know what you're referring to."

"You do?" I inquired, relieved.

"Yes," he acknowledged. "You have seen Anahita. I call her Mary. She has been seen by many here in the valley and goes by many different names."

"Have you seen her?" I asked.

"No, I've not had the privilege!" he answered regretfully. "So far the only ones who have seen her here are the poorest of the poor and those who still manage to smile despite their suffering. Consider yourself lucky and cherish the experience. She does not appear to just anyone."

"I will never forget this!" I said while I nurtured Anahita's glowing love in my heart. We continued our walk in silence.

A few blocks further along a small toddler sat in the open sewage in the middle of the street. He was playing with some dried leaves and sticks, and seemed to be experiencing a lot of joy when they floated away on the gray, filthy water. I could sense his innocent joy, and felt ashamed about the painful future we were allowing this child to have. When we passed him, he stared at me and smiled. I looked him in the eyes and saw his soul. I saw Anahita in him, then my own soul and that of my children. I knew right then and there, I had to dedicate my life to create a better world for these people. This was unacceptable! Even if I could only make a difference to one of these children, it would be worth more than all the money I had ever earned. That moment I swore that somehow, I would make things better for at least one of these children, and hopefully for many more.

That night, I told Peter all the details of my adventure and the encounter with Anahita. He listened respectfully without interrupting. When I finished, he walked over and laid his hands on my shoulders.

"It seems you have been called," he smiled. "Expect some drastic changes to your life's journey from here on forward."

Before we went to bed that night, Peter invited me to pray with him in the moonlight on his balcony. I did go outside, but had nothing to say in prayer. I had had my mystical connection earlier that evening. Instead I let my heart reach out under the silver guidance of the moon to all those who needed some love that night here at the end of the world.

When I finally got into bed, I recalled the face of the toddler playing in the sewage and imagined him as a well-educated young man who was engaged in setting up school programs for the children in this valley. With that thought, I fell into a very peaceful sleep.

The Passion of the Human Soul

By the time I woke up the sun was already warming the valley with its brilliant, nurturing light. Outside people hustled and bustled, all trying to find a way to obtain their next meal. Peter and I had breakfast, and then it was time for me to leave.

At around ten thirty we were driving back through the same street via which we had entered this forgotten place. Just when we were about to enter 'civilized' society again, the two little girls we had encountered upon our arrival came running up next to the car. They knocked on Peter's window. When he opened it, they beamed with pride as they showed him their basket full of eggs.

"I guess you girls are on your way to the beach again?" Peter said.

"Yes we are!" they laughed with eyes full of joy.

"You keep this up and you are going to become rich women," Peter said encouragingly, "but make sure you come and attend school this afternoon so that when you are grown up you will know what to do with all that money."

We all laughed. Just when it looked like they would continue on their way, the youngest one turned around and ran over to my window. She knocked on it and waved with a broad smile on her face and eyes that were beaming with love, passion and joy. The human spirit was alive and well in these forgotten children at the edge of the world. When I opened the window she reached out and touched my shoulder.

"Gringo!" she shouted and then, giggling, ran away as fast as she could to her friend. With twinkling eyes, and full of joy about the success of her daring stunt, they both ran away together, laughing.

Twenty minutes later, I had said goodbye to Peter and was meeting with the investor of the Salvador hotel project at the construction site. Somehow, this real-life Monopoly game, at which I was a master and had always loved so much, had lost its value.

The investor showed me the construction plans and described in detail his vision for the building. We talked about the market projections and the required economics to make the project work. But all of it felt empty. "What value does this project contribute to society?" I questioned in silence. For a few minutes I started to justify to myself the employment it would create. And it would! But at what cost? What kind of salaries would it generate for the locals? Would it change anything for the people in the slums? Maybe some might be hired as cleaning ladies or maintenance men, and it might help those few find their way to their next meal. But would it really change something, or would this project be just another vehicle to funnel money and profits into the pockets of some already rich Brazilian businessmen and the giant multinational corporation for which I worked?

I kept the meeting short and to the point since I had a lot of soul-searching to do. After a nice lunch in the old town of Salvador the investor dropped me off at the airport. A few minutes after three I looked down from the plane's window over this colonial city which had once been the door into a new world that civilized mankind wanted to discover in its strife for gold, power and wealth. Now it felt like the end of the world, a forgotten place which civilized mankind would rather hide than look in the face.

The whole flight to Sao Paulo I looked out of the window admiring this great country we call Brazil. Here the opposites of the world were extreme, staring me right in the face. There was violence and caring, fear and love, poverty and extreme riches. But it was also here that the passion of the human soul was alive and screaming to develop to its full potential.

Later on that night I boarded my return flight home in Sao Paulo. I was glad to be on my way to my family. But at the same time I realized a piece of my heart would always stay here with the poor, but very human, souls in the slums.

I did not plan to sleep a lot on this flight. I had a lot of thinking to do. How could I give meaning to my job after what I had experienced? Was there something more meaningful I could do to help provide some balance to the world? If there was, could I spend my time on this and still provide for my own family in the world I had raised them in? All these questions had to be answered, if not on this flight, then at least in the months ahead.

Confused and Civilized

I started to read the in-flight magazine in an attempt to focus on something else. An article about Egypt and the construction of the pyramids caught my interest. I read about the large number of slaves that had built these massive monuments of Egyptian civilization, and wondered how the history books would read about our society five hundred years from now: 'During the late twentieth and early twenty-first century America, Europe and Japan developed an advanced industrial and informational society which led to great technical achievements as witnessed in the monuments of that time. Billions of slaves were used, concentrated in vast parts of the world, to support their civilization...'

Obviously my strategy of putting my mind onto something else was not working, so I decided to concentrate on the problem at hand. "What are the two most important things we should change about our way of living so that we can change the course of our world?" I wondered.

The thought, "Be one, and trust diversification! It is essential for you and the survival of the universe," entered my head. It was my thought...or was it? Where were my thoughts coming from in the first place?

Deep down I knew my current thought was part of the One's thought. This journey had brought me closer to the Source, and therefore I could expect my thoughts to become more creative as a result.

"What do I mean by 'trusting diversification?'" I questioned.

The answer came. "Diversification makes the world go around. It is out of differences that new things are created. It is the uniqueness of things that provides protection against large-scale attacks and allows species to survive. That's why, right now, centralization is one of our key problems. In order to create a more harmonious world, we need to decentralize: Decentralize production, decentralize sales, decentralize control, decentralize power, decentralize our activities, decentralize religion, decentralize living, and trust each other's uniqueness. Honor diversity, respect it, build on it and benefit from it, together."

"And what does it mean to 'be one?'" I asked myself, and the answer came again. "There is no such thing as a 'business life' and a 'personal life.' There is only life. Therefore, each time when you use the excuse, 'This is not personal; it's only business,' you betray who you really are. Either things are personal and there is no reason to use the excuse, or deep inside you know that what you are doing is not respectful of life and not really adding incremental value to the world, and so you find it necessary to excuse yourself. Add *real* value! Let your business be about incremental creation rather than a zero sum game, where your gain results from another's loss or the destruction of our environment. Show respect for life in all you do, even in business."

"Why did we let things get so out of hand?" I questioned.

"Because we are afraid." The answer came again. "We have made an effort to improve things, but have only been exploring those areas that do not threaten our own way of life. We are afraid to change our lifestyle and potentially get by with less material possessions. However, if we do not start to think in this direction, sooner or later the decision might be taken for us, and we will not be able to co-direct the development of our world anymore. Why are we so concerned with material possession anyway, if it is happiness we seek rather than wealth?!"

Eventually I fell asleep and only woke up when we were about to land in Chicago. At eight o'clock on Sunday morning I finally boarded my last flight on this trip. I was now on my way home to Calgary.

This time it was not difficult to keep my mind on something else: I had missed my family, and I occupied myself with loving thoughts about them and the plans I had for later on that afternoon when we would all be together again.

A Time to Give!

In the days that followed I shared all the details of my journey with my beloved wife and wonderful children. I wanted to reveal my insights and experiences so that they could expand and challenge their personal perspectives. I wanted to make sure they understood our society's, often unconsciously supported, hidden poverty and economic slavery so that someday they might help with harmonizing our world.

Soon my wife and I decided to stimulate our three children's social responsibility by letting them each sponsor a Plan International child. Given my frequent work-related travels through Central and South America my children each chose to help a child in Peru, Brazil and Guatemala.

I wrote up my report on the Primus hotels, and called Mario in Salta to share my adventure and insights with him. He was elated that I had not forgotten about him, and promised to help me in my quest to bring more balance to the world.

One evening in the spring, when the first leaves appeared on the trees and the first flowers decorated the pasture, my son Tom and I were enjoying the sight of the setting sun.

"Thank you for asking me why people have to pay for food, Tom," I said. "It is a very important question. I have learned a lot since you first asked me this, and I am saddened to say that it is only because we do not care *enough* about each other. Not that people intentionally are bad or want to be cruel to each other; we are just too preoccupied with acquiring more money, a nicer car or a bigger house, and so we do not think about those who live at the edge of our world.

Those who make it possible for us to drink our coffee and eat our bananas. Those who let us enjoy our fruit salad made from their fruit. Those who ultimately allow us to live the way we live. I encourage you to keep asking questions like that, for it will keep you aware of the connection between everything in the universe, and it will awaken people to their personal power and happiness."

Tom just smiled in response and hugged me. When I looked into his eyes, I could see mystery, the power of questioning and creation and the passion for life.

Later that same year, I was out bow hunting deer in the mountains. I had already had a few close encounters on previous hunts, but each time when the deer would be close enough it would smell me or see me. Once I took a shot but my arrow hit a branch and missed. This time was different.

I was focused and yet detached, ready to receive, in flow with the moment. I was grateful and without judgment. Suddenly, a big, mature doe walked out from behind the trees. Her trail led through an open spot some twenty yards away from me, so I drew and aimed my arrow at her vitals as she made her way through the clearing. Right in the middle of it, when she was just under twenty yards away, she stopped and looked directly at me.

I looked her in the eye and there She was. In the darkness of her eye I saw passion and joy for life. I saw gentleness and caring, and a readiness to offer the ultimate gift: the gift of life. For a split second I became one with the deer, one with Anahita. I paid my respect and thanked the deer for its precious sacrifice. The next moment the connection was broken.

I aimed and took the shot. My arrow hit its heart. The deer took a few steps and collapsed onto its side. The kill was made. A life had been given, and I respectfully accepted the gift that would feed my family for the next few months. The deer would live on as part of us. I walked over to the fallen deer and laid my hands on it. I paid my respect and thanked it for its precious gift.

Then, all of a sudden, I knew what to do. It was time for *me* to give. Time to give something from my life, to provide for those at the end of the world.

"From now on I'll direct my actions to serve the forgotten ones, like they have done for us throughout history," I thought. I only had to decide how I was going to do this.

"Write down your story!" I heard the voice in my head.

"That's it!" I thought. "I need to challenge the status quo. I need to make more people aware of the world's imbalance and their potential in harmonizing it. I need to push the boundaries and encourage others to do the same."

I decided that day to start by writing a book. From that moment forward my actions would be focused on creating awareness and developing more empathy and joy in the world.

My business practices now are guided by respect for life. Fair trade and social and ecological responsibilities are as much part of them as is providing for my family. Whenever these things cannot go hand in hand I know I am not really creating *added value*, but am only playing a zero sum game. And that I will not do anymore!

By directing my actions in this way I have found internal harmony and a deeper experience of happiness. I have learned I can make a large amount of little differences. As a consumer, I can buy from socially responsible and fair trade companies instead of just looking for the cheapest deal. As an investor I can choose to invest in companies that honor life and understand the interconnectedness between all things. As a writer I can challenge others to create a more harmonious and sustainable society. And as a businessman I can be an example of integrity and fair trade.

The world cannot be changed all at once. But all change starts with a single, small step. We *can* make a difference, as a student, as a consumer, as a parent, as a banker, as a lawyer, as a politician, as an investor, as a voter or as a lawmaker. We have a choice to co-create and direct our future. We can live and be our dream. I have chosen to make my contribution to this world, my verse in this great play, an exemplary one. When this life is over, I want to look back on it like I appraise a piece of art and be in awe. Why settle for anything less? I don't just want to be satisfied. I want to be ecstatic and be able to say, "I have done *my* part and it is good!"

What will *your* part be?

Appendix 1:

Resources for conscious decision making and active co-creation in this world:

T hose of you who want to explore how *you* can make a difference and co-create a green, fair and harmonious world, will find a resource list below, which can get you started. It was by no means the intention to create an all-inclusive list and while the author is a member or sponsor of several of the below organizations, they are not listed according to his preference. Most certainly there are a lot of other very important and valuable organizations that currently make a difference in this world and all are saluted for their vision and efforts. The movement towards a humane and sustainable society is like the sea, and consists of a lot of little raindrops. This is your chance to add yours.

1. Human Rights Organizations

www.amnesty.org: Amnesty International (AI) is a worldwide movement of people who campaign for internationally recognized human rights.

www.madre.org: MADRE is an international women's human rights organization that works in partnership with women's community-based groups in conflict areas worldwide.

www.hrw.org: Human Rights Watch believes that international standards of human rights apply to all people equally, and that sharp vigilance and timely protest can prevent the tragedies of the twentieth century from recurring.

www.hrweb.org/resource.html: This page contains names of human rights organizations, other organizations doing substantial amounts of human rights work, and resources (such as libraries and internet-based information) of use to human rights activists and researchers.

www.cartercenter.org: The Carter Center, in partnership with Emory University, is committed to advancing human rights and alleviating unnecessary human suffering. Founded in 1982 by former U.S. President Jimmy Carter and his wife, Rosalynn, the Atlanta-based Center has helped to improve the quality of life for people in more than 65 countries.

www.motherjones.com: Mother Jones is an independent nonprofit magazine whose roots lie in a commitment to social justice implemented through first rate investigative reporting.

2. Organizations that help improve life circumstances in developing countries

www.oxfam.com: Oxfam International is a confederation of twelve organizations working together in more than 100 countries to find lasting solutions to poverty, suffering and injustice.

www.plan-international.org: Plan is a humanitarian, child-centered development organization working with families and their communities to meet the needs of children around the world.

www.care.org: CARE is a humanitarian organization fighting global poverty. CARE is dedicated to helping the world's poor children and their families to solve their most threatening problems.

www.doctorswithoutborders.org: Médecins Sans Frontières (also known as Doctors Without Borders or MSF) delivers emergency aid to victims of armed conflict, epidemics, and natural and man-made disasters, and to others who lack health care due to social or geographical isolation.

www.redcross.int: The International Red Cross and Red Crescent Movement is the world's largest humanitarian network, with a presence and activities in almost every country.

3. Environmental Organizations

www.wwf.org: World Wildlife Fund is the world's largest independent conservation organization dedicated to the conservation of nature.

www.davidsuzuki.org: The David Suzuki Foundation works through science and education to protect the balance of nature and our quality of life, now and for future generations.

www.greenpeace.org/international_en: Greenpeace exists because this fragile earth deserves a voice. It needs solutions. It needs change. It needs action. As a global organization, Greenpeace focuses on the most crucial worldwide threats to our planet's bio-diversity and environment.

www.webdirectory.com: Earth's Biggest Environment Search Engine.

www.envirolink.org: EnviroLink is a non-profit grassroots online community that unites hundreds of organizations and volunteers around the world with millions of people in more than 150 countries and provides comprehensive, up-to-date environmental information and news.

www.greenhouse.gov.au: The Australian Greenhouse Office (AGO) is the world's first government agency dedicated to cutting greenhouse gas emissions. Very informative and action oriented site with ideas that could also be implemented elsewhere.

yosemite.epa.gov/oar/globalwarming.nsf/content/index.html: The EPA Global Warming strives to present accurate information on the very broad issue of climate change and global warming in a way that is accessible and meaningful to all parts of society—communities, individuals, business, public officials and governments. (do not include www. in web address)

4. Fair Trade organizations

www.ifat.org: The International Fair Trade Organization's (IFAT) members represent the whole Fair Trade chain from product to sale. IFAT's mission is to improve the livelihood and well being of disadvantaged producers by linking and promoting Fair Trade Organizations, and speaking out for greater justice in world trade.

www.fairtrade.net: The Fair-trade Labeling Organization is the worldwide Fair-trade Standard setting and Certification organization. It permits more than 800,000 producers, workers and their dependants in more than forty-five countries to benefit from labeled Fair-trade.

www.fairtrade.org.uk: The Fair-trade Foundation U.K. exists to ensure a better deal for marginalized and disadvantaged third world producers. The Foundation awards a consumer-label, the FAIRTRADE Mark, to products that meet internationally recognized standards of fair-trade.

www.maketradefair.com: Make Trade Fair is a campaign by Oxfam International and it's 12 affiliates, calling on governments, institutions, and multinational companies to change the rules so that trade can become part of the solution to poverty, not part of the problem. The site provides a report that analyses international trade rules, and presents a powerful case for change. Oxfam works from the realization that change will only come when large numbers of people demand it - in rich countries as well as poor.

www.transfairusa.org: TransFair USA, a nonprofit organization, is the only independent, third-party certifier of Fair Trade practices in the United States.

www.eftafairtrade.org: European Fair Trade Organization.

www.bsr.org : Business for Social Responsibility (BSR) is a global organization that helps member companies achieve success in ways that respect ethical values, people, communities and the environment.

www.fairtradefederation.com: The Fair Trade Federation is an association of fair trade wholesalers, retailers, and producers whose members are committed to providing fair wages and good employment opportunities to economically disadvantaged artisans and farmers worldwide.

5. Socially & Environmentally Responsible Consumer Information

www.coopamerica.org: Co-op America provides practical steps to use your consumer and investment power for social change.

www.greenpages.org: The GreenPages is an online directory of qualified green businesses.

www.responsibleshopper.org: The Responsible Shopper investigates companies on their social and environmental behavior.

www.newdream.org: This is the site of the Center for a new American Dream—Caring for our world, our families, ourselves.

www.organicconsumers.org: This site deals with crucial issues of food safety, industrial agriculture, genetic engineering, corporate accountability, and environmental sustainability.

www.faireconomy.org: United For a Fair Economy is an organization that strives for more equality in the world.

www.newleafpaper.com: New Leaf Paper leads the paper industry in the development and distribution of environmentally superior printing and office papers. The company focuses on producing paper using high post-consumer recycled content and most of their papers are whitened without chlorine or chlorine compounds.

www.oldgrowthfree.com: The Markets Initiatives—Ancient Forests, New Initiatives—is committed to working with companies to help them develop and carry out policies and practices that will shift business away from ancient forest products to ecologically sound alternatives. The site provides an easy nine-step program to become part of the environmental solution rather than the problem.

www.buildinggreen.com: Building Green is an independent company committed to providing accurate, unbiased, and timely information designed to help building-industry professionals and policy makers improve the environmental performance, and reduce the adverse impacts, of buildings.

www.greenhouse.gov.au/yourhome/about/index.htm: Your Home is a site of consumer and technical guide materials and tools developed to encourage the design, construction or renovation of homes to be comfortable, healthy and more environmentally sustainable. Fabulous Australian site with environmentally sustainable solutions for home construction worldwide.

6. Socially and Environmental Responsible Investment Opportunities

www.soyouwanna.com/site/syws/socinvest/socinvest.html: Learn what socially responsible investing is.

www.socialinvest.org: A national nonprofit membership organization promoting the concept, practice and growth of socially responsible investing.

www.sustainablebusiness.com: An internet community for businesses, investors and employees that integrate economic, and social and environmental concerns into their core strategy.

www.goodmoney.com: Good Money, Inc. is a multi-media information provider for socially and environmentally concerned consumers, investors and businesspeople.

www.investorhome.com/sri.htm: Trends in Socially Responsible Investments.

www.socialfunds.com: SocialFunds.com features over 10,000 pages of information on Socially Responsible Investment mutual funds, community investments, corporate research, shareowner actions, and daily social investment news.

www.greenmoneyjournal.com: The Green Money Journal provides investment information for the socially responsible investor.

www.investorscircle.net: Investors' Circle (IC) is a non-profit national network of angel and institutional investors, foundation officers and entrepreneurs who seek to achieve financial, social and environmental returns. Since 1992, Investors' Circle has facilitated the flow of over $90 million to 147 socially responsible companies and small venture funds.

www.goodfunds.com: Specializing in serving socially, environmentally, and financially concerned investors since 1986.

www.lightgreen.com: LGA manages Standard & Poors 500™-based investments for environmentally-conscious organizations and individuals interested in supporting companies with the best track records in their industries.

www.socialinvesting.com: Prentiss Smith & Company allow their clients to enjoy consistent performance while having their money reflect social values.

www.trilliuminvest.com: Trullium is the oldest and largest independent investment management firm dedicated solely to socially responsible investing. It's been a leader in socially responsible investment and beliefs that investing can promote social and economic justice in conjunction with returning a profit to investors.

www.domini.com: Domini is an investment firm specializing exclusively in socially responsible investing. They manage more than $1.8 billion in assets for individual and institutional investors who wish to integrate social and environmental criteria into their investment decisions.

www.socialinvestment.ca: Established in 1989, the Social Investment Organization is a national non-profit organization dedicated to the advancement of socially responsible and environmentally sustainable investment in Canada. The SIO's mandate is to promote the practice of socially responsible investment (SRI), which includes screening on social and environmental issues, shareholder advocacy to improve corporate responsibility and community investment to help local development.

7. Socially Responsible Mutual Funds

www.newalternativesfund.com: The New Alternative Fund is a socially responsible mutual fund concentrating its investments in Environmental Investment, Renewable Energy, Fuel Cells , Recycling and Energy Conservation, Organic Foods.

www.ethicalfunds.com: The Ethical Funds Company™ is Canada's most comprehensive family of socially responsible mutual funds with approximately $1.5 billion in assets under management. Our family of

Funds provides professional money management while investing in a way that reflects the commonly held values of our investors.

www.meritas.ca: Meritas is Canada's newest socially responsible mutual fund company. They help people join beliefs with deeds using the tools of socially responsible investing.

8. Experience the world outside of your borders first hand.

www.usservas.org: Servas is an international network of hosts and travelers building peace by providing opportunities for personal contact between people of diverse cultures and backgrounds.

Appendix 2:

Discovering Your Purpose

The author believes that everyone comes into this world with a specific life-purpose. While one might argue about whether that belief is right or wrong, it is undeniable that if one can identify a clear focus in life it significantly facilitates conscious decision making and deliberate co-creation in our world.

Lots of people find it difficult to discover their life's purpose and throughout the years the author has coached numerous people to discover their personal mission in life following the exercise described below. In order to achieve a successful outcome, it is important to perform this four-step exercise in the right sequence. At no time during step one through three, should one try to discover any links or patterns. It is important to focus on each step separately and to only search for connections and patterns in step four.

1. **Examining your past: What has life been teaching you?**

Reflect on your life and list all the things you have learned. Apart from your formal education and work experience include the knowledge and wisdom you acquired through people and events that crossed your path. Don't forget that there are lessons in both positive and negative experiences.

2. **Formulating values: What drives you?**

List the values you live by. Then examine what makes you emotional—angry, sad, frustrated, happy, elated—and try to discover the value that pushes your emotional button. It appears that under each strong emotion is a passionate value.

3. Examining your life and legacy: What do you want to contribute to the world?

Imagine you had a good and healthy life, well into old age. You're at *your* funeral. Someone close to you is about to read the eulogy, what would you like them to say about your life? What kind of person do they describe? Which of your accomplishments or traits do they celebrate? What contributions did you make for which they express thanks? Write your own eulogy.

4. Discovering Purpose: Is there a pattern emerging?

Life's lessons prepare you for your mission and provide you with the tools to be successful. The values you passionately adhere to reflect what is in your heart. And a life's examination from your deathbed helps to eliminate clutter and to get a glimpse of your soul's mission. When you now put the results from the three first steps next to each other, a pattern should emerge: Your life's purpose!

If you are in your teens or early twenties, it might be difficult to discover a clear pattern since more pieces of the puzzle have to be contributed to your life in order to create a clear pattern.

In any case the exercise should help in providing you with a better sense of direction. If you are older than thirty and cannot find a clear pattern, go back to steps one through three to make sure you have included all your life's lessons, values and essential elements in your eulogy.

The discovery of one's life purpose and values helps in releasing the passion and joy for life which most of us had as a child and into our teens. It facilitates prioritization and decision-making, and invites the universe as an accomplice in creating your life's artwork.

Enjoy the journey and make it an awesome one!

About the Author

Hugo Bonjean was born in Antwerp, Belgium. As a critical thinker with a strong sense for humanitarian issues and justice he decided to study Social and Political Sciences at the University of Louvain. However when he realized that a world revolving around money could only become sustainable through understanding and adjusting its driving economics, he changed direction and graduated in Antwerp with a B.S. in Accounting and completed his M.B.A. at the European University. While studying, Bonjean worked full time as an account manager for De Ster, an international plastic manufacturer. Just before he finished his graduate work, Holiday Inn Worldwide asked him to help them with their European expansion. Holiday Inn was the beginning of a career that would eventually take Bonjean all over the world.

After his ten year long career for Holiday Inn and Bass Hotels & Resorts, Bonjean was offered the position of Vice President of Operations & Development for one of the divisions of Marriott International, Inc. in Latin and South America. Firsthand experiences with poverty there rekindled the humanitarian values of his teens. His passion for bringing out the best in people led him to create The Company Coach: a leadership development company that helps companies to develop sustainable business models and become more socially and environmentally responsible.

Bonjean currently lives in the foothills near Calgary, Canada, with his wife of nineteen years and three children. He spends much of his free time developing youth leadership skills in his community and helps rescue injured wildlife as a volunteer for the Alberta Institute for Wildlife Conservation. He recharges his batteries while riding his horse in the Rocky Mountain foothills.